Shaun Meeks lives in Toronto, Ontario with his partner, Mina LaFleur, where they own and operate their own corset company L'Atelier de LaFleur. Shaun is the author of *The Dillon the Monster Dick* series (*Earthbound and Down* and *The Gate at Lake Drive*), as well as *Maymon, Shutdown* and *Down on the Farm*. He has published more than 50 short stories; the most recent appearing in *The Best of the Horror Zine, Midian Unmade: Tales of Clive Barker's Nightbreed, Dark Moon Digest, Rouge Nation, Shrieks and Shivers from The Horror Zine, Zippered Flesh 2, Of Devils & Deviants* and *Fresh Fear*. His short stories have been collected in *At the Gates of Madness, Dark Reaches* and *Brother's Ilk* (with James Meeks).

To find out more or to contact Shaun, visit www.shaunmeeks. com.

T0118835

Shaun Meeks' Dillon the Monster Dick series published by IFWG Publishing International

The Gate at Lake Drive (Book 1, 2015)

Earthbound and Down (Book 2, 2017)

Book 2:
Dillon the Monster Dick series

EARTHBOUND AND DOWN

by
Shaun Meeks

Earthbound and Down

All Rights Reserved

ISBN-13: 978-1-925496-41-3

Copyright ©2017 Shaun Meeks

V1.0

Stories first publishing history at the end of this book.

Printed in Palatino Linotype and Arno Pro.

IFWG Publishing International
Melbourne

www.ifwpublishing.com

Acknowledgements

Whenever I'm writing a new book or short story, there are so many people in my life who help out in one way or another. Even when they think they aren't doing a thing, they really are. Of course there are people like Mina, who is one of my toughest critics. She's made me a better writer over these last few years by not just saying something was good enough, but showing me what to change and how to change it. I also want to take a moment to thank all the editors over the years that've helped me see the ways I could change my writing for the better; Jeani Rector, Weldon Burge, William Cook, and of course Gerry Huntman, who edited this book. Without these people, you'd think I didn't know how to even use spell check.

I also want to thank the people who read my very unpolished work and offer feedback. When I'm writing a story, I understand the flow of things, but I need to make sure everyone else can make sense of my gibberish. A huge thanks needs to be given to my brother James, Sherry Hastings Conroy, and Jimmy Koumis.

I also want to thank all the Toronto Police officers and detectives who I've worked with over the years. I've been lucky enough to work alongside so many amazing people who've taught me a lot about police work and investigations. Of course I don't always put proper procedures in my stories, but I know when I'm breaking the rules, so that should count for something.

Lastly, I want to thank everyone who read these first two books in the Dillon series. I always have such fun writing them, and there is more to come. Dillon has some dark times in his future, but also some fun and crazy ones too.

For Kaleb. My first born and the one who showed me what an old soul is.

This one is also for Adam. Thanks for being there when I was growing up and doing everything you could to make me a better person.

Wednesday

Some days, you have to just stop what you're doing, reflect on the direction your life's turning and say, *have I been making the right choices*? I do this from time to time, but lately, I think things have been going better than ever. Sure, I'm here, trapped in a locker with an insane monster trying to eat me, but other than that, I've never been happier. I have more than enough money, my job is rewarding—despite this current predicament—and I'm in a relationship with a beautiful, smart and talented woman. I know that parts of my life aren't perfect, but whose life is without flaw? I'd rather focus on the good, which for the most part outweighs the bad tenfold. What more could I ask for?

Okay, so there's the whole part of my life that's my job. It's hard work and, if you want to get technical, I put my neck on the line on a regular basis. I have monsters, demons and other beings who want nothing more than to kill me so they can stay on Earth. I face off with things not of this world more days in a year than not. That's not so different than a lot of other people in the world. Cops and firefighters put themselves in life or death situations all the time and they're still able to find happiness; to pick out the silver lining in an otherwise crazy and hard life. So is it any shock I want that too? I mean, despite the nightmares that wake me up from time to time—six or seven times most nights—my job doesn't really bother me at all. Most of the things I deal with are easy enough, but there are times when I do question it all.

The Hellion.

The Shadow People.

1

The fact that I nearly lost Rouge and my own life.

These are things that keep me awake at night. Those images pop into my mind as I try and sleep and keep me from drifting off sometimes, and other nights they cause me to wake up screaming, sure that the nightmare isn't over. That's not something I'm used to. I don't usually get this stressed out after a job. Maybe it has to do with the fact that I feel as though there's more to live for now; like my life is a little more precious than it was this time last year. I try to tell myself that it's all okay, I made it out of there in one piece and I'll just have to be careful next time, but still the nightmares persist. The unease won't go away.

I can't tell you how many times I've woken up in the middle of the night with Rouge's screams echoing in my ears. Or there's the cold feeling as if one of the shadow people are inside me again. These are the things that haunt me. I feel the tentacles of the Hellion around my chest in my sleep and I wake up gasping for air, only to find myself in my own bed, or Rouge's—safe and alive. After that, it's a struggle to shake off the way I feel and if I manage to get back to sleep, there's more of the same waiting in the great, dark ocean of my dream world.

"I know you're around, Hunter. I can smell you."

This one that's after me now, he's not as bad as what I faced up north a few months back. In fact, he's not really that big of a deal at all. Of course he is huge, with a body size that reminds me of Andre the Giant, and he smells of old cabbage and dirty socks. But in the grand scheme of things, I've dealt with worse. He's known as a Caaraan and normally they like to hang around garbage dumps and swamp areas. Being this deep in the city is a little out of the ordinary for him. Seems to me, things being *out of the ordinary* is starting to be the ordinary and that sucks. Big time.

Their race isn't something I normally deal with. When I got the call to come to the high rise in the downtown area of the city, I really had no idea what I was going to be up against. My client, Dan Sartell, told me some of his workers complained about a man dressed in old rags and who smelled like death had crawled over him, loitering in the building. Dan said the guy is hanging in the stairwells and breaking into lockers in the basement. A normal thing, according to him. Usually it's just crack and meth heads, but he knows it's something different with this guy. He said he saw videos of the guy and he's huge and looks off. He went on to say that some of his employees that have been close to the ragged man describe the smell around him as feces and wet dog. Being here now, they're so wrong. This is so much worse than that.

I asked Dan why he was contacting me instead of his security or the cops, and he was straight with me. He told me he had and both attended, but refused to offer any real help. He said one of the guards looked as white as a ghost after going into the basement level where the stinky man was and quit the next day. I asked him if it was normal. Did people ever quit after seeing a sight like that?

"He'd been working for the building for eight years and then just quit. It was like he saw a ghost," Doug told me, and I thought he wasn't far off.

The beings that cross over into this world sometimes appear to be just that. Some of them look like mist; blue, white, red; it all depends on where they come from. Many of them don't want to be like that though. They want a real body, a real form and are able to call forth inanimate objects to them to form their bodies. Whether it's rags, dirt, feces, clothes or even someone recently deceased, they can take over these objects and in the case of anything other than a dead body, reform it to make something that resembles their old selves from their home world or realm. I didn't tell him this. It's always harder to explain, so I let him think what he wanted and I got ready to come here.

From the description of the odour, the area of the city and where the creature was hiding in the building, I narrowed it down to one of three things; a Krant, an Obbile or a Zern. None are too much of a hassle, and all can be dispatched almost the same way. I checked my weapons supply. Seeing I had what I needed, there was no need to stop off at Godfrey's. I packed up and headed out.

As soon as I got here, I knew it was none of the creatures I had assumed. It's a reminder of the old saying of how not to assume or you make an *ass* out of *u* and *me*. I should really try and remember that more often to avoid mistakes like this.

Right away the smell alone told me what was currently hiding in the cleaner's locker area was not some small, timid being which had escaped their home planet or realm. Many of the creatures who end up here are no more than that. They are simply frightened, harmless creatures looking to escape their terrible homes. I can sympathize, but there's no political asylum to be claimed for their likes on this planet. It goes against the rules set up by those above me, the people who I answer to. All they get is a visit from me or some other hunter, and then it's a one-way ticket back to whatever shithole they tried to escape.

On the other hand there are demons and more malevolent things that come here, just like the Caaraan I'm currently hiding from. They come to this world not as an escape, but for darker reasons. Sometimes it's only to wreak havoc or make gluttons of themselves on items they can't get on other planets or in other realms. Other times, there are much more nefarious reasons, such as a desire to hunt and kill humans. There are also those that have much bigger plans, like my last run in with a Hellion. He had a much grander plan to destroy an entire planet and rule the ruins. I doubt one single Caaraan could do what a Hellion could, but who's to know these days.

I've seen stranger things.

When I got to the locker room, and smelt the unmistakable reek of the damned thing, I went straight to my bag and pulled out spellbound gloves and my Tincher. The gloves can hold and paralyze almost any demon or spirit it comes in contact with and the Tincher is a knife that's carved, blessed and branded with as many curses and spells as one person could imagine. It has the ability to do away with almost any of the beings I might come into contact with. My Tincher is the go-to weapon when dealing with most of these otherworldly creatures. I should call it *Old Reliable* and I know for a fact that it can and will dispatch a Caaraan.

At least, I think it can.

Well, I certainly hope it will.

With those in hand, I began to walk around, checking in

lockers, behind boxes, anywhere I thought a demon might hide. The room itself was messy, but I doubted that the trespasser had anything to do with that. The grime looked old and worn in, like it had been there for a long time. It's amazing that the building's cleaners were so comfortable to live in such filth as this. There are old, dusty pop cans on the floor, a bowl on the table that seems to be growing some sort of green and grey hair, and stacks of magazines. Beside a couch that looks as if it's covered in a layer of black oil, is an old tube TV that has been changed into a spot to melt candles and collect even more junk.

I tried not to pay too much attention to the mess and instead focused on the task at hand. I needed to find the demon and dispense with him or her. The faster I do that the quicker I can get my money and go see Rouge. We have a date later tonight, if I manage to get out of here in one piece. Since our date nights always make me happy, that's what I thought about as I searched through the dust and dirt. Just the thought of her in one of her spectacular dresses, smiling at me the way she does, put a little pep in my step and I moved quickly around the room.

As I walked towards the bathroom, the smell became stronger and I knew that's where I'd find it. Lucky there was only one room that the male and female cleaners shared. I went through the door, knife in hand and I thought I was ready for anything. But it's always when you think you're ready for anything that something you could never prepare yourself for shows its face.

The Caaraan was in there, dead ahead in one of the two stalls. The door to it was wide open and the demon was hunched over the toilet. The creature had made his body up of old rags the cleaners must've discarded close to where he'd passed from his world to ours. This is how so many of the creatures look when I find them. They are a hodgepodge of discarded items and garbage. It's really rare to find one in a human or animal body, but it does happen.

Of course, if they happen to have a Porter, then they can just cross over in full form, but that's another story altogether.

This Caaraan had used grey rags to make up his very large, very ample body, though as he knelt by the toilet, he didn't look very big. To me he seemed to be shorter than my six-foot frame, maybe closer to five and a half feet tops. I thought he'd be easy to handle, even easier if I could move fast and get to him before he could really notice me. After all, he seemed very busy with the treasure he was stuffing into his makeshift mouth from the porcelain buffet.

Turns out, I was a bit too late for a sneak attack.

Just as I thought I'd caught him unaware, the demon turned his head. The feces he'd been eating were smeared across his fake face and right there I felt a rumble in my stomach as though my lunch wanted to make an escape. These visitors tend to have some weird tastes. I've seen them eat paint, glass, semen, tires and now, feces. I have no idea why you'd want to escape to this world only to eat human garbage of all shapes, sizes and consistencies.

I took a step back and the Caaraan began to rise. And rise. And rise.

All said and done, when he stood at full height the Caaraan had to be seven feet tall. And that might be a conservative estimate. His shoulder's touched either side of the stall and looked as though he'd be wider if he had enough room to stretch out. The monster attempted to wipe the poop off his face with the back of his hand, but did little more than smear it on the rags making up his face. He looked like a drunken woman who'd tried to put on her makeup while in a Jeep that was driving off road.

He stared at me for a second and then let out a deep burp. I'm glad there was distance between us, because I can only imagine the stench.

"Who are you?" he asked, his voice was deep and guttural.

I said nothing right away, but his eyes looked down and I'm pretty sure the Tincher gave it away.

"Hunter!" he yelled, and slammed his fist hard against the metal wall at his sides. Even from where I stood I could see the deep dent and knew if he did the same to my face, getting that mess on me would be the least of my worries.

He was no doubt about to run at me, but I'm pretty fast on my feet and was out of the doorway and heading to get out of there before I could feel his crappy mouth on me. There was no way I'd make it to the door and out into the hallway in time, so I did the next best thing which was to find shelter before he could get out. I needed to regroup and come up with a plan.

And that's why I'm here now, in a locker. I still have no plan, but need to come up with one soon. I can hear him roaming out in the room, sniffing the air as though he'll be able to somehow smell me over his own stench. Maybe he can, but I doubt it. For now, I need to figure what to do when the eventuality of him turning to my hiding spot comes and he finds me hidden away.

He's not at the lockers yet, but soon he will be and when that happens, I need to do something before he can grab me. I know the gloves might work on him, and the knife definitely will, but I'd rather not get beat to a pulp while I fight to stab him. I keep my breathing low and slow so he has no chance to hear it.

"Come on out, Hunter. Maybe I will let you live. Or maybe I will suck your insides out of your ass. I wonder if you'll taste half as good as these humans do."

I cringe at the thought of my guts and waste being sucked out of me. I can't help but picture a disturbing scene of being bent over with a straw up my butt as though I'm some fancy cocktail drink. Silly as it might sound, that would be a shitty way to die.

"I know you didn't leave. I know you're still here," he continues to call out as he searches. "Let me see you. Face me and try to do what you've been sent to do. Are you afraid? A coward? If not, come out and let's see who will walk away from this."

He's at the lockers now. He doesn't seem to be opening any of them, just standing there. I can hear him moving, breathing as though he might be no more than ten lockers away from me. I can't see him though. I look through the small grate at the top and there's nothing but the messy room. Yet I know he's there. Close, so I better think fast. I could easily—

RINGRINGRING!

Oh damn!

My hand shoots down to my pants, but it's too late. I hear the footfalls of the Caaraan who heard the ringing of my cellphone.

I should've turned it off or at least set it to silent, but sometimes I just forget. What a great time for me to have a slip. I know that cellphones are supposed to be convenient, such a helpful technology, but there are times when they're a real pain in the ass.

Right now is one of them.

I pull my phone out and Rouge's number and contact picture pop up. Usually I love to see it, but right now I have other things on my mind. The Caaraan is going locker to locker, opening each one no doubt trying to find the source of the noise, to figure out where I am. I want to ignore it, but it's Rouge after all. I need to make this quick.

"Hey sweetie, I'm right in the middle of a job," I whisper as quietly as I can.

"Sorry. I just wanted to know if you made plans for tonight."

"Yep. I'll call when I'm out of here."

"Okay. I just wanted to know if it's a dressy thing. So I know if I should set my hair."

The locker door in front of me flies open and shit breath is right in my face, hulking over me, mouth open wide as though he means to eat me. The smell of caked on feces and urine wafts at me from the dark, black hole in the middle of his raggy face and more than ever I hate cellphones.

"Set it. I love the Victory Rolls."

As I say this, I lunge outward. The hand holding the knife goes forward and upward, straight into the Caaraan's mouth. I have no idea if this will work, or if he'll just bite my arm off, but there's no other choice. I've already made a ton of bad ones today—what's one more.

There's something close to shock I can clearly see registering on his face. Maybe he expected me to be curled in a ball, terrified of him, or he thought I'd plead with him and try to make some deal so I could save my ass. He's clearly never dealt with Dillon the Monster Dick before. It's a mistake so many others have made in the past.

The knife slides easily thought the rags he used to make his body, the razor sharp edge making it tear like paper. Before he can even close his mouth, the Tincher's blade goes right through and out the back of his head. He stumbles backwards and green light begins to spill out of him.

"Okay then. I'll go start fixing my hair up now. Stay safe and see you soon. Love you," I hear Rouge say, and can't believe I still have the phone to my ear.

"Love you too," I say before I hang up and toss the phone onto the disgust couch that's close to the lockers.

Then I go back to work.

As the Caaraan moves away from me, grasping at his head, I know he's already done, but I need to get out of there and soon. Right now, the first part of the soul that's come here illegally is spilling out. It won't be long before it's all out and heading back to where it belongs thanks to the spells on the Tincher.

I kick the giant monster in the chest, and push him so he tumbles over some mops and crashes to the floor. I pounce on him, grab the demon with my gloves and confirm they do in fact work on Caaraans. He tenses up, like someone who's just been punched in the temple and has been knocked out. His eyeless sockets go wide and I see more light is bleeding out of them.

"P-p-please," he whimpers, as he chokes on the light spilling from him. I have no sympathy for him. Even if I wanted to, I can't feel bad for them. These creatures aren't supposed to be here. There are rules and laws they must follow. I have to follow them too.

Well, I do try from time to time, but it's not always easy. Rouge makes following the rules hard, among other things.

I bury the knife in his throat and move the blade down until it comes out where his crotch is. I quickly get off him as the last of his spirit light explodes out of him and dwindles to nothing, to the point where I know he's gone back to wherever he came from. There is a sizzling sound as the light blinks out and then all that's left are the old rags and a pile of shit the Caaraan had eaten. I look down at it and shake my head.

Some days I really wonder if I've made the right choice to come to Earth and do this crappy job. At least I don't have to clean that up too.

SHAUN MEEKS

I wash my knife off in the bathroom, grab my phone and my bag and then head to the management office to get paid. I know getting a nice cheque will make me feel a little better and seeing Rouge tonight will make all that doubt slip away.

But some days…

I'm nearly home. I feel exhausted as usual right after a job like that. I'm really looking forward to getting there and just passing out. The streets aren't as busy as they would be if it were the weekend. That's something at least. There's not much worse than driving home in Friday or Saturday traffic to ruin your night, especially when you're tired. I pull into the parking lot and click my alarm on when my phone rings. I can't help but to curse before I even pull it out of my jeans pocket. I know who it is and I feel like an idiot.

"Hey, Rouge," I say as soon as I answer it.

"Please tell me you're not still at work."

I can hear the annoyance in her voice and I'm mad at myself because I forgot to call her back like I promised. Even the plans I'd made had slipped my mind so I have to mentally kick my own ass for that one. It seems idiotic and it is. She even called me at the job to ask about it, so you'd think it'd be at the front of my mind. Yet, when I finished with the Caaraan and then had to deal with trying to get paid from the stingy Sartell, I just plum forgot. It actually slipped from my mind because all I wanted to do was get home, take a long shower to get the feel of that dirty room off of me, and fall fast asleep. Once the idea of curling up in my bed and resting weaseled its way in there, it was nearly impossible to think of anything else.

"Just left a few minutes ago," I tell her, half lying. "I'm going to head home and get changed and I'll be right over."

"Hurry. My stomach is eating itself and I don't want my face to start melting. I put a lot of working into getting dolled up for you, Mister."

"I'll hurry. I promise."

"Well, I guess I'll sit in front of the fan and eat some chips until

10

you get here. Hurry!" she says, and laughs. "If I eat too many of these medallions of deliciousness, I won't be able to wear this corset tonight. Your haste is all that will save me from popping like a container of Pillsbury dough."

I chuckle. Even though I really wanted to go to sleep, I'd rather see her. I'm sure I'll feel more awake once I get to her house.

"You're always gorgeous and there's no way that would ever happen. I'll text you when I'm back in my car and on the way."

We say our goodbyes and I walk into the building where I live. The apartment building is small, not one of the skyscrapers that litter the skyline. This one is only nine floors. It's pretty quiet and for the most part, bug and homeless-guy-sleeping-in-the-stairwells/lobby-free. I've worked in buildings with hallways that reek of drugs and urine, stairwells and elevators covered in blood and/or feces, not to mention lobbies full of thugs or prostitutes looking to spread their legs and their diseases. The city seems plagued with these kinds of properties at times. There are days when I go out for a job and see how much of a downward spiral the city is in and I have to wonder how long before it all implodes on itself.

Even where I live isn't the best. I'm not sure you could find *the perfect* place to live here anymore. I certainly haven't found one like it, but at least I've been able to find somewhere half decent. My building is a little grimy, but when you compare it to many other areas in Toronto, it's not all that bad.

I walk up the stairs. I never take the elevator here. It's not that I'm afraid of enclosed spaces, though I'm not a huge fan, especially after hiding in a locker from a monster with poop smeared on his face. It's just one of the small things I can do to stay in shape. So, as I head up the stairs, something catches my eye on the third floor. There's a shadow I see through the frosted glass door and, at first, I think of ignoring it and walking by. Yet there's something there, a thing I'm sure I know. It's a little tickle on the back of my neck and it sparks my curiosity, so I have to see what it is now.

Slowly, I open the door, bracing to find some woman or man going door-to-door selling long distance, God, or the opportunity to buy a tree in a rainforest. I know if that's what's there, I'm going to quickly shut the door and run. There's nothing worse than solicitors. I've always wondered if the Hell Catholics and Christians always talk about is full of door to door sales people, allowed to go back to Earth just to keep working. Or perhaps it's some afterlife punishment. No lake of fire, just the worst job ever. I do feel bad for them sometimes, and the way people look at them or just straight up yell at them. That feeling usually fades when I open my door to one and they start off with their *I'd like to talk to you about* fill in the blank here.

There are no solicitors of any kind there. In fact, when I open the door, I don't see anything at all and I breathe a sigh of relief. Letting the door go and I'm about to turn back to walk up the stairs. It's only then that I see it from the corner of my eye in the hall. It's small and it's fast. Even before I can realize what it is I feel something hit me from behind and the world in front of my eyes gets a bit darker. I can't let myself go down and yet the strength in my legs is draining and I feel my body sag.

"He ain't gone down, hit 'em again, idiot!"

The voice is coming from in front of me, yet when I look towards where the source should be, there's nothing but hallway there. I squint, but as I do, I'm hit again. And it's a hard one. The first blow had struck me in the back of the head, but this one bounces of the side of it, close to my ear and most of the force hits me in the left shoulder. I cry out and know that if I don't move and do something fast, I'm not going to be conscious enough to see what comes next.

My hand fumbles at my belt where I have my Tincher attached. I can hear the voice from hall ordering another hit and something behind me shuffles. I act fast. The sound of whatever it is hitting me whistles through the air. My ears pick it up. Before it finds a home on my aching body, I move. I roll to the right, away from the hall, and try to get to my feet. I fail at that.

With one foot on the ground and the rest of my weight balanced on my knee, I turn away from the hall to meet with my attacker. I don't know what I'm expecting, but to be honest, I did think it would be some monstrous beast with a club. Instead, it's a ragged looking man with a taped up baseball bat in his hand and a lost, dead look in his eyes. There's little doubt this man is a junkie. His eyes aren't on me though; they're on the spot I was, where his bat had struck. I can only guess he's trying to figure out how he missed.

I press my empty hand against the wall and use it to help me get to my feet. Once on them, as shaky as they are, I hold the knife forward and whistle to get the junkie's attention. He turns to me, his mouth open and his eyes are slightly vacant. Not sure what this guy's drug of choice is, but if his plan is to rob me, he has another thing coming.

"You have two choices," I say though gritted teeth, as my head booms and throbs. "You can drop the bat and run like the wind, or I'm going to see how much jerky I can make out of your flesh, asshole."

He's not moving. Well, his lips are moving, as though he's talking, but no words come out. I wonder if he's talking to himself, or if he can even speak at all. He looks at me, standing in front of him with my Tincher in hand. Slowly he looks at the hallway, the door still hanging open. His eyes turn back to me again for a moment. Before I can say any more to him, he drops the bat and runs down the stairs. I think he made a wise choice.

I breathe a sigh of relief, but I know there's still someone else there. Well, unless they've run off too. I move as quickly as I can to the hallway door. My head is spinning slightly, but I want to try to catch the one that had barked the order, whoever it is on the other side of the now closed door.

When I yank it open, the hallway is empty and I'm pissed that they've taken off. I curse to myself and then something hard hits my shin. I wince and yell out. As I go to look down at the injury, I see the source of the pain and the one who'd been ordering the junkie to hit me. I'm holding back the urge to laugh.

"I should've known it'd be a damn Skell!" I blurt out, and all but stagger towards the small creature.

Skells come from a distant world. Their planet is on the edge of a galaxy, which lies on the edge of this one. The planet, like its inhabitants, is small and dim. When these creatures cross over, they tend to be confused with the mythical leprechauns. He's short and stubby looking, thick around the middle with a blunted square head. Looking at him, in the dark or at a distance you might think there's a rainbow and a pot of gold close by, but I know better. I've dispatched plenty of the little cockroaches before and this one will be no different.

"Back away from me, meat sack," the Skell nearly cries out, and steps away. His body is small and compact, comprised of dirt and grass. He smells earthy and a little bit like there might be dog shit on him. Typical for his kind.

"I don't think so, Skell. I don't know how you found me, but you should never hunt a hunter. Didn't your mommy knock any sense into that pea brain of yours?"

"Shut your mouth, traitor, and don't you dare speak ill of her," he says, and I think he almost sounds offended. I have to hold back laughing at him. Luckily, my bleeding head is spinning enough that I can disregard the humour as I try to stay upright.

"I won't. Instead, I'll send you back to her so she can teach you some damn manners."

At that, he spins and goes to run. I won't be able to catch him if he gets away, so I can't let him. The way my brain is feeling, the fact that I'm close to being sick from the swaying of the world around me lets me know I won't be any good in a chase, so I have to think of something better.

He gets four steps into his fleeing when I throw my Tincher at him with precision aim. I watch as the blade sails through the air and hits him dead in the back. The little bastard cries out and falls to the ground. I limp over to him, the hall in front of me still spinning a bit, and I hold back the urge to stomp on his makeshift head. As I've gotten older, I've managed to bite back my temper quite a lot. There were days not that long ago when instead of just sending him back, I would have tortured him a bit, gotten answers about the weak spot he came through or anything else I wanted to know. It wasn't nice, and I'm not proud of how I could prolong the pain if I wanted, but it was a different time and I'm a different man now.

The Skell is trying to crawl away. His tiny arms and legs are moving, making him look like he's swimming on the carpeted hall. I know it can't be easy for him. The curses and spells carved into the blade cannot only kill, they help to incapacitate anything I stab or cut long enough for me to do my job. I'd say it's a little like being anesthetised, only there is still quite a bit of pain involved. In order to send it back, I can't just stab it, I have to breech the creature and release the mist within. Then it goes back.

Now, if I use the Tincher and go deeper and actual pierce the core of the mist itself, well, let's just say the creature, demon or monster will soon be no more than a memory.

I stand over him, put my foot on his ankle and he cries some more. Carefully, I crouch down and flick the handle of my knife to send a tremor through the trespasser's body. I wonder briefly what it must feel like. Does it burn? Itch? Or does it simple throb with every false breath he takes? In the end, I just don't care.

"So, Skell, you want to tell me how you found me?" I ask, and doubt I'll get an answer.

"Will you let me stay? I'll tell you anything you want if you let me stay here. You have my promise."

Should I consider it? Do I want to give this turd a break so I can find out? I've lived here so long and never once found any creature not of this earth close to it, so I do want to know. But do I make a deal with some low being to find it? It's a conundrum.

"Fine. Tell me what I want to know and I'll take the blade out of you."

He's not saying anything and I don't doubt he's questioning whether I'm lying or not. I can't blame him really. If I was in the same position, and I have been once or twice in my time, I'd want some sort of reassurance. Bad luck for him because I'm not going to do anything to tell him if I'll live up to my promise or not. Sometimes, you just have to take a chance.

"Okay, I'll tell you, but you promise, right?"

"Sure," I agree, and wait for the answer.

"Since you stopped that Hellion, word is going through the universe, to every realm what you've done. Some are more scared of you and the hunters than ever before, but not everyone. There's a group out there, spanning numerous planets, realms and planes of existence, that are coming together and want you dead. They're paying any cost to get you, rid them of the last Treemor. They thought they already had, yet here you are. And it's not going to stop there. They want the Authority brought down too. You and the other hunters are just the start, the beginning of a bigger plan to make all planets, universes and realms free."

"So, who is this group?"

"I can't say. If I do, I'm better off dead. So if that's not enough to spare me, well then—"

I tear my Tincher through his false body and split him in two without letting him finish his thoughts. I know when someone is done telling me what I want to know, and he was at that point. I wouldn't have spared him anyway, but holding back made me mad. If I could, I wanted to extinguish his light completely. After all, he was trying to kill me. I guess he can count himself lucky when he gets back to his little hellhole deep in the stars.

The Skell's shell of a body deflates as his essence is sent back to his pit of a world. I lift it up, just to make sure and watch as particles of dirt and grass rain down on the hallway floor. I drop it and try to stand up. My head is still spinning and I reach over and grab the wall. With my other hand, I reach up and touch where the junkie had hit me on my big old melon. When I pull my hand away, there's blood on my fingers. Not too much, but enough to know I may need to patch it up. I'd go to the hospital and get stitches, but that might be more trouble than it's worth. I'm sure they'd be confused by a few things when it comes to any test results or x-rays. I always keep a low profile, and for good reason.

My phone is ringing.

I wipe the blood off on my jeans and pull it out. Damn, it's Rouge. No doubt she's getting a little mad at this point.

"Hey, sorry," I say right away before she can get a word in. "Had a little run in with some nasties when I got home. I swear I'll be there soon."

"Seriously? This is supposed to be a special night, Dillon."

There it is. The frustration in her voice. We've never really had fights or anything close to arguments since we made this whole crazy thing official, but there are times where I'm sure she's bordering on yelling at me. Times like this, I can't blame her. I'm late getting home, and now this. I guess the patchwork will be next to nothing so I can get out of here fast.

"Don't worry. I'll be there really soon. And when you see what happened, maybe I can get a sympathy kiss."

"You wish. You'll be lucky if you get a high five tonight at the rate you're going, buster. I guess it's back to the old chips, chump." At least I hear her chuckle a little as she says this.

We say our goodbyes and then I cautiously head upstairs. With each step my head is pounding as though a thrash metal band just started to play one of their extra-long, super loud sets. The light in the stairs is hurting my eyes a bit, but after a minute I manage to get into my apartment. I have to change quickly, but before I do, I grab some Advil and wash it down with a bit of cola. I found out years ago that taking ibuprofen with Coke or Pepsi really makes it work faster. I'm sure nine out of ten doctors would not agree, but to hell with them at this point. I've never needed quick relief like I need it now.

As I'm changing, I pull out an ice pack from the freezer and put it on the back of my head, wincing at the pain. It's intense, but some of the throbbing goes down right away. That's something. Another good thing is that my shoulder the junkie hit isn't also cry-out in pain right now. I use a bandana to hold the ice pack in place and continue to change. I need to be fast if there's going to be any chance of a good night. I know once she sees the injury, she will feel a little sorry for me, perhaps enough to make her frustration at me disappear.

I have to hope.

I'm changed and ready to go. I use a baby wipe to get rid of the blood and sweat on my hands, arms and face, letting it do the work of an actual shower. Not the classiest thing in the world, but better than going out with a layer of monster hunting filth caked on me. I'm not too ashamed to admit I have to do it from time to time, no more than I would be to say I've used the inside of my shirt to brush my teeth. I'm a busy hunter and desperate times call for desperate measures.

Before I head out the door, I go into the medicine cabinet and pull out some very special cream I have. Over the years I've managed to stockpile some good supplies to use whenever I get hurt a bit. I have items for stabs, gunshots, and even a near fatal mauling. What I pull out this time is more of a simple ointment that will stop the bleeding and dull the pain around the gash on my scalp. I'll do more for it later. For now, this'll have to do.

In my car I check the time. Good. It only took my five minutes to get ready and back out. It's faster than I thought. I pull out and start to head towards Rouge's house and turn on my Mp3 player. My car fills with the not so relaxing sounds of NOFX as I drive. At a red light I text Rouge and let her know I'm five minutes away, and if she wants she can come out and meet me in the driveway so we can get a move on the night. I end it with a well-deserved apology on my end. All I get back is the letter K.

Boy howdy is she upset.

She knows that my work is pretty serious. Hell, she was there on the beach when I faced off with a monster bigger than my building as it crossed dimensions using a Porter. She knows better than anyone how things can go insane when I head out to a call. So does that mean she doesn't have the right to be irked? Not at all. This night isn't just date night and I know it. We haven't been out for a real date in over a month. I shouldn't have even taken the job and I think when it comes down to it, that's one of the biggest things getting to her. I know it would be a thorn in my side if she'd done the same. If she had taken a gig to work one of her burlesque shows instead of coming out with me tonight, I'd be right pissed too. She has every right to want blood.

She might get some too.

My head is aching again. I wish I had more Advil with me, or a knife I could use to carve out the asshole with the jackhammer that's clearly trapped in my skull. I rub my temple with one hand and keep the other on the steering wheel. The aching is making me think about the Skell in the hall and what he'd said. It's something I haven't even been thinking of since he said it, but there it is. It could be he just wanted to live, wanted me to let him go, but the idea that there's some organization out and who've put a price on my head is terrifying. If it's true, that is. For all I know it's just a load of crap and the Skell got lucky, crossing over into a building I lived in and got some junkie to attack me with the promise of drugs or money.

So my choices in this are: the Skell was lying or I have a lot to worry about. And what about the idea of these things trying to bring down the ones I answer to? Could they? Is the Authority actually vulnerable? I wouldn't have thought so. I always looked at them as one of those Godly entities; the kind of all knowing, all seeing force that religious people follow. How could anyone attack them?

Worrying can come later. Up ahead I see Rouge at the edge of her driveway, waving at me. Through the pounding headache I smile and go to flick my lights at her since she won't see me wave back. I reach over to do just that, but I suddenly can't believe what I'm seeing.

There's a tree in the road, and it looks like it's running right at my car.

It's not running, you're speeding towards it. My inner self tells my stupid self, and before I can even hit the brake, I hit the tree on Rouge's neighbour's lawn and know this is going to be bad. I close my eyes and just accept the darkness I know is waiting for me. All I can do is hope it doesn't kill me.

It's one of those days.

Thursday

When I open my eyes, I know where I am and this Dillon is not a happy camper. It smells like antiseptic and death here. I can hear someone crying in the distance as my eyes struggle to focus. All I want to do is just get up and run. I hate hospitals. Even to visit one of them sucks, but to be admitted to one opens a whole new can of worms. If I'm ill or hurt, I have items in my apartment to deal with it. These items can even pull me from the brink of death. Nothing here in this hospital will help me. Of that I'm almost certain. I've been on the brink of death once or twice in my life and if I'd come to the hospital then, I wouldn't be in this body any longer. All they would do is piss in the wind and hope for the best. What's worse, is if they look too close at me, delve too deep into who and what I am, there are going to questions.

A lot of them.

Sure I look human on the outside, but I'm not of this world. I'm a Treemor, an alien to this world and even this universe. This body I'm in is one of many I've inhabited since coming to Earth so long ago. I'm pretty sure if they test me, they'll be able to tell something's rotten in the state of Denmark. It'll raise a lot of eyebrows and then how long until I become a guinea pig and pin cushion to doctors, scientists and eventually the government who will want answers to who or what I am? It's the reverse alien probe.

Just thinking about the truth about me and this body right now makes me realize I need to sit Rouge down and have a talk with her. We've never really gone into it all. The whole who I am, my true age and the facts about my current physical form have just never come up. I don't want to keep secrets from her; it's just a tricky subject to get into. Well, if things don't hit the fan while I'm here in the hospital I guess we'll have a talk when I get home.

"You awake?"

My eyes are still unfocused, but I can hear Rouge ask me, her voice drifting towards me from my right. I slowly turn my head and confirm it's still pounding. I wince and nod before I blink a few times to clear my vision. It's nice when she's the first thing I get to see, even if I don't fully get how I got here.

"I was starting to get worried. The doctor thought you might've slipped into a coma."

"How long was I out for?" I ask, and can see her face a little better now.

"About sixteen hours."

I feel like I've been hit again when she says it. Sixteen hours out. That's a record for me. "Jeez. Sorry about the scare, and the night. I guess the junkie hit me harder than I thought."

"What junkie?" she asks, and puts her hand on mine. "I thought you were going after one of your regular jobs last night."

"I was," I say, and then explain about the attack in the stairwell. I leave out the whole part of what the Skell said about the organization, figuring it's nothing she needs to be concerned about. I'm not even sure I should care too much. These things that cross over aren't always the most truthful of beings. "I guess when he hit me he gave me a slight concussion. I really didn't think it was that bad. Head was throbbing, but I could see fine and I made sense when I called you, I think. The last thing I remember was a tree running at my car, and then I woke up here."

"That's not what happened, Dill. You flicked your lights at me when I waved to you, and then jumped the curb and ran at one of my neighbour's trees. If you'd been going faster or didn't have your seatbelt on, I doubt we'd be talking right now."

I nod, but don't go into it. Even if I had died in this body, I still would've been able to talk to her. Sure, she might not believe it was me at first, but she'd come around to knowing it was me eventually. Accepting it, well, that's another story I guess.

The door to my room opens up and as it does, I see a familiar face. It's not one I expected, but since it's a friendly face I'm happy to see it.

"Mind if I drop in for a second, Miss?" he asks from the doorway, looking right at Rouge.

Rouge turns to me and no doubt sees me smiling. I look up at her and nod. "He's an old friend."

"Well then, you're the first friend of Dillon's I've met to date," she says with a smile.

"Dillon doesn't play well with others. If you are close to him I'm sure you know that, Miss," he says, and walks in and heads over to where we are.

"I do. And enough of the miss business, just call me Rouge," she tells him, not even bothering with the name she was born with. She never does. She doesn't even like me calling her by it.

"It's a pleasure to meet you. I'm Father Ted."

"Father?" she asks, and she comically moves back as if struck. "As in Dillon's dad or a priest?"

"Priest. I'm not wearing my collar right now because I just had an x-ray, so I'm hopping around here like a virtual hobo. I do apologize."

"Oh stop it, Ted," I say, and sit up so I can see him better. "You've always hated wearing the collar. You told me so yourself. No need to lie in the house of pills and machines that go beep." I look up at Rouge who's smiling at the man. "He's a Catholic priest, so he's a bit jaded and snarky at times. Which means you should make fast friends with him."

"You watch it, Dill," she says, and squeezes my hand. "Or I'll give them a reason to keep you here for a few more days."

I get the point and turn back to Ted. "How did you know I was here?"

"I was just walking through the halls, on my way out, and ran into a detective who attends my church. When I asked him what he was doing here, he said he was stopping by to see some half-wit detective that claims to hunt down monsters and demons, so I knew it was you. He said you'd been drinking and driving and nearly killed some people. Since I've known you for so long, I asked him to let me talk to you first, assuming the story was wrong. Please tell me it's wrong."

Drinking and driving—is that what they think? I guess they might. Who knows what my blood test results came back as. There's not a whole lot of natural order flowing through this body. For all I know, the blood in this body could easily show up as someone with a high blood alcohol level, or it could even give results that there's no living cells in it. I have no idea. This is the first time I've ever been unlucky enough to end up in a hospital without being conscious. I guess I'll just have to wait and see what they have to say about it.

"They're very wrong. I had a concussion. I was smacked pretty good in the back of the head by a junkie of all things." I explain to him the details as best I can, giving him the same story I gave to Rouge and leaving out the same little bit. I've known the priest for a long time and I don't need to pull any punches with Father Ted. His church has been a source of work for me even before he started working there. It's one of those places, a sort of crossroads for different realms and dimension. Houses of faith tend to be like that. Anywhere people gather and pour their hopes and faith creates weak spots in the fabric of this reality. It's the same where great tragedies happen, though in the latter cases the weak spots are closer to the places where demons live. It's one of the strangest parts of how this realm works.

"Well, I think it's an easy thing to explain to the detective. I know he's not going to buy into what you do, but since it was a junkie who did this, you may want to leave the rest of it out. Tell him about the attack, but not the…Skell was it? Just to be on the safe side, Dillon."

I know he's right. Ridged people tend to have a very hard time when it comes to hearing about the world outside this one. Or worse yet, the hidden one that lives right under their noses. Most people would rather live their lives as happy and as blissful with their heads in a cloud of ignorance, without the knowledge they aren't alone in this world. Sure, they pray to a higher power or look to the sky and hope one day they'll see an alien, but when they find out these things are real, that something exists outside the world they know or see on TV, it drives them mad. I've dealt with the police before, and many of them live in a world of black and white, right and wrong, truth and lies. Trying to explain to them how there's so much they don't know or can't comprehend is a little like explaining quantum physics to a toddler.

All you get is a dumb look and drool.

Father Ted excuses himself and says he's going to call the detective in. As soon as he's out the door, Rouge turns to me and I see fear in her eyes.

"This isn't good, Dill," she says, and I can hear the tinge of panic in her voice.

"How so?"

"What if they check your apartment, or find out you're not even human. They could, right?"

"Yeah, I guess," I tell her, wishing more than ever that I'd explained to her more about me than I have; although I'm pretty sure she'd worry even more in that case. At least I've told her I'm not human. Well, I didn't really tell her. She heard the Hellion say it to me as he went about trying to kill me. I just admitted to it after the fact. I think that still counts though.

"You crashed your car on my neighbour's lawn. Normally not a big thing, but if they investigate you, aren't you worried what they could find? Seriously, you have a pretty messed up life."

"Don't stress out, Rouge. I've dealt with the cops before. Heck, I've even worked with them on cases. This will be no big deal." Well, I hope it won't. I give her a smile and hope it's convincing, but the fact is I'm not all that sure it'll be cut and dry. Sometimes, especially with certain types of law enforcement, you never can tell.

Less than a minute after Father Ted left, he's back, this time with a very stern faced man in an inexpensive suit. It's not cheap or ill fitting, but you can tell he's paid by the government somehow by the look of it. The man's hair is dark brown as are his eyebrows which are currently pushing down on his eyes as he gives me the once over. I've seen that same glare before, people who think I'm full of shit, the ones who call me despite the fact that they don't believe what I do is real. It's as though he's holding a sign in front of him that says *I'm not going to make this easy for you.*

When he turns his attention to Rouge, that hard look softens a bit and it's no wonder. People tend to take a look at her and see a walking bombshell. I see it all the time when we go out, eyes turning to her, many linger for longer than they should. They see the red hair, the pale skin, the hourglass figure and the very ample breasts and it's as though they can't control themselves. Males gawk, and so many women sneer. Rouge once laughed as a woman stared at her cleavage and made the nasties face at the sight, and asked the stranger if that grimace was because she was lactose intolerant. It was funny at the time, and usually I can just let it all slide. Not always though. Some days it really irks me. Not because they stare. To look at something nice or lovely is natural. It's the fact that so many only see her as a gorgeous woman and they have no idea that her beauty is only a small part of how amazing she really is. Her looks pale in comparison to how amazing and sweet she really is.

Some days, I sound like a real sap.

"Detective Garcia, this is Dillon," Father Ted says by way of introducing us. "I'm sure he can explain everything."

"Good," Garcia says with a low, mean voice that immediately makes me feel small and weak, as though I'm about to get scolded. "He better because I have way more important things to deal with than some drunk driving idiot who fancies himself..." He trails off as he looks at his notes. "It says *Monster Dick* on your card. What the hell's that? Are you a detective or some sort of porn guy?"

Great. This again.

"Neither really, but if you have to pick one, I'd guess you'd say I'm a private detective."

"Of monsters, right? I think I saw your flyer once."

"Monsters, spirits, demons. Anything that shouldn't be on this planet."

His eyebrow goes up and I know he's not buying it. This

guy is too stiff for it. I'm betting he wears tighty whities, has sock suspenders, listens to talk radio and has every book ever published by Rush Limbaugh. He's the dude who straight and narrow guys think is too uptight. I can look at his face and see that he wants to call out poppycock, or balderdash, or some other ridiculous word that only means bullshit, so I decide to stop him.

"It's not what you think. I've even done jobs for Father Ted and a few other churches. If you want, you can call me a spirit cleanser if it makes more sense to you."

"Sure. That's so much better. Do you work for the psychic network hotline on your days off too?" He laughs, but there's little humour in that sound. "Is that why you crashed the car then? Are you going to tell me you weren't drunk, that some monster or spirit was in the car with you and you were doing your impersonation of Ghostbusters with it? Come on pal. Don't give me any garbage here. Just be honest."

"It wasn't anything like that. I was jumped in the stairwell of my building and got hit in the back of the head by a junkie. Cracked me with a baseball bat. I didn't think it was that bad, but I wrapped it in an ice pack and with a bandana for a bit and then put some ointment on it before I headed over to Rouge's house. I didn't think it was that bad. I didn't feel sick or anything, only my head was throbbing. I seemed fine as I drove over and I was good right up until I sort of blacked out and crashed."

"A junkie, eh? Well, you don't live in the best of areas, so I guess that makes sense," he says, but he doesn't really sound convinced. Maybe he's the type to say he only believes what he sees.

"Weren't there any notes on a cut to the back of my head that doesn't make sense for the accident?" I ask, hoping that will show up and be enough for him.

Garcia flips through the papers, grumbling something to himself, but I know there's got to be something there. I wasn't drunk. The story I gave him is all true. I only left the Skell out of it to save time and having to explain it to him. There's no way this looks like a drunk driver issue, unless there is a problem with my blood test. That could be an issue. Even I don't know what would show up. What happens to human blood and DNA when a Treemor host is introduced to host body? I couldn't answer that on my best day.

"Junkie, hmm? Did you get a look at him or her?"

"Sort of. Male, five foot eight, bald head, light complexion and maybe a hundred and fifty pounds. He was wearing a green trench coat too."

"Fine. Not my department, so I don't really care," he says, and closed his folder quickly. I'm sure he's upset that he couldn't slam it shut as he clearly seemed to want to do. He appears to have some anger issues.

I also wonder about why he's here to do the interview. He just said that a junkie assaulting me wasn't his department, but I've never known of a detective that gets sent to interview possible drunk drivers. Usually they work in narcotics and homicide. This seems like it's more of a uniform cop's job than one for a detective. Grunt work.

"Come now, John. There's no need to be like that," Father Ted says gently, and puts a hand on the man's shoulder. "Dillon here is a good man. I know your current case is a burden and your bosses are a little mad at you right now, but there's no need to take it out on others. In fact, there's a chance Dillon could even be of some help. It's worth a shot."

Bingo. He's in trouble at work.

"Right?" He nearly chuckles and gives me a look that borders on disgust. "A guy who pretends to hunt monsters down is going to—"

"John! Remember what I said in counselling. Sometimes you have to ask for help. Not every problem in the world is on your shoulders alone."

So, the detective's in counselling. I wonder if it's for his marriage or if there's a little anger management there. I'm sure he could use both, though whatever Father Ted is doing seems to be helping very little. Especially if it's the latter. I've never seen someone who just has walking grump face as well as this guy does.

"Okay. Sure." Garcia pulls out his cellphone and starts flipping through some things. I can't see it so I'll just assume they're angry memes he uses to keep himself as chipper as he is. After a few more swipes, he turns the old iPhone towards me. "You ever see anything like this before?"

On the screen I see the outside of a house with something dark painted on the siding. I can barely make out what it is he wants me to see. As I squint, Garcia enlarges the picture and there's definitely something written on the wall. It looks like a letter or a symbol, but it's only vaguely familiar. I stare at it for a moment and I can feel the answer hidden somewhere in my memory. It's old, I know that much, but I can't put my finger on what it is. Something is tickling the back of my mind, but a tease is all I get and I feel a bit defeated.

It's hard. In my life I've seen and learned to read so many languages. Some are as easy to learn as Earth types, others are no more than colour variations that speak in ways words can't. Some languages are told in rock or structure forms, while others are told in drawings or symbols. There are millions of worlds and planes of existence and each one has their own way of communicating.

"Off hand, I'd say no," I say, reluctantly admitting defeat. "I don't know what it is, but, give me a day or two and I can probably find out."

"How?" Garcia asks, and there's the scepticism again.

"I have books and people who know things. If this is something real and not just kids trying to pretend to be into black masses, I'll find it for you."

"It's real all right," Garcia growls, and pulls his phone away. "Kids messing around don't steal kids from school playgrounds or their beds and leave things like that behind as a joke."

"Kids?"

"Yeah. Four so far. This is what we find at each of the scenes."

He looks at the screen of his phone and for the first time I see something other than anger or sternness. It's faint, but it's as clear to see as the throbbing in my head is to feel. The detective looks lost and sad, as though something was taken from him each time one of these children were taken. I get that. Even in my job there have been times when I didn't do what needed to be done right away and the results weighed heavy on me. Even with my recent bout up in Innisfil I had that happen. I watched a good man, a local sheriff, die and in the end I felt as though it was my fault. Somehow I'd failed him and the result of my failing was his death. It's a guilt that is hard to live with, but one I've come to know very well. We can't save them all, no matter how hard we try.

"I can't make you any promises, Detective, but at least I can try. And who knows, if I find something there's a chance of stopping any more kids getting taken or hurt. But it's up to you in the end. I'm willing to try."

He looks at me and even though his brows are down and he looks as though he's ready to punch something, he nods. "Anything is better than losing another one. Even if it means working with someone who calls himself a monster dick. Seriously, you ever think about changing that. It's not very PC."

"There's nothing really PC about me, Detective."

Friday

Rouge stayed with me overnight in my hospital room. Father Ted somehow managed to get her cleared to stay, which shows me just how awesome the man is. It's not every day a priest talks a doctor in letting your girlfriend spend the night, sharing a bed. Guess there's nothing in the bible about that particular sin.

The doctor told me I have a pretty serious concussion and some bad bruising on my shoulder. To help me sleep he gave me some drugs, but I don't bother with them. The pain was hard to sleep through, but aside from a few shots of some hard stuff here and there, I find it best to keep my senses about me. These days it feels more important than ever.

When I wake up it's already morning. Rouge is beside me, her arm draped over my chest and it feels so good it's hard to disturb her stillness and wake her up. I lay here for a while, just looking at her and feeling her breath on me and I can't help but smile. I don't think I've ever felt so happy with anyone. All these years since I first came to Earth, living as a loner, I forgot what it felt like to be this close to anyone. For a while, my life was a lot like Mister Rogers. All my friends were make believe.

Oh, there's Godfrey, but how good of a friend is he really. That relationship has had more ups and downs than a rollercoaster. He's ripped me off on more accounts than I have fingers and a few of those times have nearly cost me my life. Then again, he's also given me items I could never do without like my gloves, my Tincher, and a few others that have saved my ass. He's a strange and complicated man, but to class him as a friend is a tricky thing I'd rather just avoid altogether. In a pinch, I guess I would say he was one of the only real friends outside of Father Ted and now Rouge, but that's not saying much. I wouldn't trust him further than I can throw him and he outweighs me by fifty or sixty pounds.

Rouge is nothing like that. She's a beautiful, smart and lovely woman. She's the kind of person you'd look forward to seeing at the end of every day, the one you want to rush home and be with. She's silly, serious and super smart all at once. There's also the fact that she has an affinity for horror movies and comic books, which only makes her cooler than I can ever claim to be, and I'm pretty awesome. The fact that she stayed with me last night, even though she could have gone home and slept in a nice bed with her little puppy curled close to her proves the type of person she is.

I don't want to wake her. She looks so peaceful here on me, but like a hotel, check out is at eleven sharp. I shift a little and she opens her eyes and looks at me. Her smile is enough to make me feel better. I sit up a bit and give her one back.

"How you feeling?" she asks, and moves her hand lightly across my face.

"A bit better," I admit, and it's true. My head's still pounding, but for the most part it's less than it was when I went to bed. "When I get home I'll have one of my baths and that should do the trick."

I have a special concoction at home. It's a strange mix of fluids, salts and things not really of this world. Lay in a bath of that and water and within a day I can heal gunshot wounds, stabs, cuts or other injuries including dismemberment. Aside from getting my head cut off or a hole blown straight through me, I would be right as rain after a healing bath. She's seen this first hand.

"I hope so. Especially since you're going to go help that cop out with the kids. That kind of stuff is terrifying."

"I hope I can do something, but it doesn't really sound like my line of work."

"Sure, but you have connections, right?"

"A few," I say, and think about the ones I know. There's

Godfrey, a man not of this world either who is a bit of an encyclopaedia when it comes to that kind of stuff. There are a few other people I've met over the years; scholars, nerds, and dark souls who tend to hide in shadowy places and read books about things of nightmares and impossibilities. One of them should be able to help me in this, which will maybe in turn assist me in making another connection in the police department. "I'm sure someone will be able to lend a hand and stop whoever is doing this."

"Good. I had nightmares over it. Just the thought of some kid being snatched up when they feel safe and taken who knows where and subject to who knows what is scary as Hell."

Rouge reaches over and wraps her arms around me and I move closer for a hug. I need it as much as she does.

"Sorry about the date," I add, whispering in her ear.

"You should be. The things I had planned for you. Guess it just wasn't your day. Poor you."

"What things?"

"If I tell you," she says with a smile, "you'll only feel worse over it all. But trust me; it was going to be a hell of a night for you, Mr. Monster Hunter!"

I bet it would've.

After a few more words and a kiss or two, we get out of bed and get changed. I'll be glad to get out of here, and I'm sure she will too. There's nothing very comfortable or romantic about having to spend the night together in a plastic wrapped, adjustable bed. I still feel a little woozy and my head feels like it's pounding with each beat of my heart, but I'll feel better once I get to breath some fresh air and take a nice, long healing bath.

We walk out of the hospital and standing in the emergency driveway is Detective Garcia. He's leaning against an older, tan sedan and drinking a coffee. He's scowling at everyone walking past him. He looks them up and down as if he's assessing them, judging them for whatever reason. He seems so miserable; a true curmudgeon. When his eyes meet mine he looks even less cheerful, which I wouldn't have thought was possible. I point him out to Rouge.

"Oh yeah, Mr. Chipper," she whispers, and as we get closer she smiles the fakest smile I've ever seen. "Hello, detective. Did you miss Dillon?"

"Not even close. I was told you were getting out and since time is a little of the essence I figured I'd stop by to give you the case file." Garcia goes into the open window of the car and pulls out a small, beige file folder. He rifles through it, as though he needs to check the contents and make sure it's the right one. Not sure if he's doing that for my benefit, Rouge's, or it's just an affectation. Whatever the reason he soon sees everything is in order and holds it out to me. "Please don't share this with anyone. The things in there are sensitive, items we haven't even released to the press. That's in case —"

"In case people call in and try to take credit for the kidnappings. I get it. It helps weed out the false calls from the potential suspects." Hey, I've spent enough time watching Law and Order and The Wire to get how these things work. TV has taught me so much in my life. I don't share that with him though.

I can see cutting him off or acting as though I already know the deal has upset him. Then again, I think the colour blue and cute puppies might make him look the same way. Such a sour puss. I'd love to see this guy in a bar drinking. I think after six or seven he might even get more severe, working the opposite it would on most people. I take the file and go to walk away.

"You two need a ride anywhere?" he asks, and at first I'm about to say no, that I'm fine driving myself home. That's when I remember I don't have my car here. In fact, I may not have a car at all if the tree won the fight I put the old brute through. I'll have to ask Rouge about that when he drops us off.

"Sure," I say, taking the offer.

"I'd love to, Dillon, but I have to go pick the puppy up. My friend's watching her and she lives just up the street. She'll drive me home after I'm sure." I see the look on Rouge's face right away and know there's no friend close to here watching her dog. Normally she'd just leave the little puffball with her neighbour, not bring it all the way down here when she was coming to see me. I don't blame her either. A car ride with Mister Sunshine should be a delight.

"Maybe I can come with you then?" I say, and hear Garcia huff as though this is boring him somehow.

"I'd say yes, but she doesn't know you and to tell you the truth, you look like hell. I'd rather not this be the way my friend meets you for the first time." I'm almost insulted, but then I look down at myself. My clothes are wrinkled, there's blood on my pants and shirt, so I can see what she means. Not the best way to be introduced. Though, it now means going in a car with the grump Garcia and no doubt listening to talk radio or better yet, some self-help tapes. Oh, how much fun can one person have in a day? "Plus, I bet you and the detective here have a lot of stuff to talk about that my ears shouldn't hear."

"You coming?" Garcia all but barks at me and I'm so tempted to say no, I'd rather walk all the way home naked, but I really need to get back to my place and do something about the way I feel.

"You sure you don't want to come with me and Chuckles?" I whispered to Rouge as I give her a hug.

"I'd be happy to say yes, but I think you two could use some alone time. And I'd rather be stuck on public transit than in there with him." She chuckles.

"I figured as much. I'll see you later then?"

"Not soon enough."

I turn and begin to get into Garcia's car then call out to Rouge.

"Miss me already?" she calls back.

"How bad is my car?"

"It's not that bad," she says, and for a second I breathe a sigh of relief. "That is, if you like a front end that looks like an accordion."

I feel a cold hand in my stomach. My poor car. I never even took the time to give it a name. It seemed like a silly tradition at the time, but now that it's gone I feel bad for not taking the time to do it. It was a good, reliable one, lasting nearly fifteen years and that's the longest I've ever owned anything. I'm going to have to get a new car now, something I'm not really looking forward to. Car sales people are usually worse to deal with than monsters, but I guess I'll deal with it later.

I say goodbye again to Rouge and get in the detective's car. It smells so clean in here. From the outside I was expecting a mess and the stale odour of cigarettes, onions and patchouli. The outside of it is covered in a layer of dust and there's thin lines of rust veining along the sides near the bottom. It comes off as someone who uses it a lot, but doesn't take the time to give it the care it needs and deserves. So, to me the expectation was a matching inside. Instead it smells like cleaner and air freshener and has the appearance of a car that's vacuumed every day. The seats are spotless and there isn't a speck of dust on the dash. The only thing in there that didn't come with the car is a rosary, which hangs from his rear-view mirror. Very nice. I wish I could say the same for my dearly departed vehicle. That interior was a mad disarray of old coffee cups and receipts as well as some blankets and bags of things I don't even remember buying. This is a great example of how different the two of us are. This should be even more fun than I thought.

As we pull out of the hospital, there are a few moments of uncomfortable silence, and then it starts.

Question time.

"So, how did you and Big Red there meet?" he asks, and pulls into traffic, already knowing where he's going since he has my address.

"On the job. And her name's Rouge, not Big Red."

"Oh, sorry. No offense. Not that Rouge Hills is her real name anyway. Do you even know it?"

"Of course. She just prefers Rouge, so that's what I call her," I say, and think that I have a lot in common with her. Nobody calls me by my real name either.

"It's a good stripper name." He all but laughs as he says it, though the words are more mean than humorous.

"Look, if you want my help like you say, maybe you can kill the disrespect," I say, and am a little more than irritated. I'm pissed off. I don't appreciate his tone or the asshole-ish way he's coming off talking about her. He doesn't even know her, or me for that matter. "First, she's not a stripper, she's a burlesque dancer. There *is* a difference. How would you like it if I say you're pretty much a meter maid or an over-paid security guard?"

He nods and from the stern face I see something I'm guessing is his form of regret. "Sorry about that. I'm normally not this much of a prick. Sometimes, cases like this just eat away at me and get under my skin. Can we pretend like I never said any of that just now?"

"Sure," I say, but I'm not so convinced that he's not an asshole on a good day.

Then again, I guess it's a good enough reason for the crap coming out of his mouth. Stress can do crazy things to people. I haven't even had a chance to look at the file, but the fact that Father Ted brought him to me means something. I go back quite a ways with the priest, close to ten years in all. He called me out of the blue, long before I'd set up my website and said he'd gotten my name from Godfrey and that alone had me intrigued. The old seller of strange goods had never once sent me a client, so why this one, and why a Catholic priest of all things. Before then, I had rarely had any dealings with religious groups, and never once a Catholic.

Father Ted claimed there was some sort of porthole in the basement of the church he'd been asked to take over. It was just opening, but wasn't actually new. It was to him, but far from new in the grand scheme of things. The grey stone building had been constructed back in the late 1890's in the High Park area of the city. Set off a side street, the church had been shut down during the 1940's when three nuns were found in the basement carved up and naked. It was a gruesome story I read after meeting Ted and it haunted me a little. One of the local papers posted pictures of one of the dead women, laying in a bare, dirt-floored room in the lower level of the gothic structure. It was no wonder the place had been closed down. Who would want to be in the same place as those who'd been murdered in such a terrible way?

Yet, like the pages of the newspaper, memories fade with time and one day in the early 2000's, the higher ups decided it would be a good idea to re-open the place. A crew went in and cleaned it up, but as I said before, tragedy is a great way to weaken the thin wall between this realm and other worlds. Soon after the doors were open, Father Ted and a few others began to see things. At first he thought it was nothing more than a trick of the shadows, being under-slept and in a new place. It didn't take much longer for him to see differently.

What happened in the church years before, an unknown assailant assaulting and brutalizing such innocent souls, not only weakened the veil, but attracted the worst of the worst. What came through was not the spirit or soul of some creature or entity looking for a better life, one trying to escape pain and torture. This type of horror left a stain, a scent that attracted the lowest of the low in the demon world. It called to and opened up for a beast known as a Wredth. In demonology—which gets some things right, but not much—these would be known as low-level demons; bottom feeders. Nothing in the ether world cares for or respects a Wredth, and neither do I. These things love blood, violence and all things rotten. The one I found in there was small and twisted and had made her body up of old tree roots she called forth from the earth floor of the cellar.

She was hungry and had been going up to the church to try and feed off the parishioners. She'd hide under pews and scrape their ankles and then lick the blood from her gnarled, makeshift fingers. As soon as I heard the story I knew what I was up against and this time, unlike so many others, I was right. I'd brought the right tools for the job and went at her without a thought.

I went into her place, into the cellar of the church and told Father Ted to wait upstairs. I found her hiding, partially buried in the dark, terrible smelling earth where the nuns had once been laid out and offended. I used a Cufter to pry her from the ground. This is a tool made for her kind. To someone who might find one, it looks a little like an old metal fan blade with three triangular grooves taken from it. She screamed as the curse metal touched her and I yanked her out. Soil rained down from her body as she struggled and cursed in a language most humans never have to hear. I pulled out another weapon, a bottle of yellow water that is believed to have come from the pools between life and death.

As soon as she saw it, she calmed down.

"Please, sire, I do no more wrongs," she pleaded, and held her hands together as if praying to me. "I am Middia, and I only want to stay in this rich earth and smell the spilled blood of the Jesus witches."

"Shut your mouth, demon!" I barked, and uncorked the bottle of vile smelling liquid. It looks like it'll come close to being a urine type smell, but it's closer to that of very unwashed feet and spices. Either way, it smelled horrid.

"No. Don't send me back to the ether place. I will stay and help you hunter. I can be thy side kicker."

"Right," I said, and stepped forward. "It's a nice offer, but I work alone."

"I can make dreams come true for you, give you lusty things. I just need to call a new form. A soft, wet one for you to find satisfaction. Let me stay and a play thing you will have for life."

I cringed right then and there. I'm pretty sure I nearly puked at the idea of it. The only thing that helped was when I tipped the bottle over her and poured it on the nasty little demon. The thick liquid spread over her, false flesh bubbled and popped and filled the air in the basement with the acrid odour of burnt hair and garbage. Her screams echoed in the small room. I let her drop from my hands and thrash about on the ground. She was coming as close to dying as she can in this world. It's something like death, but it does no more than send her back to the ether world.

"My Lord, Dillon, is this what you do?"

The sound of the priest's voice nearly scared me to death and I spun around. He stood there on the shadowy stairs, his cross clenched so tight in his hand his knuckles glowed white. His eyes were not on me though. They were on the Wredth who was dying on the floor in front of me. He looked horrified, confused and disgusted.

"You shouldn't be here," I told him plainly, and looked down to make sure it was still going the way it should. No problems there.

"And what of that? Should it be here?" he asked, and stepped off the stairs and made as if he wanted to come over. I held I hand up to him to warn him to stay back for the moment.

"No. That's why I'm sending the damned thing home."

I turn back towards the dissolving demon and see there is no way for her to come back to life anymore. The roots that once held together to form what resembled her body had begun to fall apart and at that point she was no longer in this realm. Mud and loose earth oozed and fell from the form and pooled under the collapsed body. It was one of my favourite types of job; fast and easy. Any case where I walk away without a scratch is a good one in my book. I'm not always so lucky.

Behind me, I heard footsteps and knew it was the priest.

"Don't you have any pity for them?" the priest asked from behind me as I kicked apart the past of her remains.

"I can't have pity for them, Father. I have a job to do. These things that find their way through are breaking the law and I'm here to send them home. If I let them stay here, not only am I breaking the rules, but I'm risking so much to how this planet is. It's a simple as that. There's no time or place for sympathy or apathy in my line of work."

"There's always time, son. Everything in God's world deserves understanding and pity," he said, and his voice was low and solemn.

I couldn't understand how he could feel bad for something like the fallen thing before me. It was the equivalent of the devil, a demon who represented evil spoken about in his own Bible. Catholics can be a strange group at times.

"You'd think so," I tried to explain, "but these aren't creatures of the God you pray to. There's nothing natural about them. Some seem harmless and pathetic, sure, but they're not. Think of what they could do to the faith of your flock alone."

He considered the words and then shook his head as though he couldn't see my point. "We all know evil exists."

"That's just it, Father, not all these things I send off are evil. Some are children, others are parents. Some of these things were tortured and abused back where they come from. They come here to escape, to get away from it. Others come here because they imagine it's a better place than their own home. Many of them just want to come here because they're told they can't. Sure, there are evil ones like the demon I just got rid of for you, but that's not all that's out there." I walked across the compact dirt and stood in front of him, wanting to get this across to him even better than I could. "If people here find out about these other worlds and planes, most will question everything they know. How can one God exist when there are millions of different worlds and dimensions out there? How unimportant would they all feel if they came to realize they're not alone in this universe, but they're no more than a speck in the grand scheme of things? How does it make you feel knowing that?"

He was silent and even though I hated telling him the way I did, he'd already seen too much. Most people can't handle the truth of it all, but when someone sees a demon dispatched or nearly gets gutted by a monster made up of bog moss, you might as well take the kid gloves off and give it to them straight.

"So, you're saying my belief is nothing, that I'm wrong in all of it? Is every follower of God, Buddha, Allah wrong in what they choose to believe?" he said, and I hated that he jumped to that right off the bat.

"I'm not saying anything like that, Father. We all need faith in something. Never let that go. Faith is a good thing. So many people sleep better with the idea that something bigger than them is keeping watch, and they're not wrong. There's something out there. Just believe that and you'll be fine. Even if it's different from what you picture in your mind, doesn't make it any less real. If a child is born and smells a rose, maybe they get an image of what it looks like and that's enough to make them happy. Do they need to be told they're wrong, that a rose looks different than they think it does? Does it make it any less real? Not at all."

After that, we went up to the rectory and had some tea and talked for hours. We spoke about the universe, spirituality and belief. I told him bits about myself, but nothing of how inhuman I was. That might've been too much for him to absorb. We really hit it off and I decided to stop by twice a month just to have tea and chat with him. He never spoke to anyone else about me, promised not to say what he'd seen in the basement. There were other cases at the church after that. He'd call me right away, but he never came around when I was at work. I'm sure seeing one demon was more than enough for him.

In all that time, there'd never been a time when he passed on anything outside that church that might interest me. I know I've done jobs for some of the people that go to his church, but none of them were sent to me by Father Ted. I don't know if people never spoke to him about it, or if he just didn't want to share my particular talents with his flock. Either way, for him to have told Detective Garcia about me meant this was something he felt was important, or at least that's how I take it. Breaking secrets isn't something Father Ted is known for.

Instead of flipping through the file right then and there, I decide to ask the detective himself about the case. I could get some details from the pages, but I want more than that. I want to hear how it affects this man, how deep the crime runs. Just from the sound of his voice I will be able to pick up more of the severity than I ever will from the folder sitting on my lap. There are details in this no doubt, but I want more than that. I want to get a sense of how the case is taking a toll on the detective.

"Can you give me a brief rundown of what I'm going to be looking at when I read this?" I ask.

"There's nothing really brief about this, but sure. When I spoke at the hospital, I held a lot of it back. I didn't want to say too much in front of the Father, or your lady friend."

"I'm sure I'll appreciate that."

"Oh, you will. Trust me," he said, and I could see that stern look returning to his face. "The first case was about a month ago. A young boy, five years old, was stolen from his own bed. His window was wide open. The perp pried it open with some sort of tool, and then climb through and snatched the kid. There was some weird stuff on the ground, almost like slime, and outside the window. Lab says most of it is human waste, mixed with some other fluids, but there's nothing really definitive there. On the side of the house was this symbol or pattern. It looked like it was written in grease. There was also blood on the floor in the kid's room, his blood type. We found nothing really of use, aside from the blood. The symbol is meaningless, the grease was from the boiled fat of a cow.

"The second abduction happened three days later. This one was a girl, nine years old, taken from a school playground right next door to where she lived. Parents let her go play in the park and when they went to get her thirty minutes later, she was gone. More of the slimy stuff was found on the scene and the symbol in grease was under one of the slide. No blood found, but her shoe was found half a mile away with blood on it. No witnesses to any of it.

"The next two were more of the same. One was taken from his mom's car as she ran into the grocery store. She left her six-year-old daughter in the car with their Labrador. When she got back, the dog was dead and the girl was gone. Side of the car was smeared with the slime and the symbol was on the outside of the passenger's side door. After that, same day, another boy was taken, this time from his babysitter's house. Just like the others. All this in less than a month. No hair, no fibres, just this nonsense that makes me feel like we're chasing our tails. I don't think I've ever been so frustrated in my life."

Now I get the stern look on his face all the time. He's been soured by the case. You can hear it with every word, feel the anger and hopelessness pouring out of him. I know it can't be easy, but I have to hope there'll be something I can do to help him. So far it all sounds strange. It has the tinge of something ritualistic, but nothing I'd ever heard of. Some of the things that really stump me are the symbols and the slime. I have no idea what either of these pieces of evidence mean.

"Well, I will get a hold of people I know right away and hopefully I'll be able to have something for you in a day or two."

"I won't hold my breath," he says solemnly, and pulls over to the curb. I saw I was home. "Want me to walk you upstairs, in case there's another junkie waiting to jump you in the stairs again?"

"I think I'll manage."

"I'm sure you will," he says, and for a moment I feel as though he isn't buying the story I'd given him. It wasn't a lie really, so I'm a little offended.

"Hey, I'd invite you up, but I never put out on the first date," I joke, as I do my best to make light of his distrust.

"Sure, joker. How about you just get out of my car and call me when you get something I can use. If you can at all. I won't hold my breath."

I step out of the car and nearly slam the door, but hold back. I'm not going to let him get to me. Maybe I can help him with the case and he'll be less of a dick. That'd be nice.

"My number is in the file. Call when you get anything," he says, and before I can say anything, he's driving off. I'm not going to hold back the hope that he'll be less of a dick. Hard case or no, he needs to learn some manners.

I take more Advil and have one of my special baths. What I put in the water are things of this world and more that are not. After a two-hour soak and meditation in the healing waters, I feel a little better, but my head is still a bit of a wreck. It's fine if I'm sitting still and keep my eyes and head facing forward, but if I bend over or turn too quickly the throbbing returns along with a little bit of vertigo. Not good. Usually the bath heals almost anything. I guess this is the first concussion I've ever had. It sucks.

I put on some clothes and sit down with a coffee and some music as I look over the file Garcia gave me. It's grim reading, but there's not much new here. What Garcia told me on the drive over is more than enough. The only thing I can get out of this are the photos. There are clear pictures of the symbol and some of the slime at different crime scenes. Then I get to the heartbreaking ones; blood in the kid's room, the dead dog and the lost shoe. There's also one of a blue blanket laying on a lawn with blood on it and after reading a little more I see this is from the babysitter's house; it was the little boy's favourite blankie. I'm not really used to this. Part of me thinks I'm not really cut out for it. Normally I deal with monsters and creatures from other worlds, beasts in horrific looking forms. Hell, I even fought a giant, tentacle monster without batting an eye. But this kind of thing is way out in left field for me and is not really my forte. This is some vile crap that makes my hairs stand on end. Leave it to a human to show me what a real monster is.

I pick up my cell and dial a number I have stored. It's picked up on the second ring.

"What you need now, Dillon?" Godfrey asks with his thick Jamaican accent, despite the fact that he's not even from this planet. I've always wondered if the accent came with the form or if it's a bit of a put on so he seems more human than he is.

"I don't need anything really. I want to stop by and show you something. You're a fountain of information. I know you love the Earthly occult stuff, so who better to ask than my good friend?"

"Mon, you're so full of shit, you're teeth are turning brown. Why you buttering me up so much? Is this some kind of joke you want to pull on me?"

"No joke here. I'm helping some people out. Let me just say that some sick people are out there and the people hunting them down are looking for some help."

There's a pause and I knew there would be. He's considering what I'm saying because he could get in trouble for it. We both could.

"Look, Mon, I'm not looking to go start anything with actual humans." His voice is low and serious, something I'm not used to. It's almost as though he's actually afraid of what it is I might want help with, and in a way, I can guess why. "You best not either. Hunting down humans is not allowed. I don't need that kind of heat on me, Dillon."

"Don't worry," I say, and hope to make him feel better. I know the rules about getting involved in human affairs or even hunting one down, so that's not what this is. I need him to know it's all good on my end if I want him to help me with this. "I'm only consulting for this one. Helping out an old friend and a cop I'm hoping I can use as a resource later on."

"Oh, fuck the police!" he blurts out in a near growl. "Assholes come here every now and then and call me voodoo man, or devil worshipper! The devil worships me, not the other way around."

He laughs at that and I go along with it.

"I'm sure he does. So, can I stop by and just ask you your expert opinion? Maybe this guy can help get the uniformed a-holes to lay off you too?"

"I'm sure he won't, but for a good customer like my friend Dillon, I will do what I can. When will you stop by?"

"Fifteen minutes. I need to get a cab."

"You ain't driving that old shit box?"

"Afraid not. My car is no longer part of this world," I tell him, and feel something close to sadness and loss at the thought of my long, lost baby.

"Ashes to ashes and all that. More like good riddance. That thing was an eyesore and a death trap."

"Yeah, well, I liked it and that's all that mattered. I'll see you soon, Godfrey," I say, and hang up. How dare he insult my car. It was a classic. That thing had been with me for longer than anything else in this world. It had seen me though countless jobs, meals and many a lonely night. It knew my favourite radio stations and I knew all of the bumps and curves of it's less than perfect body. Now, it's gone and I feel sad to know I'll never see it again.

In a way, that car was my first love. So if Godfrey keeps it up, I may have to put a foot up his ass and teach him not to speak ill of the dead.

The cab I take smells like sour milk and Cool Ranch Doritos. I like eating those chips, but man do they have a funk to them and this cab is ten times worse than that. I open the window to try to breathe some fresh air, but all that comes in is the exhaust of other cars and I start to miss my old beauty even more. At least it was my own kind of stink and I had A/C.

On the way I text Rouge and tell her I hope everything went well picking up the pup and I hope to see her soon. She sends one back almost instantly saying she can't wait and not to work too hard. She then asks how the ride with Garcia was and I tell her it was more fun than an open casket funeral. She isn't surprised.

The cab pulls up to the curb and I quickly hand him the cash and get the hell out of there. I worry for a second that I'm going to bring the odour with me, but luckily I'm safe. I don't smell like old sneakers filled with stale chips.

I walk over to Godfrey's store, if that's what you want to call it. It's pretty nondescript. There's no sign over the door, no way to look in and see what to expect. Today he has dirty sheets hanging in the window and another covering the glass to the door leading inside. You'd think it was an empty space, somewhere waiting to be leased, but that's the way he runs it. Back when I first met him I thought he just wanted to be left alone, but he explained he goes it to keep all the lookie-loos out. Even so, there have been plenty of times I've gone in there to find some hipster or other lost soul getting ripped a new one for coming in and wasting Godfrey's time. He has little patience even on his best day.

There's a brass bell over the door that jingles a strange tone as I enter and within seconds the tall man with a huge frame comes out, looking as menacing as ever. Lucky for me, I'm someone he wants to see so a smile unravels on his face, shining overly white teeth at me. He walks towards me, arms outstretched and hands open.

"Dillon, my favourite customer, and as you said, my good friend. I like the idea of being friends with a man like you." He embraces me and his squeeze is so tight, he makes my head start to throb again. Just when I thought it was going away too. Thanks for that, buddy. "We are friends, right? You weren't just buttering me up? Hoping to get something from me for free?"

"Damn right we're friends, but I'd appreciate a little less in the way of anaconda hugs," I say, nearly gasping.

"Of course, of course," he says, and laughs as he lets me go so I can breathe again. I take in a long deep breath and the room grows dim for a second, and then brightens to the way it should be. I hope this goes away soon. This is getting ridiculous. "You must still be in pain after the attack and the accident."

"How did you know that?"

"How does the wind know to blow? How does water know to be wet? Things just are. I have a way of hearing about things. You should know that by now Dillon, especially if you're my friend."

He does have a knack for finding things out that he has no right knowing. I have no idea how either. The man not only runs this store, but is kind of imprisoned here. He's not actually allowed to leave it. Godfrey once did some very bad things in the worlds beyond this one, and this store, this placement was where he was sentenced to spend many centuries. He's trapped in here, like a prisoner, but he still has arms and ears that reach out and gather not only items I need and he wants for his collections, but information. I'm sure it helps him pass the time.

"I guess so. How've you been?" I ask.

"As good as I can, no more, no less. But enough of this. I have a special guest coming to see me soon, so we should keep this as quick as possible. Friend or not, my next appointment is a little shy."

I'm curious, but I know better than to ask. He loves his secrets and his privacy. I'm the only hunter he works with since I'm the one who works this sector of the world, but he has dealings with a lot of others. Some bring him items I end up using, others obtained illegal items to Earth, which he collects. I'm sure he also has his fingers into other things that might be even worse, but it's not my business what he does here. As long as he doesn't ever burn me again like he did in the past, or leave here, he's good to go in my books. If he were to go out of these walls, then I guess the friendship I offered him would be over. He'd be just like any other that shouldn't be here.

Hunted.

"So," I begin, and hand the folder to him. "There are four missing kids, presumed dead, but none of their bodies have been found as of yet so there's no way to know if they're dead or alive. Investigators didn't find very much evidence at the scenes other than some blood that was from the kids, slimy stuff that looks like human waste, and a symbol drawn in cow fat. Looks ritualistic in a way, but I'm not sure. There's something familiar about it, but I can't put my finger on it. What do you think?"

He's got all the photos out and I see a look on his face. Even though he's intently staring at the pictures, I can see it clear as day. It looks like a mix of concern and worry; maybe something bordering on fear even. I can tell he already knows what it is, but he keeps flipping through the pictures, back and forth. He won't look up at me. So much for being in a hurry. I guess he'll keep his next client waiting until he has the balls to look up.

"Spill it, Godfrey," I say, and he shoots a glance at me.

""What do you mean?" he says, and even though he's playing coy, I can hear a slight shake to his voice.

"I know you recognize it. Your eyes went all shifty as soon as you looked down at the one with the symbol on it. So, tell me what it is so I can pass it on to the cops and be done with it."

"I might know what it is, but it doesn't make sense. Even if it's what I think it is, you need to drop this now. This goes beyond you."

I don't like the way that sounds.

"Just tell me. I have a cop worried and wanting answers. I'd like to give him something at least. If it's a cult group, he needs to stop them before any more kids get nabbed. If it's something more than that, maybe he can be better prepared to go after it."

He slams the folder shut and pushes it at me hard. He starts to shake his head and mumbles something under his breath. I can't make out what it is, but whatever he knows is not a good thing. I still need it though. Anything would help at this point.

"Come on, Godfrey. I thought we were friends." I can see right away that those words get to him and he slumps a little.

"You aren't going to like this, Dillon. I know you well enough. But you can't pursue this thing. It's bad enough you're dating a human. That's a huge law to break. This will just be the straw that breaks the camel's back. If I tell you this, it's going to get you moving down a path that will get you exiled from Earth and maybe imprisoned somewhere far worse than this store."

I'm more than curious now. I already knew I could be in all kinds of trouble for dating Rouge. The higher ups have a whole set of rules for beings like Godfrey and hunters like myself. We are all here for a reason, a purpose and one thing we are never supposed to do is get involved with or have sex with any human or other creature which originated here. I know the law and am fully aware of the consequences that could include being yanked from the planet and locked in a deep dark hole in the coldest reaches of space. Sure, I know this very well, but I know other things too. The main one being that I am a good hunter, maybe one of the better ones. I hold onto host bodies given to me longer than most, have a great capture rating and after finding and closing a porthole in the middle of Lake Simcoe, I think I've earned a few Brownie points with them. The fact that I'm still here tells me this.

So what else could I be threatened by?

"All right, Godfrey, you have me interested. Spill the beans."

"Come to the back with me," he says, and I follow him through a curtain of beads to a room more expansive than the store. Incenses burns all over the place and the air is so thick with rich smoke that it's almost hard to breathe. "Sit down while I find something."

I look around and see only two chairs. One is huge and ornate; something an old king of England would look right at home in. It's behind a desk so I assume that one is Godfrey's. Over across the room is another, small and less impressive chair, which is leaning against a wall painted black. I grab it and pull it over to the desk just as he comes back with a huge book in his hand. I sit down and he drops the book. The weight gives it an impressive sound and dust flies up from it. Godfrey drops himself in his throne and looks about as happy as a man who just found out he's dying.

He flips through the book and then asks for the picture of the symbol.

"I knew it was the same," he says, and turns the book to me. "Do you see it?"

I look and there's no doubt it's the same. A weird hooked cross surrounded by two circles. The book looks old so I'm guessing the symbol is too. There's no writing on this page, so I have no idea what the thing means.

"So, that's the symbol. What does it mean?"

"What does it mean? You don't know what this is at all, do

you? My spirit, Dillon, you need to do more research on this planet, Mon."

"If I did, I wouldn't be here. So, what is it?"

"It's the sign of the Golgotha," he says, as though I know what the hell he's talking about. I clearly don't. Name doesn't even ring the smallest bell, so I shrug. "Didn't you study any of the old Earth lore before you came here, or after even?"

"I guess I missed this one. I know what a Leprechaun is, an Igopogo, a golem, and a few others, but not this one, so enlighten me."

"A Golgotha is a demon born from rot and human filth, but not from another realm like anything you've dealt with before. This is an earthbound demon, a creature called forth and born here of human waste and decay."

"You mean an earthbound demon made up of piss, shit and rotting flesh? That's what stole these kids?"

"Usually they're just made up of shit, but yes, the others too. The first one was called forth during the death of Christ. At the foot of the crosses of all those crucified on the hill the first was born. A witch, a follower of Christ cursed those who killed her Lord and called forth the unspeakable demon. It rose from the piles of rotted blood, piss and shit, and then killed the Roman soldiers who had tortured the God Prince."

"So, what you want me to believe, or whoever is writing the symbol really, is that a Golgotha has been called by someone to rise up and steal kids? Sorry for the pun, but that sounds like a load of shit, Godfrey. When was the last time someone did anything like that?"

"There's no record of anything like that, but the symbol, the slime as you call it, it all points to a Golgotha."

"How would anyone know how to call one up though? There's no hills of the crucified anymore. Is there even anyone who'd have the skills to bring one of these demons back?"

"There are all kinds that could, and so many other ways than the way the first one was called. Just leave it alone, Dillon. You know you can't do anything about this. Go and tell the police you're sorry, but there's nothing you can do. Don't even make mention of the demon to them at all or you may cross a line you can never come back from."

"I can at least tell him what you think it is that took the kids."

"What good would it do? If you involve yourself in this, you run the risk of breaking one of the biggest laws set up for you to follow. You must never kill any earthbound creatures, or even have a hand in one dying. It's the law."

"I've done it before. When I was up north alone I killed things that had turned into zombies after they ate Gloudian flesh."

"They weren't human any longer when you did that, Dillon. They'd changed, became something not of this earth. A Golgotha is not the same thing. Go after it and there will be a price to pay. Even if you assist the police with information you can be violating it and in turn, I will be too for telling you. It may not be just your life and freedom on the line, but mine as well."

I get what he's saying, I really do, but there are other things to consider here. I'm not going to only think about myself in this one. There are kids out there that could still be in danger, ones that feel nice and safe now, but could be the next victim for this demon. Or maybe there's something else, or someone else behind it. Does the demon have to be called forth like the first one, or can they rise up on their own? I ask him that very question.

"They can't do it on their own. They need someone to call them forth."

"So what are the chance that there won't be any more victims, that the person calling the demon forth or the demon itself will just up and go away on their own?" I'm hoping there will be an answer I like, though as soon as the words leave my lips I can see there won't be.

It figures.

"They're low. As long as the person who's conjured the demon keeps doing so, it can just go on and on. Sorry, Dillon."

Well, that seals it for me. There's no way I can allow this to go on. I'm not really thinking of hunting down some shit demon and dispatching it, that's not really ideal. I know there could be some serious repercussions if I were to kill this thing, assuming I could even figure out how to without any tools from Godfrey.

Without his help, I wouldn't even ask for it if I was going to do it, there's no saying what tools and weapons I would need to get rid of the smelly thing. Assuming it stinks, seeing as what it's made of.

But I can't not tell Garcia about this and that what he's dealing with might be bigger than a nut job with an occult fetish. I know he'll have that look on his face that says *Dillon, you're full of shit*, but he needs to know; no matter what I suffer after this. I may be a selfish ass in so many ways, but I don't dig the idea of kids being hurt by anything. I'm going to chance it, no matter what.

"I wonder what's going on in that pea brain of yours, Dillon? No doubt you're thinking of some way to tell the detective or of even hunting the demon yourself. Am I right?"

"You know me so well, Godfrey. I guess that's why we're such good friends. And as a friend, I could use some advice I could pass on to the cop on how to kill this thing." I smile, but there is no humour on the man's face. In the years and years I've known him, I've never seen such rage on the man's face.

"I'm not getting taken from here," he growls, and balls his hands into fists. "There are worse punishments than being trapped in this store for an eternity, you know. You're not the only one to think of here."

"That's the point. I'm not just thinking about me. I'm thinking about the kids who are going to be killed if I sit on my hands and do nothing."

"No! I won't allow it!"

At this, Godfrey jumps up from his throne and there's something in his hand. I'm out of my chair before I even see the jagged blade rising into the air. I back away as he comes around the desk. I have no idea if he means to scare me or split me in two, but I need to get out of the store and fast.

"Put the sword down, buddy. You know I'm not going to do anything to get you in trouble."

"You think they'll know that, or that they'll believe you if you vouch for me? Look where I am, Dillon. Stuck millions of miles away from my home, my family and for what? Stealing a few things *they* decide are more important than my own life! So you tell me if I'm overreacting."

I know for a fact there's more to it than that. Stealing a few precious items doesn't get someone exiled to Earth the way he has, but I'm not going to argue with him in this state. I'm still trying to get out of here in one piece. The big issue is how unfamiliar I am with the room so I have to either hope I'm backing up towards the beaded curtain or risk taking my eyes off Godfrey to double check.

"Where do you think they'd put me if I let you do this, Dillon? Maybe they'll put me on the dark side of the moon. Or perhaps I'll be unfortunate enough to end up on Centauri Prime where I can spend eons mining bugs from the scrotums of the cave beasts there? I've come to find a way to make life here easier, to make something suitable enough to call home and I won't let you take it from me. You either agree not to pursue this or you just won't be anymore."

I could lie here, tell him that I'll drop it, but Godfrey would see right through it. There's no question he would. He's been able to sniff out my lies in the past and whether he has some psychic gifts or I just have no poker face, it's obvious I should just forgo the effort. Better to put all my energy into escape rather than anything else at the moment.

As I pass by a table, I know I'm heading in the right direction. From my peripherals, I spot something on the scarred wood top and I turn to it a split second before grabbing it. The item is a triangle of glass with lead seams. Inside it there's a powder. It's fine lavender and grey colour dust and I know right away what it is. When I look at Godfrey, still backing away, I can see how important it is by the fear in his eyes and I know this is my golden ticket out of here.

"Put that down, Dillon, and do it gently. Do you know what that is?" he asks, and the sword lowers a little.

"Of course I do," I say, even though I'm only guessing at this point. I think I know what it is by the colour and the fineness of the dust; not to mention the container it's in. But I have no way to be sure. Only one way to find out. "It's the remains of a Nod, right?"

"Yes. And if you know that, you know to be very careful with it." His sword lowers even further, but I'm not going to let him get any closer to me. I have the Nod remains in my hand, the cremated dust of one of the holiest and most viral creatures in the history of all worlds. While they say to own it would give one good luck, to breathe it in or get any of the particles on your skin would be a slow and painful death which there is no way to recover from. This is my way out for sure. "If you put that down now, you can go. You have my word."

"I'm sure I do. You are the most trustworthy person I know," I say, and think about how wrong this could all go, but I need to get out of there and fast. "But the word of a man who's a known liar and cheat, doesn't really hold much weight with me. Hope we can still be friends after all of this though."

At that, I lightly toss the glass triangle in the air before turning and running out of there. I hear the sword clatter to the ground as Godfrey screams out, "*No!*" I'm pretty sure he's able to catch it. By the time I hit the door and run outside I didn't hear glass break or cries of pain, so he should be fine. I'll owe him big time when all this is over.

I hate owing people.

Once outside, I don't stop until I'm able to jump into a cab. As soon as it's heading off back towards my house, I can relax and take it easy. I pull my cellphone out and send Garcia a message real quick. I could call him, but to be honest I don't like to make phone calls to people I hardly know or don't really like at all. He's fitting into both of those areas right now. I tell him I found something already that might help the case, but it may sound weird. He messages back fine and we agree to meet tomorrow. I don't want to get too invested in this, though, so I hope I can stop at just giving him the information. Godfrey may be right about the ramifications all this could have, even doing this part, so in this case, less may be more. What could happen if I do nothing is something I don't want to live with.

I'm not even sure I could.

We're sitting on Rouge's couch watching Netflix and eating popcorn. I'm trying to watch the show, but there's a part of me that's having a real hard time paying attention to it all. I take a handful of the buttery mess and half of what I grab ends up on either my lap or the floor. I'm sure her pup is happy, but when I hear the incredulous sighs from her, I know she's not impressed with my lack of concentration or dexterity.

"Something bugging you, Dill?" she asks, and pauses the show.

"Nothing really. Let's keep watching. I never knew women's prison could be so interesting."

I turn back towards the TV, but nothing happens to the screen. It's still frozen, two women trapped in eternal derp face. I sigh and know there's no way I'm going to get out of this without talking to her about it. I put the bowl on the coffee table. She's already giving me a look even though I haven't even started.

"It's work," I say finally, ready to open up to her.

"So I guessed. What is it now? Not another monster in a lake I hope. That wasn't my idea of a fun weekend at the beach."

"It has to do with the case Father Ted wanted me to help the detective with."

"Forrest Grump?"

"Yeah." I tell her everything I learned about the demon while at Godfrey's. She winces as I mention the demon and what it's made up of and the history of it.

"So, like the thing from the movie Dogma with Jay and Silent Bob," she says.

"What movie?"

"Jeez, you seriously don't know who Jay and Silent Bob are?"

I shake my head and she laughs. "It's a good thing you're dating me, Honey. I'm going to have to educate you in the history of movies, I think. Anyway, there's a movie called Dogma and in it the group have to fight a thing like what you mentioned. A shit demon."

"That's in a movie? Who the Hell would make up something like that for a movie?"

"My thoughts exactly. I never really thought it was real though. Are you sure your leg's not being pulled?"

"Pretty sure," I tell her, thinking of the way Godfrey reacted to the news. I doubt he would've lied to me and pulled the sword out with the intentions of turning me into two separate people. "If you could've seen Godfrey, how mad he was, you'd be sure he was telling the truth about it."

"I guess. To be honest, it sounds pretty ridiculous. I would call bullshit on it, but I'm sure you've seen worse," she says, and eats some popcorn. "It's just I can't get the picture out of my head from the movie. The thing looked pretty silly, to be honest."

"Guess I'll have to see it someday soon," I say, and wonder if it's on Netflix. "Just curious, how do they defeat the thing in the movie?" I ask with little hope that whatever it is would work in real life.

"From what I remember, and it's been a few years since I saw it, Silent Bob knocks it out with air freshener. You think that might really work?"

Air freshener? They killed or knocked out a demon with damn air freshener? That seems so ridiculous and far-fetched. No magic, no talismans, just some *Febreze* and a hope of good luck. Should be easy then, right?

"I doubt that'll work," I say, and feel a little defeated.

"Well, how are you going to get it then?"

"I'm not sure I'm going to. I had no plans on hunting down the demon on my own. All I was going to do was pass the information on to Garcia and let him do what he has to in order to stop it."

"What do you mean you're not going to help him go after it?" she asks, and looks utterly shocked by what I said. "This is what you do; go after monsters. Detective Garcia and the local police won't know what to do, how to beat it. Most of them won't even believe in the monster you're going to tell them about. You're going to just throw them to the lions?"

"It's not like that," I tell her, and try again to explain what's going on. "If I do this, try and hunt down the Golgotha, then I'm putting a lot at risk. I'm all for saying 'fuck the rules', but this is more than just a rule. This is one of the main ones I'm not allowed to break. Killing a human is bad, killing an ancient creature or demon, well that runs the risk of having me yanked from the planet all together."

"Just like dating me?" she asks, and I feel a pull at what she's implying. "I guess I'm a worthwhile risk for you, but those lives of the kids taken and killed are not?"

"It's not that," I say, and go on to explain, but she holds her hand up.

"Of course it is. What would you do if I was taken by this thing? Would you just pass on the information and leave it to the police to come and get me? Or, would it break the rules and come after me, regardless of what the punishment might be?"

She makes a good point. I'm not sure I could sit in my place and not do a thing if she was taken. The idea of some earthbound monster having her would be enough for me to travel to the ends of the earth to find her and kill the bastard that took her. So why won't I do it for these missing kids and the others that might still be taken and harmed? Does her life mean more to me? Is it because I love her?

The idea makes me feel selfish. "I see your point. Still, I don't even know if Garcia will let me help."

"If he doesn't, well, he doesn't. But you really have to try."

"I will."

"Promise?"

"I swear on you and me," I say, and smile.

"I like the way you make that sound. Makes me feel like I'm important in your life."

"That's because you are," I say, and lean in to kiss her. As I go to pull away and move towards her ear, I say, "I love you, Rouge."

I hear her take in a gasp of air, this being the first time she's heard me say it, the first time I've had the balls to let it out. I've felt it for a while, it's just time she knows it.

"Did you…just…that…you…" she stutters, and I lean back to look at her in the face.

"I did, because I do. I love you, Rouge."

She says it back. More than once and then we go to the room and show each other how much we love one another. We forget about the missing kids and the demon and just focus on ourselves.

It's a nice, perfect night for once.

Saturday

This is not my idea of a fun way to spend the weekend. Even a few hours is kind of annoying to me, but it's what Garcia wanted. I hope this'll be fast, but these things never are. Still, it'll be nice to pass on what I found out for him so I can get out of here. I don't mind coming to do jobs at the church, but I'm not one for sticking around during service. I'm not sure if today is the day I'm going to give him my offer to join forces with him, so to speak, but I at least want to give him what I have and offer some hope to the man.

At least the pounding in my head is all but gone today.

Instead of sitting with Garcia and his family, I stay near the back, out of everyone's way. I skim through some literature they have, but it's all the same. It could be worse I guess. Instead of reading this pamphlet about the Stations of the Cross, I could be looking at one of those creepy religious tracts I sometimes find laying around the city. Those things are nightmare-inducing. There are those that show how being gay can lead you into Hell, or how lying can lead you into Hell, even how being a salesman can lead you into Hell. All in all, they're usually only about how anything you do will eventually ruin your life and damn you down below with the devil and brimstone. Not that this thing is much more fun, but it beats the heck out of that.

Once the service is finally done, Garcia side steps his family and walks right over to me. There are still too many people around for me to be able to speak freely. Once the crowds start to thin out I get ready to give him what I got. Before I can tell him

61

anything, we're joined by Father Ted.

"Dillon," he says, and shakes my hand with gusto. "So nice that you came out for the service. Does this mean you might be a regular here from now on?"

"I'd love to say 'yes', but I feel weird lying in this place. I'm actually here to see the detective. He thought it'd be a good place to meet. I must admit, I didn't even know there was Saturday mass. I thought this was a Sunday thing only."

"No, we have services here every day. But today is actually First Communion for some of the local children. You couldn't tell?"

I shrug. To be honest, I wasn't listening to anything he'd been saying on the altar, so I couldn't tell if it was First Communion, First Confession or a hoedown. I don't tell him that. I don't want to sound like a jerk.

"Is this about the case with the children then?" Father Ted asks in a low voice, and Garcia nods. There aren't that many people around us, but I feel a little odd talking about what I've found out with so many of them close by. This isn't something you want to say with others being able to overhear you.

"Is there any way we could go speak in the rectory? Maybe use your office?" I ask.

"Of course. Anytime, Dillon, but do you mind if I sit in. Some of those kids were members of this church and I feel I need to hear this too."

"Sure," I say, as I can't think of a reason to say no. This is something he might even know about. Golgothas are part of the church's rich heritage of the strange and demonic, so maybe he can give us some advice, even offer a way to stop the thing when we do find it. So, the more the merrier.

Garcia goes over to a woman I assume is his wife and whispers in her ear. She looks as serious as he does and nods to him. Before coming back over to us, the detective walks over to a young boy, maybe ten years old, and ruffles his hair. I hear the kid cry out, "*Daaaaaaad,*" and I see the man smile. I think it's the first genuine one I've seen him have in the short time I've known the detective. It's a nice thing to see; proves to me he is human after all.

"You have a nice family," I tell him when he returns, and see the sourpuss look has returned.

"Thanks," he grunts, and we follow the priest to the rectory. The back halls leading there are dark and cool, and they hold the smell of used frankincense and candles. It's a nice thing, brings back memories of all the times I've spent in this place over the years talking to the priest, to my friend.

Once in his office, we all sit down and Father Ted offers tea. We both say no and I add that I need to make this quick as I have somewhere else to get to after this. Sure it's a lie, but it's one out of respect for the time of these two. Or at least that's what I tell myself so I don't feel too guilty about it.

"So, I spoke to one of my sources and as soon as he saw the picture of the symbol, he knew what it was right away," I begin, and Garcia pulls out a small police memo book and a pen with his name engraved on it. No doubt that was a gift from his wife or son. I tell them everything I know, not bothering with Garcia's scoffing. I begin to explain the history of the Golgotha as I know it, and how someone must be conjuring the demon to come forth. Right away I see a confused look cross the priest's face.

"What is it, Father?" I ask.

"You say it's a Golgotha that did this? A demon first born on the site where Christ died?"

"That's what my source says."

"Why though? Why would one of them rise now, even if conjured? It doesn't make sense."

"I know it doesn't, but it is what it is. Godfrey had a book with the symbol inside it. He showed me the picture and then told me what it said about them. It was a bit brief, but he says there's no doubt." I tell them I don't know how to find one, or whom could be doing this, even that I have no idea why anyone would, and when I finish I see two very different faces staring back at me. "I can see you're still not convinced, Ted."

"I just don't know. I know a lot about certain things as far as demons and evil goes, where it relates to my churches dogma, but none of this makes any sense really. I just don't know."

I look over at the detective and on Garcia's face I see nothing but the words *bullshit,* and know I have a long way to go to convince him that what I'm saying is true. I don't even know I can, but I have to try at this point. People who've never been around this sort of thing, who've never experienced the world hidden under the regular world are really hard to make see the truth.

"So, you and your buddy think this demon that's made up of shit and piss—pardon my language, father—which dates back to the time of Christ, is here now, in the city, called forth by some unknown person to steal kids for an unknown reason. Does your friend live at the Queen Street Mental Hospital? Or are they an outpatient somewhere else?"

"I know it's hard to swallow—"

"You think?" He laughs and cuts me off, but there is no real humour in that sound. "Maybe if what you said made any kind of sense, I could buy it, but this is just stupid."

"Well, I don't know how I can convince you. All I can say is this is what I found out and you can work with it or ignore it, but it's the truth." It's like trying to talk to a wall, with this guy. How do you explain to a non-believer that the truth is really out here? Why couldn't this guy be a fan of the X-Files and Whitley Strieber?

"How do I know it's not a stunt by someone who wants us to think he's called up this demon? Some nutcase who's read one too many books from the occult section of the library and now suddenly they're fucking with us to throw us off the case? It sounds like bullshit."

"It could be, sure, but I doubt it. Not with how the kids were taken. This is something else, something inhuman." I want to grab him and hit him in the head until he gets it, but clearly his skull is so thick that it probably wouldn't work either. "The way the symbol is written, the slime found on the scene, and the fact that nobody has seen a thing, it's too much for it just to be some crazy person who is using the idea of an ancient demon to throw you off."

"I beg to differ," Garcia says, and tucks his book away. "I've been a cop for a long time, seen a lot of messed up stuff, things that don't seem to add up. We hunt for answers, but in the end it always turns out to have a human face and a human answer. No matter what you tell me, I know that monsters don't exist. Nor do real demons. The stuff in the bible is to teach us lessons, and this taught me one too. You're a nut, Dillon. Regular men and women are the root of the evil in this world."

Garcia stands up and makes to walk out, but Father Ted grabs his arm.

"Wait a second, Jonathan. What if there was a way to prove it? What if I could show you monsters are real?"

What is he going on about? How on earth is he going to do that? Unless he has video of one of the things that have appeared in the church over the years, this is going to be a hard thing to prove.

"There's nothing you can say to do it. Sorry, Father. I know you're a priest and all, but there are things I need to see with my own eyes. And since there are no monsters here, no demons hiding in the corner, I guess I'll never know. I'm going to go home now and spend time with my son."

Father Ted looks at me and I see something there. I know what it is too, even before it leaves his mouth and my jaw nearly drops. I'm not sure what the man was thinking, what went through his head, but I almost feel as though he might've crossed a line; at least as far as I'm concerned.

"Come with me, both of you."

We follow him and I'm looking forward to seeing what it is. I'm sure I know, but I want to see the exact nature of it.

We head into a part of the rectory I've never been in before and soon we come to a door where the priest stops. He takes a deep breath and I see his shoulders slump a little and again I wonder just what it is he's about to show us. He touches the knob, then pulls his hand away and turns to us. His eyes meet mine.

"I want to apologize ahead of time for this, Dillon. I know you might not understand it, but it just seemed like the right thing to do at the time."

I go to say something, but stop. I don't really know what to say until I see whatever is behind door number one. Father Ted gives another apology before he turns back to the door. This time he opens it with little hesitation. The priest steps out of the way and I move in first, not wanting to let the detective see what's in the room before me. I suddenly wish I had my tools with me.

As I step in, the first thing I notice is a strong smell of Jasmine. It's pleasant and I begin to try to put the smell to any name of any monster I've ever dealt with, but none come to mind. The room is cool and dark and as I reach for the light, Father Ted calls out for me not to.

"I don't want to frighten my guest."

His guest. That sneaky little priest. Now I know for sure what he's done. I never really thought he'd do anything like this. I'd like to say he's been lying to me, but since I didn't ever think to ask if he had something living with him that wasn't of this world, there's no real deceit here, other than the fact that he kept it from me. Then again, I don't tell him about everything in my life. We're all allowed to have our secrets.

"Okay, Ted," I say, and leave the light alone. "So, where is you guest. I can't wait to see it."

"What's this going to prove?" Garcia asks, as Father Ted comes further into the room and makes a strange sound with his mouth. It's like a cross between a whistle and how you'd call a small animal like a squirrel.

"Oh, I think you're about to see what this'll prove," I whisper to the detective, and wait patiently for it. Luckily, we're rewarded rather quickly. The Father has done a good job of making the tourist feel nice and safe in this world.

From the far corner that's hidden in the shadows of a dresser, a small shape steps out from the pool of darkness. It's no bigger than a toy poodle and walks on hind legs, though it's slightly hunched over. The body of the creature is small and thin, lumps here and there. As it moves further into the light I can see that whatever it is, it's made a form for itself out of what looks like discarded tea bags. My guess would be Jasmine green tea, Ted's favourite. It moves closer to us, making a cooing sound like a dove or pigeon and as it looks up at me I know right away what it is.

"So you found yourself a Quilly?" I say, and can't help but smile at the sight of the tiny thing. A Quilly is one of the most laid back, least violent, and complacent of all the creatures in the expansive universes. They live on a small, peaceful planet and have never really been involved in any wars that I can recall. I do know that some species will visit their planet and steal their kind to use as pets. Others tend to keep them as slaves to do tiny jobs such as cleaning sewer systems, or entering the rectums of giant beasts to steal organs. There are also some—mostly demons— that think the small creatures are a delicacy and steal them by the crate so they can eat them raw later on. It's easy to feel bad for their kind and I'm curious as to how it found its way here. "What's your name, Quilly?"

"Peel," he says in a soft voice, and beside me Garcia finally lets out a quick gasp.

"What in God's name? That thing talks?" The detective's voice is shaky and it's to be expected. It's not every day that your world is flipped upside down.

"It's not a thing," I tell him. "That there's a Quilly named Peel. His body is in the world he came from. Creatures may be able to cross over, but for the most part, they have to leave their true bodies behind. Only their essence can make its way over to this world. So he's made one here out of old tea bags. At least he smells better than a lot of the things I have to deal with."

"There's no way...No...I mean...this...it's a trick...a joke... You two are having me on, right?"

"No," says Father Ted, and puts a hand on the detective's shoulder. "It's not a trick at all. I found him in the basement. There's a...weak spot down there, something like a crossroads where other creatures can cross over to our world. These are the things Dillon hunts down. I normally call him when one shows up, but not with Peel here. Nothing so innocent should be forced to meet with Dillon when he's doing his job. Sorry, Dillon."

"Oh, I get it," I tell him. I understand completely. There have been times where I've let a creature or two stay on this planet, despite how much trouble I could get in. Rules sometimes have to be overlooked.

"So, that's a monster?" Garcia asks, and I have to stifle a laugh.

"No, not even close. Peel here is a Quilly. He's no more a monster than you are. Sure, he doesn't look human, so to you I guess he would be a monster. But where he's from, you'd be the same. In fact, you look way more threatening than any Quilly ever has."

"This…it just makes no sense…none at all."

"Why should it?" I ask, and there isn't any joy in those words. I can image how he feels, how so many people who call me feel. Where I grew up, we knew about so many other worlds other than our own. Our planet was only one of many in our solar system that was inhabited. The people of Earth, on the other hand, are still in the dark, blind to the secrets around them, some of them so close. They have no idea of the life that lives in the stars above them, even that on their own moon. When I work for people and tell them I removed a monster or demon from their home or place of business, they usually convince themselves it was a fluke, just *one of those things*. They called me, seeing something out of the ordinary, a sight they couldn't explain and when I tell them it was a being not of this world, they laugh it off as though it's just a big mistake. At the end of the day, it's easier to live in denial than to accept the truth. "This universe isn't really built on sense or sanity, detective. It's a mishmash of mistakes, flaws and the unbelievable. But what you're looking at—this little Quilly— he's just the tip of the iceberg."

He's floored. I can see it, as I've seen it a million times before. Only the few handle this better. I watch him and see him sort of sway where he's standing. His eyes are still on Peel, but they're not focused. He looks like he might even faint at any moment, and that wouldn't be a first either.

"So, then, you actually hunt down these…monsters?" he stammers, as I see his hands start to shake.

"Well, the things I normally get called for have a little more girth to them, but yeah, this is the gist of it. Creatures like Peel, and much freakier, scarier monsters are my specialty. Anything that's not supposed to be on this planet is what I deal with. I guess you misjudged me after all." I snicker a bit as I say this. I can't help it really. He'd been so smug, thinking I was just a fraud and a joke; well, he doesn't seem that way now. Not as pale and freaked out as he looks at the moment.

"So, are you going to send it back too, like the others?" This time it's Father Ted asking the question and I study him. His face is a mix of fear and regret, as easy to read as a *Dick and Jane* book and I'm a little torn. This is my job. I'm here to find all these creatures, good and bad, and send them back to where they should be. There are laws and as small and harmless as Peel seems, he's not supposed to be here. "Please, Dillon. Just this one time, look away. He means no harm and he's become somewhat of a companion for me."

"How long's he been here?" I ask, and try not to bring my feelings into this. Father Ted is a friend, someone I actually take the time to see and I don't want anything to come between that. Even my job. He's a good man, and I would do almost anything for him, but would I break the rules for him? That's a hard one. I'd break them for my own selfish reasons, like I do with Rouge, but this isn't about me. It's about the priest and the Quilly.

"Nearly six months," he says quietly, and my mouth nearly drops.

"Six months? You old bastard! How did you keep him a secret for so long? Do your nuns know about him?"

He nods and I'm even more flabbergasted.

"So all this time, every single day I saw you over that time you've been keeping this from me? Even when you called me to rid the place of others that crossed over, you had Peel hiding out in your room?"

Again he nods and I laugh out loud.

"Are you going to..." he trails off and I shake my head.

"Listen, Father, there are rules and then there's this. The fact that you broke your own vows to keep the little guy here means something. I guess he's harmless and if that ever changes, which I'm sure it won't, you'll call me, right?"

"Of course I will."

"That's settled then," I tell him and I mean it. I won't send the little guy packing just yet. I doubt I ever will, but I will have no qualms if things change. None at all. After that, I turn back to Detective Garcia. "So, you still think what I said is a load of hogwash? Or are you ready to listen to reason?"

He shakes his head, his shoulders slumped and he looks utterly defeated. "If that's real, I guess I'll listen. I don't know how I'll get anyone else to, but I'll hear you out. My God, this is so wrong."

"You don't know the half of it."

After that, I explain to Garcia what he's going to be up against. I tell him what I know about the Golgotha. Father Ted also adds a few things, what he knows, but that's not very much more than I do. Garcia's first question is what we can do to stop it and I have to admit I have no idea. This is an earthbound demon, an entity of this world. Everything I would normally do is either forbidden or won't work at all. I have tools and spells, curses and talismans galore at home, but those are for specific beings, creatures not of this plane. In other words, they'll be useless in a fight with the Golgotha.

I tell him the real trick and sure way to beat this thing is to find whoever summoned it and, well, there's no easy way about it. He'd have to kill whoever called it forth. Just throwing them in jail won't stop the Golgotha, it'll just come and get him from wherever they held him. Or her. It could be a woman, I remind him. It wouldn't be the first time some monster like this, or a golem was called by a woman. Men don't hold the patent on being messed up.

"So why? Why would anyone call this thing up to snatch up kids in the first place? There's got to be a reason for it," he says, and I hear the frustration return.

"If there was a reason for anything people do, I'm sure I could tell you. To be honest, every time I have to deal with someone or something that has a crazy idea in their head to become more powerful, richer or anything else, it makes about as much sense as this does. Better not to try and understand the workings of the mad, detective. How many times does some monster have to decide to try and destroy the world before they realize there's not point to any of it? Who wants to rule a pile of waste? The problem with trying to make sense is that these people, monsters and demons have something not right in the head. To them, their ludicrous ideas make total sense, but to people with sense, they come off as insane."

I wish I had more to offer, to tell him something that could lead him to the source, but this is as much as I have or can offer. I think I'm safe with the information given, that I haven't really crossed any lines as far as the higher ups would go. I'm about to wish him good luck when his phone rings.

"Hello...wait...where?...okay, no, I understand. I'm on my way." He hangs up and is moving towards the door. "Are you coming?" he asks me, shooting me a glance over his shoulder and I have no idea what he's talking about.

"Coming where?"

"Another kid was just taken. And it's only a few blocks from here, in broad daylight."

I don't say anything at first. I don't want to say yes or no, for different reasons. In a way, this is what I live for, investigating and hunting. Normally I'm called to a case and it's as easy as tying a shoe, but it's the challenge I love. This case has just that and there's a fresh scent Garcia's running to. How can I pass that up?

Easily. If I go and there's a way to track the damn thing, then I run the risk of getting way too involved with it all and that could easily lead to a bigger problem than a Golgotha. If it looks like I'm interfering with an earthbound being, especially if I kill it somehow, I'll be pulled in and up on charges. If I ever thought Godfrey had it bad living life in a store and selling goods to hunters, I can only imagine what they'd have in store for me. No doubt I'd be somewhere desolate and disgusting. Worse still, there's no way I'd ever get to see Rouge again and that's nearly enough for me to say no alone.

"Sorry, detective. I actually can't get any more involved in this. If I do, I'd have to pay a heavy price," I offer, and hope that's enough of an explanation for him.

He stops, turns to me and I see the rage in his eyes even before he starts to yell at me. Clearly it's not enough. "What do you mean you can't get involved? You tell me this is a monster I'm up against and you're a monster hunter. This is your specialty and you're just going to walk away? Really? So I'm supposed to face some shit and piss demon by myself while you go off and play house with your stripper girlfriend? I can tell you don't have any kids. If you did, there's no way you'd pass the buck to me, asshole."

Well that's a good way to convince me to come.

I hold back the urge to punch him for the stripper comment. I understand his anger, know where it's coming from, so I bite my tongue and just say sorry. I could explain it all to him, but since it would involve me telling him and Father Ted I'm not even human, I decide against it. That's not going to help anyone here. I don't think there's anything I could say at this point that would make it easier for him to understand or accept.

"I have rules I have to follow, detective. I'm sorry." That's all I offer, but I can see it's not enough.

"Dillon," Father Ted says from beside me, and puts his hand on my shoulder. Right away I know he's about to try his voodoo on me, and I'm actually worried it'll work. "You can't let him go off on his own, especially if they find this…thing. You have a gift, and a purpose. I know you might not think there's a large force at work here, one testing us in everything we do, but there really is. Whether you call it God, the Universe or just say it's a higher power; there's a reason for everything we come face to face with. Right now, this is a test for you, don't you see? You're faced with an option. You can do the right and selfless thing, or you could just turn a blind eye and ignore it all, possibly costing the lives of the child taken and the detective here. I'm not going to tell you what to do, nobody can, but you really need to look inside yourself and make a decision that will let you sleep through the night."

Bastard.

I see why this guy became a priest. If religion hadn't called to Ted, he would've made a damn fine lawyer, car salesman or politician. With that silver tongue the man could sell a freezer to an Inuit. I don't want to do this. Godfrey was right when he told me not to get involved, that I should've just let it go. I didn't listen and look at what I've gotten myself into here. A whole pile of cow dung.

"You owe me big time, Father," I whisper to him, and look down at Peel with his false face. "Actually, you owe me two times now." I turn towards Detective Garcia and walk towards him. "I guess I'm coming with you after all."

How is this going to turn out well for me?

The car ride to the scene is quiet. Before we left the church, Garcia said farewell to his wife and son. I stood and watched him bend down and say goodbye to the boy and felt strange at the way the man's face changed. In the blink of an eye he went from stone still and mean to soft and as gentle as can be. I can bet that a lot of his passion for this case has to do with that child who he clearly loves more than life itself. I wonder if every time a new one is reported he somehow puts himself in the shoes of the parents and imagines it's his own that's been taken. I know what it's like to have someone you love threatened. It's not a good feeling.

As we sit in silence, I pull my cellphone out and decide to text Rouge, just so she knows what's going on. We don't have plans today, but she'll probably want to know that I took her advice and am helping out Detective Garcia.

So, against my better judgement, I'm going to help the cops out. Don't even say I told you so.

Fifteen second don't pass before she responds.

Ha, I knew you would. Always the monster hunter, my little dick.

Little? I type back, not liking the implication. For the first time ever, I regret using the whole Monster Dick thing.

Oh, don't be so sensitive. Anyway, I'm heading out to help

one of my friends get ready for a gig tonight, and then I'm off to a show. If this doesn't take long, you should stop by. It's going to be a Lord of the Rings vs Harry Potter theme burlesque show. You know you want to see that!

Yeah, that sounds sexy and enticing. I'd love to see Dumbledore and Gandalf strip. Jeez. I think that, but don't type it. Instead I write, **For sure. Send me the name of the venue and I'll do my best to swing by.**

After that, I tuck my phone away and see that Garcia is pulling up to the curb. There's police tape up already and people are huddled all around it. I'm amazed to see news crews are already on the scene too, and for a moment I have the briefest bit of selfishness as I imagine it will be a good place to plug the business.

I shake that thought off pretty quick. I need to keep my head low as well as my profile at this point. This is a job where I need to stay off the radar, in case the higher ups are tuned in to local Earth TV. That's always how I picture them getting their information, the beings who sent me here, those I answer to. All of them sitting on some galactic couch, some sort of junk food in hand, watching to see the way those on Earth who've been hired to keep the peace and bring law and order do just that.

I'm sure that's not how it really is, but it's what I picture whenever I think of them.

And even if that's not exactly how it is, best to stay away from media. Anyone with a camera or a microphone is going to be a plague to me.

"If it's all the same to you," I say to Garcia, as he pulls his keys out, "I'd prefer to stay as far away as I can from those cameras over there. You don't mind, do you?"

"Why would I? I don't want to explain to them who you are or why I brought you here. If my Captain finds out or word gets around I'll be a laughing stock."

"So what do you suggest? I'm sure someone is going to ask who I am when the see me cross the police line."

Clearly he hadn't thought of that, but neither had I. He stares out the window as the world moves in chaos before him and

I see the gears turning. Somewhere in the distance a woman can be heard crying hysterically and I know all of this has to be a hard thing for a man like him. He has religion and he has the law; two things in his life which have always provided him answers and a sense of right and wrong. The nature of the world in the eyes of people like him is that there's good and there's evil. Very seldom does anything run the fine line between the two. Then, this afternoon, his world gets turned upside down, a double barrel of the impossible shot into his chest at point blank range. I have no doubt the very foundation of everything he's ever held true has been torn to shreds.

In the past, I've worked cases where people lose all faith in religion, unable to hold onto the idea and ideals of God, Buddha, Allah, Jehovah, Ganesh or the others once they've had a peek into my world. Not that long ago there was a single mother, very religious and set in her ways. She called me because she thought I was an exorcist and could clean her house of the demons, which were haunting it. I told her to leave, going along with the story she wanted to believe, but in the midst of dispatching five monsters made up of used feminine products and hair collected from the tub drain, she walked into the room. She saw them and knew it wasn't demons, at least not in the way she imagined them. She took a full ganger at the horrors in front of her, and at me with a bizarre tool that looked like a steering wheel, and her world was shattered right at that moment.

When the monsters were gone, she was in tears. She held a bible in her hand and was ripping the pages out as she yelled *Lies! Lies Lies!* over and over again. I made my way towards her and stopped the destruction of the book she once held so much faith in. I took her to the kitchen, made her a tea and did my best to fix what was broken in her. I explained that nothing had changed, not really. She wanted to know how there could be a God when things like that existed and people like me had to come and get rid of them. I'm sure she didn't totally grasp what my job really was, but she wasn't ignorant either.

"It's simple. There is something in charge of all this. Give it whatever name you want, it doesn't matter. It doesn't care the name, or the symbols used to give it thanks. All that matters is that you do what is right. You can still believe in that, if nothing else. Call it God or Jesus, heck, you can call it Howdy Doody and it'd still be happy, as long as you believe. Just have faith in what's right and what's good and do your best to do what you can not to be an ass, and you'll be just fine."

Is this true? Is it a single source, one that wants humans and all other kinds in the world to do good and have some sort of faith? Does it matter? Will it change how anyone should believe, or whether they believe in something or not? How do I know? I'm not here to shine a light on things I don't fully know myself, but I do know that having faith makes all kinds of beings hold on to hope and stay positive, to think twice before killing another or just being a total douche. And that is a great power all in and of itself. I told her that and for a second she was silent. Then, she sipped her tea and looked at me with a smile on her face and hope in her eyes.

I wonder if I'll have to have the same talk with Detective Garcia. More than likely I will, though it's not something I look forward to.

As I think this, the detective reaches into the backseat and pulls a duffle bag onto his lap. He says nothing, so all I can do is watch as he rifles through it. A moment later, he pulls an SLR camera out and passes it to me. I'm confused and say so.

"What am I supposed to do with this?

"It's all I can think of. If anyone stops you and asks, you're taking crime scene photos for me. You're my nephew and visiting from out of town. You're in school for criminology and forensic pathology so I thought this would be a good lesson for you. You got all that, Dillon?"

"Did you just think all that up on the spot?" I ask, pretty impressed by how quickly he came up with a somewhat reasonable lie.

"Yeah. Bullshitting is one of the first skills you learn to hone in this job. Now, wipe the dumb grin off your face and keep your head down. Got it?"

I nod and somehow I feel like a kid around this guy. The

way he's started barking orders at me, being all alpha male and all, I feel small and that's not something I'm used to. I won't do anything about this right now, but there's no way I'm going to sit in the shadows of the world's grumpiest man and let him treat me as though I'm his little submissive. I'll give him fifty shades of shut the fuck up before I bow down to him. He's going to have to learn quickly that I don't do too well taking orders, or he's going to find himself hunting down demon McPoopypants by himself.

We get out of the car and pass through the police line without any questions. Most of the officers take one look at him coming and turn away, as if they want to avoid him. My guess is that people know the type of person Garcia is and would rather just let him by than have to face his stellar attitude. I can't blame them really.

The crime scene is a house. Apparently this is a daycare for area kids, one of those private deals. It's a nice place, three stories with a big front yard that's very well kept. We walk over to where two uniform cops are talking to a woman, and I listen in as Garcia starts to run his questions.

"Detective Garcia," one of the uniforms says. "This is Annie Fletcher. She runs this daycare and owns the house." Garcia says a brief hello and returns his attention back to the officer. "Approximately fifteen minutes ago, Ms. Fletcher went into the house to get drinks for the kids. She had four of them over today."

"Usually I have more, but it's a weekend so the day is lighter," the daycare worker says, and sniffles. Tears have dried on her cheeks in white crusted rivers, but as she talks, more come out and the dried remains are turned fresh again. She breaks down and when it's obvious she won't be able to go on, the uniform officer continues again.

"When she came back out into the backyard three of the kids were crying and one was missing. There was some weird stuff all over the lawn and the kids were going on and on about a monster that came over the fence and took the little girl. They say it went to the back of the yard and back over the fence it came from. Best guess is that someone in some sort of disguise came over and scared the kids before taking the girl. We have a K-9 unit enroute to try and follow the scent."

Garcia says nothing. He looks at the woman, then towards the place where the suspect ran off. Clearly his gears are turning, but he offers nothing in the way of what that might be. He stares off and I follow his gaze. I have questions I want to ask, but I think it would be better to just stay silent until the two of us are alone.

"Where are the kids now?" he finally asks, and that is a good question. I would love to hear what they have to say too.

"They're in the house watching TV and waiting for their parents to come pick them up," the second officer answers.

"Has anyone gotten a description of the person or monster they saw?"

"No," the second says quietly. There's a look on the police woman's face, one that is a cross between *we messed up* and *what good will it do*, but she says nothing more on the matter.

"Well, when their parents do show up explain that we need them to stay and provide that. Get on the horn and have someone send out a sketch artist. I know it's not going to make a lot of sense, but if it is a mask the perp is wearing, maybe someone will know it." At that, his eyes fall on me and I know he's not really thinking that at all. If he's accepting what I'm telling him about the Golgotha, then he knows this is no man or woman in a mask. This is something shiftier by far.

"Will do."

"Ms. Fletcher, why don't you go in the house with the officers and have a tea or something else," he says gently, almost with kindness in his voice as he puts his hand on her shoulder. I'm caught off guard by this and wonder if that's the same tone he uses with his son, one where he doesn't sound like a complete grump. "This isn't your fault. You can't control the actions of others, especially someone as sick as this. Have a tea and make sure the other children are all right. They'll need a kind face to make it through all of this in one piece."

"Thank you, detective," she says, and offers the saddest smile I've ever seen. I have no way to know just how hard it must be for her, but I know it's got to be bad.

Once the two uniformed officers and Ms. Fletcher disappear

inside the house, Detective Garcia turns back the way the demon fled and his stern look returns. "Same as last time. I don't even need to see the shit on the lawn to know this is the thing we're after. What do you think, Dillon?"

"First thing is, I think you're right. But I want to go over to the fence and see if there's any signs over there that might help us out," I tell him. I have an idea of what we're going to find, but there's no point saying it until I know for sure.

"Like what?"

"I'll know it if I see it," is all I offer the detective.

We walk over and as we go, I snap photos here and there. Some are of toys on the lawn, others the disgusting slime the demon left behind. In the light of day I can make it out so much better. It's not what I am expecting. I thought it would be something more like ectoplasm or a kind of glittering, otherworldly mass, but it looks more like the scum that floats on the water on a bog. I take a handful of pictures of these. On the eighth photo, Garcia turns to me and has a confused look on his face.

"What are you doing?" he asks, and sounds annoyed.

"Taking photos and keeping up appearances. If anyone asks who I am and we give them the story you made up, it'd be good to have some pictures to prove that's what I'm doing here, right?"

"True. Guess I didn't think about that."

I take a few more shots before we head to the edge of the yard. It looks like such a nice place for kids to play. The grass is well trimmed. There are toys and swings, even a little jungle gym for the little tykes to climb on. They were probably just sitting out here in the cool of the day, waiting for some treats after a day of play when their nightmares came to life. I don't want to think too hard on how terrified they must've been, seeing the demon in its terrible form come at them and steal one of their friends. It's nothing a child or any person of Earth should ever have to face, even if this thing is from this world or not. Could their little child minds even wrap around what they were seeing at all?

At the edge of the yard is a small wooden fence, about four feet high. There's slime on the top of it, so I know this is either where it came over, or the way it left; perhaps both. I grab a tricycle sitting close by, wheel it over and stand on it. I lean over, doing my best not to put my hands anywhere near the smelly mess, and there I find the exact thing I knew would be there. I let out a long, low breath and snap a picture.

"What's there?" Garcia asks from behind me.

"It's the same symbol that was found at the other crime scenes. There's no doubt now that it's connected." None at all.

"Shit. So, now that we see it there, how do we figure out what it's for? Does the demon leave it there? Is it some graffiti thing to say 'fuck you' to us?" Garcia asks. His voice is low no doubt worried someone might hear him say the 'D' word.

"I don't think so. I'm pretty sure this is left by the person who summoned the demon, as a way for the creature to find its target. I'm not sure Godfrey mentioned it, or if this is just me speculating, but it makes sense. I think it makes sense in some weird way. At least it feels right to me."

"Well, can you call this Godfrey person and find out for sure?"

"Not really," I say, and think back to the last time I saw him, chasing me, no doubt about to kill or maim me. "We're not on the best of terms right now. It's a long story." Something I don't really want to get into, but I don't tell him that part.

"Okay, but if you're right, and the person who's summoning the demon is the one writing that, doesn't it help us in any way? Wouldn't that mean that the person is also here and writes that as the demon is stealing the kid?"

"I don't think that's it at all. We know for one that these attacks are planned somehow. I think whoever is behind this is pre-picking the targets for the demon. There's nothing random about it at all. That's more than we had before. I feel like the one who is summoning this creature is putting the symbol up as a way to focus where the damn thing should go."

"Good. Then we'll start to get the media to show the picture of the symbol and have people looking out for it. Best way to avoid other cases later on."

"Not at all," I say, and step down from the kid's bike. "If you do that, you'll have every nut job, anyone who hates someone in the slightest putting the symbol up all over the city and you'll never get anything but a headache. Not to mention we don't even know when the symbol's put up for sure. It could be days before, hours or mere minutes. There's no way to know for sure."

"So in other words, this really gets us nowhere?" he says, and there's a clear sound of defeat and anger in his voice. "More of the same."

"It's more than we had, Detective. At least we know this is part of the same case, and not some other random sort of abduction. And knowing something about the symbol is better than knowing nothing at all."

"Yeah, that makes me feel *so* much better," he says, and the sarcasm in his voice isn't lost on me.

"Detective Garcia?" a voice calls out from the direction of the house. We turn and there's the female uniform cop walking towards us. "The K-9 unit's here. Should we bring the dog straight back here?"

"Sure, then we'll go around to the other side of this fence and track the bastard."

She walks away to go grab the officer with the dog and now I'm a bit worried. If we all go as a group and we're are able to track this demon down, what then? We can't very well turn and say that their help is no longer needed and send them on their way. These people are the police and they have protocols when it comes to these things. Even bringing me along might raise some eyebrows; if not now then later if things perhaps go sideways. Yet, I don't know what else to do. A dog is the best way we have to track the thing down. It'll be easier for an animal trained to pick up and follow the demon and the child's scent than any other choice currently on the table. The only other way to do it would be for me to do my best Native Tracker impersonation as I follow the bits of slime this thing leaves behind in hopes of locating it. And since I don't have any skills hunting that way, best to use the dog.

I tell Garcia about my concerns and he agrees that it's a lose-lose situation, but as there's a child hanging in the balance, he chooses the side of do it now, deal with the consequences later. I think it's all we can do at this point.

After the dog and his handler are brought out back to sniff around, we head out of the yard in hopes of finding the missing child and the demon. The dog is leading the way, followed by the K-9 officer, Daniels, and the two uniform officers I already met—sort of—Jen Platanov and Jon Tham. The five of us move along, the dog clearly has a scent and is pulling forward. I don't really know the area, so I have no idea where it's leading, but I have this feeling in my stomach and a tickle in a small part of my head that we're running headlong into something we should take more time with. These other three police officers have no idea what they could potential face, if we can find the demon at all. Who knows what they'll do, how they'll react when they come face to face with it. To be honest, I'm not even sure just how Garcia will handle it. Sure, he saw the Quilly back in Father Ted's room, but that'll be small potatoes compared to the monster we could find. Then again, I don't even really know what one of these damn things will look like. I've never actually seen a Golgotha before. Maybe I should've watched that movie Rouge had told me about.

Time will tell.

But that's not the only thing I think I'm worried about. There's still the fact that what Godfrey said could be true, that I could face some serious problems by killing this thing and/or the person who summoned it. I don't want to think that way, but I'm sure that's part of what's making me want to hesitate a little more than normal.

"I think the trail's leading us to the creek," Daniels calls out, and then tells the dog what a good girl she is.

The creek? I guess that makes sense. If the thing is a Golgotha and made up of shit and piss, the creek would be the perfect place for it. Seeing as it's less of a body of water and more of a sewer runoff, where else would a fecal matter monster feel at home?

"Should we call this in?" Jen asks, and Garcia immediately shakes his head.

"No time to waste, Platanov. Who knows where this sicko will be or what he does to these kids. I don't want to take any chances. We move and we move fast. The only thing that matters is bringing this scumbag down and getting the child back in one piece."

Again, I don't really know police procedures, but I'm thinking what Detective Garcia's doing violates more than one of them. Yet they don't stop or question him. Whether it's the right thing to do by the rules or not, it must be the right thing to do for themselves, their consciences, and the child. That's a feeling I can relate to. Sometimes, you just have to say to hell with the rules and do what you have to do. Do the right thing trumps following the rules any day of the week in my book.

We continue on.

We move from the side streets and go off the beaten path and through a thicket of woods. I'm guessing this is part of High Park now. I want to stop right then and there, sure that we are going to see a bug or eight million, and to be honest, I really hate insects.

Yes, I'm a monster and demon hunter. I've seen death and horrors the likes that would turn most people green, or at the very least give them nightmares for months. That doesn't stop me from hating those creepy, crawly, mindless and disgusting little things. Just the thought of some beetle or spider crawling on me is almost enough for me to turn and run like a coward, but I know I can't. There's no time to be selfish, not with the child missing, and yet there are going to be worms and ants and all kinds of wrong all over the place.

Some days it sucks to be me.

So I keep going, we all do. I can smell the rank sewage water even though I can't see it yet. The air is thick with the foulness of waste and for a moment I think of some of the vile beasts I've fought over the years. A few of them have smelled this bad with their bodies made up of rotted things and human waste. I try not to open my mouth, not wanting to taste the way the tiny particles of smell hang in the air. All things we smell are particulate. That means whenever you smell a fart, you're actually breathing in microscopic bits of poo. Not a pleasant thought; even less so when I smell what's in the air around here.

The dog turns sharply to the left and after a few minutes of pushing through the woods, happy that no bugs are crawling on me, we get to the slow moving creek water. It's not very deep, but it's as murky as anything I've ever seen before. It also looks a lot like the slime from the crime scene.

The dog is panting, barks here and there as we move south along the shallow bank on the edge of the water. I look around at people jogging, walking their dogs and sitting on benches and see shocked looks on their faces. I'm sure they're wondering what's going on, but now I'm starting to wonder how a giant poop demon could get past them without the same stares. The dog is clearly following the scent of the Golgotha. If that's true then this would have to be the way the monster came, yet it's so out in the open, so close to a very well-traveled path. Someone must've seen it or else we're following a dead end.

I'm starting to feel less hopeful.

That is until we stop and the dog begins to bark wildly and pull towards a very dark tunnel that is spewing out all sorts of filth. It's part of the sewer system, one of the run off pipes. A rusted shopping cart sits in front of its five-foot high mouth and there is no part of me that wants to go inside. The smell wafting out of there is horrendous. My stomach clenches just standing there.

"Any of you have a flashlight?" Garcia asks, and moves towards the opening. All three officers in uniform pull small LED flashlights from their duty belts and hold them out.

"Are we going in there?" I ask, although to be honest I don't want anything close to the truth here. I'd prefer Garcia turn to me and say *of course not*, but I know that's not going to happen. Some days I feel as though if it weren't for bad luck, I'd have no luck at all.

"This is where the de...sicko took her," he says, no doubt catching himself before he can say the word demon. "We need to get in there and find her as fast as we can if we have any hope of saving her. Unless you have a better idea?"

A shake my head.

"Who is this guy anyway, Detective?" Jen asks, and to be honest, I'm surprised it took this long for someone to wise up.

Here's some guy standing there in jeans, a t-shirt and hoodie, and their boss is asking me advice. It must be weird for them. Luckily Detective Garcia explains it flawlessly, speaking the lie as easily as if it were the truth, and from the looks on their faces, they've bought it. That or they just don't want to argue with him. "Well, maybe it would be better if he stayed out here. No point taking someone in that's not armed or trained for this."

Garcia's eyes make a strange move, almost as though the idea of going in there without me scares him, but there's no way that's what it is. What's he got to be scared of? Anything he has on him, like a gun, would be more effective than any of the weapons I have at home or the Tincher that's tucked into my belt. My weapons and tools are made to go up against creatures and beings not of this world. Sure my blade could kill something of flesh and blood, but what about something made up of poop and piss? I don't think my cursed and spellbound blade would have any luck at all. So in a way, I feel like going in with him would be useless. Not to mention I'm betting dollars to donuts that the tunnels is loaded with rats and cockroaches.

More damn bugs! The day just keeps getting better and better.

"No, he's coming too. Give him a flashlight and he can walk with me. Daniels, you and Kodo go in first."

The K-9 officer nods and turns his light on and walks slowly towards the mouth of the tunnel. I can see the man and the dog feel the same way as I do about this. Bugs, the dark and small spaces are not the makings of a nice Saturday afternoon in the park. The fact that we're going after a demon born from human waste who steals children is just the fecal icing on an already rotten cake.

"Dillon, you come with me. Platanov and Tham, you take the rear."

This can't be a good thing. This can't be a good thing. No, this can't be a good thing.

That becomes my mantra as we step into the circular mouth of the tunnel and follow Daniels and his dog to my very own kind of Hell. As soon as I take a second step in, icy water finds its way up and over the top of my shoes and I'm sloshing through the neighbourhood's memories of meals past. I can smell the water going into my shoe and know that as soon as I get home, these are going down the chute. They're garbage. There's a lesson in this; I need to start buying waterproof boots similar to what these uniformed officers are wearing. Since I never know what I'm going to be stepping in, it'll save me time and the urges to puke my guts up on jobs like this.

Sounds echo around us as we go. I'm trying not to notice the cries of rodents or the way the walls of the tunnels seem to be moving. Garcia's close to me and I can tell I'm not the only one stressed out. His breathing is as rapid as mine. I don't know if he's as squiked out by bugs as I am, but something is getting to him.

"Damn there's a lot of fucking roaches down here," Jen says from behind me. I want to say *Hey, thanks Captain Obvious*, but I hold back so that a scream doesn't come out of my mouth instead. I never said I was a tough guy.

"That one looks like it's the size of a bird." Tham all but chuckles, as if there's something funny about a huge ass bug. Well, there's not. Nothing funny about something like that at all. I make sure not to look over at the one he's talking about, but in my attempt to avoid it, my eyes fall right on the one he must be talking about it. I really want to get out of here.

"Are you seeing this?" Detective Garcia whispers beside me, and I shake my head.

"I don't want to see it," I whisper back. "I don't like bugs. Not at all. In fact, I'm doing everything I can not to turn tail and run the fuck out of here, Detective. So, nope, I see nothing at all."

"Not the bugs, Dillon," he says, and grabs my hand that's holding the flash light and moves it up the side of the walls. "Look there."

I see it right away and it's weird. The strange symbol that's been at the crime scenes, the one we found on the fence just a little while ago, is on the walls of the tunnel. It appears every fifteen feet or so. What makes it strange is the fact that where each of those markings are, in every single spot, there isn't a bug near it. I watch as a swarm of them run towards one of the symbols, but four or five inches before they get there, all the bugs swerve and change direction. The same thing happens again and again. If I didn't know any better, I'd say the bugs were afraid of it.

But why?

I guess it's something I'll want to find out afterwards, if I can for my own sake. Not that I plan on ever dealing with anything similar to this again, but I do like learning new things whenever I can.

This gets me thinking of Godfrey and I wonder if things will ever be the same between us again. For a long while we were on shaky ground. He's ripped me off in the past; given me weapons he promised would work only to nearly get me killed when I try to use them. He claims ignorance on his part, always has, and I let it go as that, but I've never been totally sure. Since I let that be water under the bridge, I can only hope he'll feel the same way after this is all over. Assuming we're not both in some serious shit.

Well, I'm already in that. Literally.

"You still there?" Garcia asks, and I'm pretty sure I missed something he said.

"What?"

"I asked if you have any idea why the roaches are avoiding the writing. Can they sense something wrong with it or is it written in something they're somehow afraid of?"

"I really don't know," I tell him honestly. "This whole thing is a little out of my normal area of expertise. I told you that. This thing, these symbols are all from this world. I don't really make it a case of studying up on monsters that are allowed to live here. At this point, your guess is as good as mine."

I shoot a glance behind me, just in case the two officers back there heard me say the *M* word, but neither are really paying attention to us. And no wonder. They're looking down at the water at our feet and when I do the same, shining the light downwards, I see a river of waste and bloated bodies of rats floating along the surface looking like hairy, dead schooners.

"That's just great," I mutter, and try not to notice any of them bumping into my ankles. I hadn't before then, but now that I've seen their bodies, there's no way I can't not notice. Can this day get any worse?

"Detective?" Daniels calls out from up ahead, and all I can think is I thought that way too soon and things are about to show me how worse they can get.

I move up to where the K-9 officer is standing along with Garcia. I have no idea what it could be, but I'm hoping for the best at this point. Something has got to make the day get better. To think I could be relaxing at Rouge's house, sitting in the backyard and enjoying the beautiful day instead of hanging out in a sewer with cops, hunting a demon I have no right hunting.

Once we get to him, I see his concern. Ahead of him is a break in the sewers. It's like a crossroads. There is a large center area with a ceiling height of about fifteen feet and at least five other tunnels to choose from. The dog seems as confused as we do, sniffing the air in front of each, but unable to choose the way to go.

"Any ideas?" Garcia asks me, and all I can do is huff.

"How would I know?"

The dog is whining now. I don't know if he's afraid of what's ahead or perhaps saddened by his own confusion at what to do now. The dog's been trained to follow his nose, a canine version of Toucan Sam, but now he's stuck. That's when my brain finally kicks in a little and I come up with an idea.

"The symbol," I whisper to Garcia. "If one of the tunnels has it, then it will be the way to go. Maybe it acts like a path for the demon to follow, like a guide for the thing. It's worth a shot, right?"

Garcia nods and it does make sense to me. If the symbol is being put on areas where kids are to be taken, perhaps being used like a beacon to call the demon, then it would make sense that a path of them may be created to lead the creature to the goal. It doesn't fully fly with me though. Unless each symbol is done slightly different than the final one left where the kids were taken from, how would the demon know when to stop following and when to grab. If we find one in the tunnel ahead, I will check out for any variations before we go, instead of checking those behind us. There has to be something different in them though, a way to lead the monster or why else have them all through the sewer to begin with? What would the purpose be to it if not to guide the beast?

Garcia motions me over and as I walk across the highest part of the crossroads, I hear something to my left.

Oh damn!

There's a growl. A low rumble that's building up and as I turn to see what it is, I hear the dog barking and whining seconds before it runs past me. Daniels is calling out to it after the animal tears his leash from his handler's hand, but the dog is the smart one here. Something's coming, and I think we all should run. It sounds big.

"What the hell is that sound?" Tham asks, but maybe he shouldn't have.

As the words leave his lips, something huge and dark reaches out from the tunnel behind him and pulls him backwards into the shadows. He lets out a small scream, but the sound is cut off as his head smacks off the top of the tunnel's mouth with a wet whack. I see his head slump forward as though he's already knocked out, and then he's gone.

"What the fuck was that?" Platanov asks Garcia, as I pull my Tincher out from my belt, tossing Garcia's camera to the side.

"I don't know," the detective tells her, and all the cops now have their guns drawn. The flashlight beams pointed at the tunnel Tham was sucked into are shaky and the sound of everyone's breathing has become laboured with fear. Mine is no different. Things had escalated pretty quickly.

"Something grabbed him. No way a person could do that," she tells him, as though we all don't already know the same thing. "What the fuck was it? Did anyone see what took him?"

"No, but whatever it is, made Kodo run off too," Daniels adds, but there's no help in pointing that out either, other than the fact that maybe we should do as the dog did and get the hell out of there as fast as we can. I consider saying it, but right now my mouth is dry and tastes like shit as adrenaline pumps furiously through me.

We all stand there. Flashlights aimed at the tunnel where the young, Asian cop was pulled, and say nothing after Daniels' last useless statement. I know what I'm thinking; mainly that everyone should run and that Godfrey was right, but I wonder what's going through the heads of Daniels and Platanov. They have no idea that what took their fellow officer, what they might have to face themselves is a demon. They're totally ignorant to the fact that a monster just grabbed their co-worker and no doubt is killing the man in some horrible, disgusting way. They're oblivious to the fact that their guns might be about as useful against the thing in there as a Band-Aid would be to a shotgun wound. Should I tell them this? Should I warn them even though there's no way they'll believe it?

Why bother? They'll see it soon enough, I'm sure.

There are noises echoing around us and I don't like it. It reminds me of the sound someone makes as they sloppily go to town on some very rare, extremely juice steaks; a mouth slobbering on wet, bloody meat...but there's something else as well. I stop in the dead center of the opening, and Garcia is backing towards me, his gun pointed to where Tham is no doubt being eaten.

"Did you see it at all?" he asks, and there are no whispers this time. "Is it what you said it was?"

"I couldn't see anything. Just a dark blur," I tell him, and Platanov turns her head when I say it.

"What does that mean? *Is it what you said it was?* Do you know what the fuck is going on here?"

There's panic in her voice and if I say yes or try to explain to her what's going on, that panic is going to go nuclear. I say nothing instead and shrug and she forgets about the tunnel and stalks towards us, her gun at her side. I see anger in her face, something I see way too often these days, and I try and think of something, anything to say fast and easy. There has to be some way to calm this down and get the rest of us out in one piece.

Before I can get the words out though, it's already too late.

From a different tunnel, one to my left, a monster is born, a second one comes from my right and jumps on top of Daniels.

The cop's gun goes off and my eardrums are ruined; the world turns into the sound of being underwater. I step back and trip. I fall ass first into the water and bounce down so hard that it shakes my head something fierce. My headache reawakens and I doubt it's just the fall though, but instead the left overs over the concussion I suffered the other day. The mix of my ears blown out and my head pounding makes me feel sick. The smell rising from the water I'm sitting in isn't helping all that much either. I'm covered in filth. Right now I'm so glad I didn't wear my leather jacket.

Through the dense muffles I hear Platanov scream as the first monster wraps its hideously gigantic jaws around her waist. Teeth that look like a burnt down village or blackened driftwood bury themselves in the side of her stomach and blood bubbles out from her mouth, gargling her scream. I look at the thing and know two things; this is an earthbound monster, and it is not a Golgotha. Not even close.

A Golgotha is a demon made up of human waste. If that's so, then these creatures should be slimy piles of disgusting, but they're not. They're beasts, solid and muscular. The monster's head is twice the size of its body. It has a nest of red eyes covering the coarse hairs of its face and its chin melds and melts right into its chest as if it's all one body part. The creature's arms are dark and shiny, covered in human waste and now blood, but that's only because of the slaughter. The arms are huge, close to the height of me—and I'm six feet tall—and nearly as thick. The creature's back legs are smaller, looking more like a toad's than anything that should belong on the rest of it. Parts of the skin look more like shells of a sea creature, especially running down the back where small worm-like strings dangle down. As I stare at the monsters eating Platanov and Daniels, I know these things aren't what I thought, not what Godfrey claimed they were. These aren't demons at all. These are something else entirely; earth-born monsters and my Tincher will do little more than piss them off and make them eat me slowly to get even.

I stand up from the muck and run to Garcia.

"We need to get out of here," I tell the detective, and pull him by the arm, but he's frozen, eyes stuck on the slaughter. I look over and see blue ropes pulled out from Daniels' stomach. The dying man reaches out and tries to grab at them, begins a tug of war with the monster, but he's already dead. He just doesn't want to admit it. "Seriously, if you don't want to end up like them, we need to go. Now!"

"We...can't just—"

"We can and we will, if you want to see your kid again."

That snaps him out of it. He looks at me and there's nothing left of the man I first met there, fear has swallowed his anger. He keeps saying *my son* over and over, and I know I need to drag him or push him out.

A bone snaps in the direction of Platanov. From the corner of my eye I see her body split in two and gore showers from her. That's it for me. I pull Garcia with all my force towards the tunnel we came through and then get behind him once he's in. He doesn't seem to want to go, but I don't stop. He has to get going. Once those things are done with the cops, they'll be coming after us. We've only gone ten steps or less and I feel his resistance let up a little. Good. He needs to run. I tell him that and he turns to me.

"What about the child? We need to save the child."

"If it's still alive, yeah, sure, but we don't have the power to do that right now. Maybe we can—"

"HUNTER!"

A booming voice echoes in the tunnel and cuts me off. A cold shiver runs down my spine at the call. Those monsters shouldn't be able to speak and even if they could, how would they know who or what I am. Earthbound beings, humans and monsters know nothing of hunters and the fact this something behind us does, makes me terrified.

I stop pushing Garcia and chance a look back. In the dark behind us, three monsters are there. I still can't remember what they are, but that's not what I'm focused on. Instead of the beasts, my eyes fall on a human figure, shrouded in darkness, with arms raised out to me. This must be who called out to me.

"You can't run from me forever, Hunter. I know who you are.

I know what you are. And in the end, you'll be mine."

The man laughs and the monsters roar along with him. It's time I just get the hell out of here. I start to push Garcia so hard, I'm afraid he's going to fall, sure they're coming to get me. If he does fall, I can't even say for sure that I'll help him up at this point. I'm actually scared. I've faced off with some crazy things in my time, beasts of all sorts that would make anyone's blood run cold, yet I can usually keep a level head. Usually.

But what I saw there, and knowing that nothing I have can hurt these monsters is something different. The person calling out to me, calling me a hunter as though he knows who I am hits me on such an irrational level that I'm starting to feel dizzy with panic. The throbbing in my head doesn't make any of this better.

I've forgotten about the bugs around me now, no worries about the floating, bloated dead rats. My only concern is getting out alive, in one piece so I can live long enough to make sense of all of this. I'm breathing heavy as my feet splash through the murky water and I'm muttering something under my breath, but I have no idea what the nonsensical words mean. Maybe I'm praying to someone or something for help.

Through all the fear and all the panic, through the nausea and the pounding head, one thing I fail to notice was the fact that there was no sound of them giving chase. As we hit the light and fresh air of the outside world, it finally hits me that nothing came along after us, as though the creatures never even thought to bother with us.

We move away from the sewer tunnel. Garcia is breathing hard and after a few steps he bends over and pukes. I almost join him. I tell him we need to get away from the opening, just in case, and he wipes his mouth and nods. We keep going, for another forty or fifty feet and then I figure that's good enough and I collapse onto the grass.

I'm out of breath. My head is spinning and pounding at the same time. As I stare up at the clear blue sky above me. Things feel as though they're getting darker. What the hell is wrong with me? Is it the fear, the excursion, or the leftover effects of the blow to my head? Does it even matter?

Beside me, I think I can hear Detective Garcia sobbing. I try and tell him it's okay, we're safe and that we'll find a way to figure out what's going on, but even as I say it out loud, I don't really believe it. So why should he? The words fall weakly out of my mouth, trembling the way the rest of my body is. This is not the way I pictured the day turning out at all.

"How are we going to stop them?" he asks, his voice little more than a whisper. "How do you stop anything like that?"

"I don't know." This is all I can think of at the moment. I really have no idea. Until I can remember what they are, I have no way to figure this out.

👏 · 👏

It takes a while for us to get up and moving again. Once we both calm down, Garcia realizes he has a whole new set of things to worry about. He just lost three officers and a K-9 in the sewers and now has to go try and explain it all to the higher ups. I know this won't be easy and I tell him the only thing he needs to do is keep my name out of it. He doesn't like that idea at all. He's clearly one of those people who might cross the line now and again to get things done, but in the end, he's a stickler for the rules. Keeping my name out of it all makes things easy for me, but he thinks it will make it hard for anyone to believe what he saw down there.

"Well, then don't tell them the whole truth," I say, and right away he's shaking his head. "Oh, you think it's a good idea to be up front and honest, right? You think if you tell them there are three huge ass monsters in the sewer and someone controlling them, that's bound to help the situation?"

"No, but—"

"But nothing. You tell them the truth and you'll be locked in a padded room in no time. This isn't even what we thought it was at first, so let me try and do something to figure it out before you get a ton of cops killed."

"What do you mean, not what we thought?"

"Those things aren't Golgotha, not by a long shot."

"What are they then?"

"Damned if I know. A Golgotha's supposed to be made of feces and piss. So you'd guess they should look more like something made of mud and debris. Those things looked like humans crossed with spiders, crabs and frogs. Nothing even close to how a Golgotha should look. And there was nothing demon-esque about them. No horns, no hellfire. These things are born of the earth, possible within the crust."

"But you said—"

"Yeah, I know what I said, Detective. Godfrey saw the symbol and the muck and thought it was those things. Not that this changes much, but if we have any chance of stopping them, we need to know exactly what they are." I don't even bother telling him I'm more concerned about the person or thing that called out to me. I want to know who or what that was even more.

"So what do you expect me to say about it then? These people had families, so I can't just ignore it as though it never happened. Am I supposed to say I just lost them, or maybe that we were attacked by a wild animal or I could say a single psycho stealing kids took out three cops and made a trained dog run away while I did the exact same, coming out of this totally unscathed? Sound good?"

Great, the angry cop is back. I take a deep breath and slowly stand up, hoping my head doesn't suddenly explode.

"I can't tell you what to say, Detective. But, if you tell them what really happened down there, you'll get one of two results. The first will be spending some time in a rubber room peeing into a diaper until you admit you're nuts. The second is a whole bunch of cops go into the sewer and never come out. And if you mention me in all of this, let's just say nobody will be stopping these monsters any time soon. So, I don't care what you say, just keep me out of it. Okay?"

Garcia says nothing to that. He just sits on the grass looking off into thin air. I can't imagine what he's feeling. Those were his people, officers he knew on some level and he'd watched at least two of them get eaten. I've never lost any friends like that before. Well, that's not totally true. I was still around when my whole family and all my friends were been taken or wiped out, but that was war. This, well, it's really not the same thing at all.

"You'll have to come up with something, Detective. I wish I could offer you more, but I can't. All I can do is promise it's not over." This gets his attention and he looks up at me with hope in his eyes. "I'm not going to lie, this might end badly for us if we pursue it, but I can't let it go. Not now."

"Why? Is it the kids, the monsters?"

"That and more. Something else was there with them, and he knew who I was. Didn't you hear him call out to me?" He shakes his head and I let it go. He was in a state when the shadowy man called out to me, so it's no wonder he didn't hear it. "You will have to handle this end of it while I try to find out what I can about what those things were and how we can kill them. I'm making you a promise right now that I will do everything I can to stop this, as long as you do your part, Detective."

"I will. I don't know how, but I will."

Good, we have an understanding. Now, I need to find a way to get home and start figuring out the next step here.

I cab it back to my place and run up the stairs with my Tincher in my hand. I don't know why I pulled it out, other than still being afraid from what was in the sewers and cautious because of the attack here in the stairs the other day. The headache's still pulsing like a heartbeat only serves to remind me of it and that gets me to quicken my pace. When I get to the floor where I was hit I nearly stop and check the door to make sure nothing's there, but I'd rather get home. There's safety there. My apartment is full of weapons, curses and hexes to offer protection. Best place to be right now is on my couch with an arsenal, my laptop, and my cellphone.

I open the door and let out a small, sad yelp as something grabs for me. My Tincher falls from my hand as I flinch backwards and look like a fool.

"Hey, muffin, why so jumpy?"

"Jesus!" I gasp, and nearly feel the urge to grab my heart in case I go into cardiac arrest. I look at Rouge standing in front of me, dressed in a pair of her yoga pants and a Pantera t-shirt of mine. She looks all relaxed and cute. Clearly a rouse she's using to sneak up and kill me. "You nearly scared what's left of my breakfast out of me."

"Oh charming as ever," she says, and then winces as she steps towards me, covering her face right away. "You sure it was nearly?"

I didn't even notice or think about the sewer smell that must be hanging to me. My mind has been so wrapped in what happened there and what we're going to do about it that I all but forgot about walking through the disgusting water and falling in it. Now that I'm aware of it, the smell is one step away from the gates of Hell. Good thing the cabbie didn't notice either.

"Sorry, I know it smells like it, but you have no idea what I've just been through."

"Well, it smells like you were fishing for used diapers in a sewer if you want me to be honest. You, Darling, need a shower."

"That I do."

"And when you're done, you can tell me all about it. Want me to put on some coffee or tea, a warm glass of Febreze perhaps?" she asks, and smiles, but I know when I tell her what happened the humour will drain out of her, so I will wait and enjoy the smiles for now. I could use them after all.

"Coffee would be great. Some toast too, if you don't mind. And some Advil."

"Headaches again?"

I nod and head to the bathroom. I run the water and just get in full clothed, figuring I can peel the disgusting outfit off and leave it to soak in the tub. Not the classiest thing in the world, but I'm not a very classy person. Also, it's better than leaving the soiled and possibly ruined clothes just lying there on the floor.

The water is hot, hotter than I usually like it, but I feel so gross. The water pooling by the drain reminds me of chocolate milk. I imagine how many different asses have made the wonder soup I'm coated in.

I stay in the shower until the colour of water is just the colour of water again. The heat of it feels great and some of the throbbing in my head melts away with the filth. As I stand here under the flow from the showerhead, I close my eyes and can't help but relive the day. Of course the images of the officers being killed comes back time and time again, but it's always the voice calling out to me, yelling out the word *hunter*. That echoes through my mind the most.

"You okay in there?" Rouge says, as she knocks, pulling me from my thoughts.

"Yeah. Sorry. I'm just trying to smell better than some dirty old socks," I tell her, trying to make light of the way I feel.

"Well, you've been in there nearly an hour. I don't think you're going to get any cleaner, lover."

An hour? It didn't feel like that long. It's amazing how time flies when you're worried. More so than when you're having fun.

I dry off and walk to the bedroom to get some clothes on. The apartment smells of fresh-ish coffee and I'm dying for a cup. I throw on some clean jeans and a Municipal Waste t-shirt and then head out to see Rouge and my caffeinated beverage. Once I have both, we sit on the couch, eating toast and drinking and I tell everything that just happened. I can see a look in her eyes as the story unfolds that tells me she is terrified and worried. I can't really blame her. She was up in Innisfil with me not too long ago where I nearly died more than once. She was there when so many people in the town were turned into something that resembled zombies and a gaunt monster from a hellish nightmare had me seconds away from the big goodbye. Yet she looks as if she might cry when I tell her what happened there.

"So they're dead," she says quietly when I'm done. "What about the kids? Are they dead too?"

"I have no idea," I tell her, but to be honest, I have to assume they are. Why else take the kids at all. "I hate to say it, but I think they might be."

"But you're not sure, right? You didn't see them dead?"

"No, but assuming they took them as food, I'm placing my bets on the fact that they must be dead." It sounds terrible coming out of my mouth and I regret the tone almost right away. I'm clearly not in the best of moods and really, I'd rather have a nap than talk about it. "Sorry, that came off as jerky. It's not something I want to think about. I hate the idea of them being dead, but why else take them if not to kill them?"

"To get to you, stupid!"

"Why to get to me?" I ask. "How would they know taking kids would draw me out?"

"Well, it did. And you said the person with them, the one who called out to you, seemed to have known who you were, right?" I nod. "Then, who's to say this wasn't all a ruse to get you there in the first place."

"It doesn't feel right, that's why," I tell her, and in all honesty it doesn't. "There's way too many things that had to come together to get me there in the first place. I wouldn't have met Detective Garcia if I hadn't gone to the hospital, so I needed to be attacked first. Then, whoever set this up had to assume I would be willing to break all sorts of laws that govern me on this planet. They'd also have to hope that Garcia would believe me enough in order to go down into the sewer with him. That's a whole lot to bring together."

"Sure, but that's assuming there's no other play after that. You said the monsters didn't chase you out, right?"

"Yeah."

"Well, why not? Why didn't they run you down and take you out right then and there? There were three of them, plus whoever's controlling them, yet there was no pursuit. Sounds like there were no plans to kill you right then and there at all. It's more like they wanted you down there to see what you were up against and terrorize you, more than anything else. Or they have something worse planned for you, God forbid. Is someone pissed off at you?"

Everyone's pissed off at me, but I don't say it. I'm sure by now Rouge already knows it. What she said makes sense too. Maybe this all has to do with the attack in my stairwell after all. Look at it all separately, and nothing makes sense. As I lay each piece of this out beside the next, it's starting to make an actual picture and I don't like it at all.

"So, you think there's going to be more to this?" she asks

me, and I nod and reach over to grab my laptop. "What are you doing now?"

"Trying to see if I can find out what I saw down in the sewers. I thought it was going to be that Golgotha I told you about, but it wasn't."

"So it wasn't the shit demon?" she says, and chuckles a little. I raise my eyebrow. "Didn't I kind of say it sounded weird and unlikely? I mean, it's something that's been in a movie."

"As usual, you're right. Now I have to try and do something to figure out what it really is and I have one idea of how to do it. Not that I look forward to the idea."

"What are you thinking?"

"Well, what are your plans for tomorrow?" I ask, and the thought brews a little more in my head, a plan that may be the best way to get some answers.

"Not much, why?"

"I was thinking about going window shopping tomorrow and I'd love you to come along."

"Is this work related?"

"Yeah, but don't worry. This won't be hands on." I tell her, though I'm not so sure about that. With the way my days have been going as of late, I could be walking into a nightmare or a fight for my life. I have to hope that it will be neither though. Something's got to go right for me one of these days. Even a broken clock is right twice a day.

"Even if it was, I'd come along," she tells me, and kisses my cheek. "Someone's got to protect you from the big bad wolf."

Sunday

We take public transit today. I'm not a huge fan, but with Rouge coming along, it's not so bad. This is what I'm thinking up until the moment a woman is across the aisle from me, clipping her fingernails as though she's in her own bathroom. *Seriously!* I have to bite my tongue as little bits of nail fly off into the air and shower the floor near me feet. I want to yell, or get Rouge to go slap her, but decide it'll just make the day start off on a bad foot. Better to let it just roll off my back and ignore it as though —

A nail hits my cheek. No, ignoring this won't work.

"Excuse me, miss," I say, and bit back my rage and disgust. I wish I had some hand sanitizer on me so I could rub the spot raw, but I don't. Rouge whispers my name and puts a hand on me and for her sake I'll be as kind as I can with the woman. "One of your little clippings there just hit my face."

"Sorry."

"Yeah, sorry is for when you bump into someone by accident, or throw away a newspaper someone was reading. Sorry doesn't cover this."

She just sits there clipping her nails and staring at me while she does. "Well, what would you like me to do then?" she asks with this indignant smirk on her face, and I suddenly want to use her face as a mop to clean the floor up. I decided to be the bigger person and let my words to the bitch slapping.

"How about we start with you putting those nail clipper away and you stop spreading your biohazard around as though this bus is your personal bathroom. Do that kind of crap at home. This is public transit, not your own car or house."

"Maybe I don't have—"

"Manners? Oh, I can see you don't have any of them. Your mother must be so proud," I say, and I know I'm getting worked up now, but I can't help it. "Look around you. Do you see anyone else clipping their nails? Hey, maybe you want to pull out your insulin and give yourself a shot in public too, rest your used needle on the seat, because you paid your fare. After this are you going to pull out a pumice stone and shave your feet down a little? That would be sweet too."

I guess she's had enough. She gathers her belongs and rings the bell. Or maybe this is her stop. I think about calling out and telling her she forgot her nail clippings, but at this point I'm just glad to see her go. It appears the rest of the bus is too because many are either laughing or quietly cheering as she departs. I can't imagine anyone finding what she was doing to be an okay thing. I turn to Rouge and see she's blushing slightly and I'm worried I embarrassed her. I'm still not an expert in this whole dating thing and I hope I haven't stepped over a line.

"Sorry about that," I say, and place my hand on hers. She doesn't pull it away and I'm guessing that's a good thing. "I didn't mean to go off like that. It's just I was kind of grossed out there."

"I don't blame you. I just don't like confrontations. Especially in public is all. Still, I'm sure if it hit me I would have gone all biblical on her and brought the wrath of my Scottish heritage down on her."

"Wrath of the Redheaded Rager!" I joke.

We laugh at that and just start shooting the shit for a bit. It's a bit of a long ride, but time can fly when the two of us talk. Eventually, the conversation gets to the incident in the sewers yesterday.

"So, do you still think those symbols are a way to lead those monsters to the victims, or are they something else?" she asks quietly in case anyone close by might overhear the conversation.

"I don't know anymore. After what you said last night, I've

had a new thought. If this whole thing was about getting to me—and I'm not saying it is—maybe the symbols weren't to guide the monsters to the kids and back to the sewer. Maybe it was to get me to follow them. Could be those symbols were nothing more than a lure to catch my dumb ass."

"Or maybe they're like the cave drawings cave people used to do before. They might tell a story or something. Is it just a symbol?"

"It is. They're the same one over and over again, so it's nothing like the cave people. Besides, I think those old cave drawings are being given too much credit than they deserve." I see the confused look on her face and I smile. "Well, anthropologists think humans lived in caves back in the day, but maybe that's because the types of homes they made didn't last through the ages. Maybe their homes were more like huts, just wood and straw; something more arcane than what was used closer to the Egyptian type architecture. That type of structure would just blow away over the millennia."

"What does that have to do with the drawings?"

"Well, we think they lived in there, those dark, dank places and drew on the walls as a way to tell tales and pass on history. What if it wasn't anything more than the fact that they used the caves as toilets? Seeing as they had no plumbing back then, it could be the art is just bored men and women doodling while they do their business. No different than today really. Back then they drew woolly mammoths and hunters, now they draw boobs, penises and tell people who to call for a good time. Makes sense to me."

"So," Rouge says, and I can see her biting back a chuckle, "you think that the old cave drawings are just toilet art?"

"Why not? I mean, their diet would have been seriously rough and they'd spend a fair bit of time in the old thoughtful squat. Why not draw a pretty picture of his or her day while they wait. It's not like there were books kicking around back in the day, so they couldn't just bare down and read a chapter or two."

She wants to laugh out loud and that's good. After my little outburst on the finger clipper, it's nice to bring some levity.

Seeing her laugh is always a treat, especially when it's a good, hearty one. She makes the most adorable sounds when she's really having a good time. And even though she's holding back the roar, it's nice to see the sweet smile on her face.

And just like that, we're at our stop.

I ring the bell and we get off. No applause for us, though. I haven't told Rouge where we're going yet, but I feel like I should tell her now that we're coming up on it. She met the man once, picking up a few things for me, but I'm not so sure she'll remember the place.

"Why didn't you tell me we were going to Godfrey's?"

Apparently I'm wrong.

"I didn't want to spoil the surprise," I say and smile, but she sees right through it.

"Wait a second. Didn't you tell me last night that he wanted to kill you because you were getting involved in this? Didn't you say he came at you and you had to fight him off? Now we're going to stroll in there, say hello and hope all is forgiven? That sounds like a *really* bad idea, Dill. What do you hope to get out of it?"

"He knows more than he's letting on. He said the symbol was for that shit demon, but it wasn't. Godfrey's not likely to make a mistake like that, so why tell me that at all? Maybe he knows what's down there and thought he'd be able to scare me off the case by claiming this was some earthbound demon."

"So you think he did it because you're a rule follower?" she asks, and I can hear the snark and I totally see her point. She's right. He knows I'm not one for the rules. If I was I wouldn't be dating her, would I? "You know that doesn't make a lick of sense, right?"

"Well, I guess we're about to find out, right?"

I push open the door for Godfrey's only it doesn't move. It's locked. That's not normal seeing as I don't think the man has ever actually locked the place up. I stupidly try again, as if it'll make a difference, but it's still locked.

So why now? Damn it.

"Well, unless you know how to pick a lock, my lady, I'm guessing this is a dead end."

"What makes you think I can't?" she asks, and brushes past me. "You know, there are many a time when we performers have to jimmy doors open to get into change rooms some asshat has locked. Lucky for me, one of the old greats who used to work in the city, Miss April March, showed me a wonderful trick with a key and a bobby pin."

"Let's see it then," I say, and move in to get a better look.

"Step back, rookie. My trick is not for newbies like you. This is an ancient secret you must earn to learn. Plus, I like the idea of big bad monster hunter needing my help from time to time."

She hovers over the lock, shifts her back so it's impossible for me to see and within seconds pushes the door to the store open with the familiar jingle I know so well. We go in quickly and I lock the door once inside. I'm impressed and let her know.

"All in a day's work, Dilly. Now, I hope you have some sort of magical shotgun hidden up your sleeve in case your buddy decides your head would look better on this dusty floor than it does on our neck."

"No need for that," I tell her, and show her my gloves. "These are enough to hold him if I need to. That's a big *if* though. Even though he came at me with the apparent intention to kill me, I'm pretty sure he wasn't really meaning to. If he did, he'd be in just as much shit than if he helped me out in the first place. It's something I was too busy to consider when I felt like I was running for my life. But since things went sideways, I've been trying to put it all together in a way that goes from A to B nice and neat. That's part of the reason I know he has some idea of what's really going on here."

We walk around the store quietly and slowly. I have no idea if I'm right about any of it. Maybe Godfrey is here, hiding and waiting for the right moment to jump out and put an end to me. It would be bad for him, unless he could convince the higher ups that he was doing it to protect this world and the creatures natural to it. They might let him slide for that, despite his record with them. So, it's better to be on the cautious side when I'm here on his home turf.

"There is some seriously cool and weird ass stuff here, Dillon," Rouge whispers, and points to something that might look like a rusted farm tool, a pitchfork with eight prongs all going in different directions. "What's that thing there? It looks like something my friend's granddad might have had on his farm, only ruined."

"That's an Amcasser. It's sort of used in ceremonies where you need to reach spirits who hover in different dimensions all at once."

"Oh, that makes sense," she laughs, and I can tell she's being sarcastic.

"Well, right now the two of us only exist in this dimension. This time, this space, so it's easy. But there are creatures so large they exist in more than one time and space, their bodies crossing into multiple dimensions all at the same time and yet staying whole. That tool helps you communicate with them all at the same time. I've never had to use one, but I know where it is if I ever do need it."

"Some days, I think I have it all down, that it can't get any weirder. Thank you for bringing me here, lover, and proving me so wrong." She kisses my cheek and we move on to trying to find Godfrey. "Maybe he's not here," she suggests after a few minutes.

"He has to be."

"Why?"

"Well, technically, he's not allowed to leave the store."

"So he can't go out to the movies or to a strip club on the weekends?"

I shake my head.

"Why not? What is this, a prison?"

"In a way, yeah. Now, I know he's left here before. I've even gotten him to bring me items in the past. I think as long as he's helping he can get away with it, but if he leaves now, he's not helping anyone but himself and that wouldn't be good for him. There's also what happens when he leaves here of course."

"Oh, do tell. I'm sure it's going to be horrible."

"If he leaves, even to help me, the spell cast on him to look like a human—a Jamaican in fact—goes away. Without the spell, people see Godfrey for what he is, and that's not something people would easily accept."

"Is he a monster?"

"Let's just say that Rick Baker would love to use him as a model if he hadn't quit the biz."

"And what about you? What would you look like outside of the spell on you to make you so damn cute?"

Here we go. This is something I've been avoiding for a while. I take a deep breath and try to figure out if I should tell her everything or just run over a half assed account to make it easier. Damn, nothing's easy about this.

"Well, there's not really a spell over me. This is a human body. Sort of a host body in a way," I tell her, deciding not to pull any punches. "If it grows too old, or dies, even if it gets injured beyond a point that my medicines and potions won't help, another one would be provided."

"So, this is just borrowed skin?" Her face is still and I can't tell how she's taking it. I don't like this at all. It's stressful on an already stress-heavy day.

"I guess you can say that. This is my real form, no matter what, I always look like this. Treemors are humanoid by nature. But, well, if this skin dies in any way, there's another body for me, sort of a clone, but not really. It's not a body that died or had a soul before. It's only a shell of a human which accepts my DNA and adapt to it as I take it over."

"So your DNA is like a virus?" I can't tell yet if she's amazed, amused or turned off by the whole idea of it all. I know it's not an easy thing to take in, and I should've mentioned it before, given her all the details, but how do you explain to someone that the skin you live in isn't the real you?

"Not really. It's more symbiotic than virus in nature. I bet this is weirding you out right now. I'm sorry."

"Well, between that and all this creepy, dusty shit that makes me think I'm on the set of the next Saw or Texas Chainsaw

Massacre movie, weird doesn't quite cover it."

I like this even less now. It reminds me of one of those movies where a woman finds a secret out about her boyfriends and then it's splitsville. I wish I could pull her to me, tell her it's fine, I'm as normal as she is, but I feel guilty and shitty as hell. I can't shake the feeling that keeping this from her is the equivalent of lying to her and she deserves better than all this. Better than me.

"If you want to go, I'd understand," I tell her, and expect to hear the doorbell jingle as she flees from here as fast as her feet can take her. When there's nothing, I risk a look towards her and see she's staring at me with one eyebrow raised and a look on her face that says *really?* all over it. "Seriously. I should have told you all that before now. I feel pretty much like a class A jerk."

"Good. You should, but that doesn't mean I'm going anywhere. I kind of fell for you, fella. Finding out you have some skeletons or in this case, spare bodies you can use in your closet isn't going to send me running. Face it, buster, for now you're stuck with this fair-skinned lady in your life. You cool with that?"

"If you're good with me, I'm more than cool with you," I say, and she gives me a peck on the cheek.

"Good. Now let's find your buddy and get out of here."

I pull my gloves out and put them on, figuring this might be a faster way to get it done.

"Why are you putting those on?" she asks.

"Just in case Godfrey's found a way to hide himself. If he's here and I touch him, these will help me know it."

"Good call."

I walk around with my hands forward to grasp the air in case Godfrey has made himself invisible. I know I must look silly, but it's the only thing I can think to do. Once this proves fruitless though, I touch objects, rub my hands along the wall. I do every aside from punch dance in hopes of pulling Godfrey out from his hiding spot.

In the end, it seems he's not here.

Fifteen minutes of this and I finally call it quits. Rouge, who stood by one of the walls looking at some tools and strange objects, seems relieved and yet somehow disappointed. I get that. It would've been nice to find him and get some answers, but at the same time it could've led into another fight and that's not something I want.

I stand there for a moment looking around the back room and I decide it's useless. We head towards the beaded curtain. It's there that something catches my eye and I can't help but smile.

"I think that book's for me," I say, and walk over it the table where a large, dusty, leather bound tome lay.

"What makes you say that?"

I turn and hold the book up to her and point to the yellow piece of paper stuck on the front of it that reads, *For you, Dillon. I'm sorry*. This is the same one he pulled out that had the symbol in it. Maybe there will be some answers in here.

"I guess you were right after all." She smiles and after tucking the book into my backpack we leave the store. "I have no way to lock the place back up."

"Who cares? I'm sure he's still in there anyway. Just because I didn't find him doesn't mean the sneaky bastard wasn't watching us."

We walk down the street and I wonder if we should take a cab and forgo any more run-ins on public transit. At this moment I'm missing my car. You never know how easy something is until it's gone and you have to rely on others to get you around. We turn the corner, on our way back to the bus stop as I'm thinking this, when someone at my feet calls out.

"Spare some change, buddy?" a man lying on the sidewalk asks, and shakes a cup at me.

"Sorry, pal I—" I trail off as my eyes fall on him and there's instant recognition on my end. "You motherfucker!" I growl, and hand Rouge my bag so I can lift the homeless junkie off the ground and slam him into the wall of a coffee shop. Just seeing him brings back the headache I almost forgot I had. "This is the piece of shit who clubbed me."

The man's eyes fly wide open as I hold him against the wall and his mouth starts to move as though he's trying to tell me something, but nothing comes out. Rouge says nothing, and I can only assume that's because she is fighting with her own thoughts of whether I should let him go or beat him senseless. No doubt she's remembering the accident and me being in the hospital. Just seeing the junkie and putting my hands on him is bringing it all back for me and the only reason I'm not yelling at him is the fact that my head feels like there's a bass drum in it. I do my best to fight it back so I can jack this guy up. This is my chance to maybe get some information from him.

"So, tell me why I shouldn't break your face," I growl, and fight back the pain in my head.

"I don't even know you, bro. Why are you being so agro? Maybe you need to step off and take a pill, bro."

"I'm not your fucking bro, asshole! Are you saying you don't remember me? How about this; I'm the guy you clubbed in the head a few days ago when you were with the—"

"Oh shit! You're the dude the man in the costume wanted me to whack."

"Man in the costume?" I ask.

"Yeah. Little dude, looked weird. He was dressed up in a messed up costume like it was Halloween. He offered me two hundred bucks to smack you and take you somewhere after that. Said he'd give me more when we dropped you off. He even had an old bat to use on you. Beating people ain't my normal thing, but two hundred bucks is two hundred bucks."

"Dropped me off where?"

"He didn't say. I was supposed to knock you out and then carry you to wherever he was going. Didn't happen though. I ran because you went all nuts and I was scared, man. It wasn't anything personal though. I...I have an addiction, bro."

I let him go and he slides down the wall. This guy is nothing and has no real answers. He hits the ground and starts to laugh wildly.

"The costumed guy lied to me too. He said he'd give me more, but he never gave me more, but then again I never knocked you out so he could take you so I guess I didn't do the job so he's never going to..."

I walk away with Rouge beside me as the junkie continues to babble on. I doubt he knows where I was going to be taken, and even if he did say something, why should I believe him? At this point I could get him to claim monkeys fly out of the Pope's ass if I offered him a few bucks to tell me. Just when I thought I might get somewhere, nothing.

"Now what?" Rouge asks, as a bus pulls up and we jump on it.

"We read the book and hope Godfrey left it there for a reason."

We get back to my apartment and make some food and coffee. While we eat, I open the book taken from Godfrey's shop. It's called *A History of Demons, Witches and Beasts of the Earth*. It sounds like something from a damn Harry Potter book, but was written in 85 A.D.

The pages are thick and stiff, yellowed, and they smell of old basements and dusty clothes. I flip through it and see all sorts of monsters and demons; creatures I've never heard of or seen before. It amazes me how blind the world is to the things that cross over when this planet has such a rich history of the bizarre. Dragons are a perfect example of that. More than a quarter of the book covers all different breeds and creeds of the ancient beast kings. How people think they're a thing of myth is beyond me. So many cultures in every corner of the globe have depicted the same kind of monster. Hasn't anyone thought this to be a strange thing? How could societies that have never spoken to one another, cultures who've never travelled outside their small circle, all draw and make stories about the same creature? If they never existed, how can they all seem to know of dragons and draw them or write about them in a way that's so similar? I guess it's easier to deny it than to acknowledge the reality of it all.

After that, there are pages of water demons, witches with the powers to seduce, plasma monsters that live underground and are as big as a large city, warlocks who have discovered fountains of life and death, and demons who can jump from host to host and live forever on Earth.

Finally, after having gone over three quarters of the book, we get to the Golgotha and I know that is not what I faced off with. No way. The thing drawn on the page looks like a melted chocolate bar with eyes and mouth and misshapen arms. There is nothing about symbols or anything else to allude to being close to what I came across in the sewers. So, that answers that.

I keep turning the pages and right near the end, I see it.

The symbol.

"Here it is," I tell Rouge, who's lying on my couch, her feet across my lap. She sits up and leans over my shoulder.

"I expected something more than that," she says.

"It's not much, I know. So let's see what it says. *The Corelux is a symbol used by warlocks, witches and masters of the dark arts to call forth the Colossus. The Colossus were once thought to be demons, but are in fact ancient creatures born in the deepest part of the ground and live on the borders of what many believe to be Hell. The Colossus can be called and controlled using the Corelux and used as guardians, protectors, hunters, or to destroy villages. Though a Colossus will not go out during the time when the sun is up, it will accomplish any deed by night.* That's weird."

"The whole thing is weird."

"Yeah, well, part of it that doesn't make sense is there's no mention of how the symbol is used to guide these things. Only as a way to call them forth and control them. So, you might be right. It could've been put there to get me involved and then lead us to the sewers." That I don't like. Someone has clearly gone to great lengths to get me involved in this and it worked. I feel as though I've been played like a fiddle. "The other part that I don't get is the whole sun thing."

"What about it?"

"Well, it says they won't hunt during the day, but more than once the kids were stolen in broad daylight." I flip the page and there's a picture of the ugly bastard, one drawn just like I saw it in the sewers. No question about it.

"That's what killed the cops?"

"Yeah."

"How on God's green earth would a thing like that be able to even sneak around? Seriously, Dillon. There's no way."

I nod and know she's right. These things are too massive,

too solid and too much of an eyesore to be walking around in the light of day and nobody notice. If it had been a Golgotha then maybe, assuming those things can change how solid or diarrhoea-like they can make their bodies. These things are more like tanks. There's nothing else helpful right off the bat, so I keep reading out loud to Rouge.

"The Colossus are loyal and fierce. Their multiple eyes can move in different direction so as to see attacks from all sides and heights. The hairs on their faces and arms are tipped with poison as are their fangs, which have barbs to hold onto their victims. The poison is a slow acting acid that eats their victims from the inside out. Many who have gone up against a Colossus and the magician who called them forth, die. Only someone with the symbol of the Eastern Mage branded on them, the sceptre of the third Pharaoh, and the hair of a northerner may stand a chance at defeating a Colossus. If all else fails to fall them, the winds of the dragon wing or the fire of Ra will extinguish the life of a Colossus." I stop, as there is nothing more on the subject. I flip through the book, rifle through a few more pages and when I see there's nothing else, I close it, using the sticky note as a bookmark. "Well, that sounds like a fun time."

"Did you actually get anything out of that other than mumbo jumbo?" Rouge asks, and I smile.

"Sure, there's a thing or two in there that'll help. I guess one of the first things I need to do is find out what the symbol of the Eastern Mage is and get that tattooed on me."

"Hopefully it doesn't look like a tattoo of a Nickleback album," she chuckles. "If you can ever get a hold of Godfrey, you think he'll be able to get you that sceptre thingy, or the hair of a whoever?"

"I doubt it. I'm not sure he has the means to get his hands on that stuff, but I know someone who might help with the sceptre part. As for the hair..." I look at her and smile, raising my eyebrow as if she'll know what I mean. She looks back and there's nothing in her face to tell me she does, so I guess I'll have to spell it out. "Your family is from Scotland, right?"

"Yeah, but that's not very north. Are you sure they don't mean Inuit or something?"

"It might, but I'm betting this means someone from the highlands. You know, in a lot of cultures, red hair holds some serious power. Even though you've...enhanced yours, it's still a powerful magic in the eyes of many."

"Really? Ginger magic?"

"The hair of the devil woman," I say, and laugh. "But that'll come later. For now, I need to get the tattoo and the sceptre."

"What about the two other things? The wind of cheeks and Ramen noodle fire," she's says.

"I hate riddles. I have no idea what either of those things are, so I won't worry about them. First things first." I put the book down and grab my laptop. I start a Google search for the symbol I need tattooed on me and once I find it, I make a call to an artist I know. I tell him I need it ASAP and he says to stop by his house in three hours. I pass it to Rouge and ask if she wants to come.

"Maybe not. I don't know if you whine and cry when you get tattooed, but I'd rather see the end result than the actual work being done. Call me old fashioned. Anyway, I should go home and see the pup and let my friend off the hook." She kisses me goodbye. It's one of those long hard ones and I savour the moment.

When she leaves, I make another call to a woman I did a job for five years ago. She's a curator at the ROM (Royal Ontario Museum) and if there's anyone I can think of that might know or be able to get a hold of the sceptre of the third Pharaoh, it's her. I find her number and dial.

She picks it up on the fifth ring and says hello tentatively.

"Hi, Sara. It's me, Dillon. I did a few jobs for you years ago."

There's a pause and I wonder if she really has to work hard to remember or if I just caught her at a bad time. In the background on her end I hear some things shuffling around, what sounds like a chair scraping across a floor and then her breath deep in the phone.

"Sorry, did you say this is Dillon?" she asks, her voice close to a whisper.

"Yeah. Dillon, the guy who got rid of those weird...things in you museum," I say. Actually they weren't just weird, they were vicious. The museum had somehow become a go-to place for a breed of demons called Thursh. Hunchbacked, gorilla-like and as smart as wood, a group of seven invaded the tourist attraction over a two month period and I was called back numerous times to get rid of them. When the Thursh first arrived, they gave everyone the scare of the century. As I've said, when things cross over to this world, for the most part, they arrive in spirit form and have to use inanimate objects to make up their forms, if they choose to. Most do. Maybe there's this need to walk in a body that looks and feels real, but whatever the reason, this is what they do.

When the Thursh came, they took the bodies of mummified corpses and the armour of medieval knights and walked about looking like ghosts of those things. Even when I got there and saw them I was a little freaked out. It took me a while to pick out what they were and then I had to come up with a way to stop them. The big thing was not to cause too much damage to the items they were possessing.

Turns out I didn't need to work too hard on that. On the first day I managed to dispatch two of them using little more than my Tincher, but over the next month there were sightings of more of them and I returned again and again. During that time, the only person who worked at the museum that I talked to was Sara, so I'm surprised she's having trouble remembering me.

"You're the monster guy, right?" she finally says, as though it's just hit her.

"Right. Look, I'm wondering if I could come and see you tomorrow. There's something I need and—"

"I don't think that's a good idea. No, it's really not."

I'm a little worried by the tone of her voice. Something seems off here, and I want to find out what it is. When I met her before, she was so warm, a little on the bubbly side, yet very well spoken. Now, she seems…off.

"Is everything okay, Sara?"

"Sure is. Thanks for asking. I should probably go though."

"Wait. I need to know if you have or could get me the sceptre of the third Pharaoh? Do you know what that is?"

Silence.

On her end I hear a strange noise again, and then she whispers something. Perhaps she's at home with a jealous boyfriend and I'm getting something going I shouldn't. I didn't even think of that when I called the cellphone, but now I feel like a jerk. I'm about to say I'll call another time when she makes a weak sound, almost like she's in pain.

"Is everything okay? You don't sound right," I say, and for a second there's silence again.

"I'm...fine...I...no, please don't...no...Dillon!" Her voice moves from fear to outright panic. "You need to call the other one...you know...no! Get away from me!"

"What other one?"

"I can't say, but remember and you'll know...please don't..."

Her voice trails off and there's nothing there. I call her name out again and again and think of rushing out to her, but I have no idea where she is. It's Sunday, so she's probably at home, and I don't know where she lives. I can hear her crying though, begging and then, there's nothing but silence and my own voice calling out to her. That is, until the phone sounds as if it's being scraped on something and someone begins to breath heavily into the phone.

"Sara? Is that you? What's going on?"

"She's not coming to the phone, Hunter. She's busy with other things at the moment."

It's the voice of the shadowy man who was in the sewers, the one who called the Colossus' up from wherever they once were. "I see you've been figuring things out, haven't you? Was it the old bastard Godfrey who led you down this path?"

"Who are you?" I demand, yelling at him so loud my head starts to pound again and my vision wavers. "Did you hurt her?"

"Your friend, or is she just a customer? Either way, yes. I did in fact hurt her quite a lot I'm afraid. She was trying to tell you about something I want, or at least something I want to keep away from you. As soon as I found out you had the book, well, I knew you were going to go to the only person you knew who might lead you to where certain items were."

"You sonofabitch! I swear when I catch you, you're going to regret every bit of this." I sit down on the couch, my head pounding and spinning way too much for me to deal with this right now. I feel responsible for Sara's death, even though I had no way to know the bastard would be there, or could know I had the book or even that I would go to her. He seems to be two steps ahead of me at every turn and I don't like it.

"You and your silly name-calling, Hunter. Now, maybe if you tell me where Godfrey is and you give me the book you can just forget this whole silly thing of trying to come after me. Let it go and maybe I won't be so mean about what's to come. Of course, I'm still going to come after you, but at least I won't be a jerk about it and kill the pretty little redhead of yours too."

"You even think about touching her and I swear—"

"Oh, stop swearing. I get it. You're a tough guy with a mean streak and I'll get mine. Sure. I'm positive we will see just how strong you are, Hunter. But, I will give you a few days to think about it, and no more. If you don't give me Godfrey and the book, well, I guess I'll see if I can make someone as tough as you cry like the bitch I'm pretty sure you are."

"Why not meet now? Let's see how fucking tough you are face to face!" I'm yelling this, but the line has gone dead and there's nothing but static. Bastard.

Yet, as angry as I am, I'm also filled with fear and dread. The threat he made is serious and there's no way I'm letting anything happen to Rouge. Not long ago I saw these things of myth known as the Shadow People take hold of her, threaten to devour her from the inside out and it was enough for me to offer myself up to them. I don't want it to even come to that this time. I have to do something now.

I dial her number and she answers it on the second ring.

"Wow, Dillon. Miss me already."

"Of course," I say, and even I can hear the shaky tone of my voice. No doubt she can too.

"Are you all right? You sound like you're about to cry or something."

"Look, I need you to go find somewhere safe to stay. Out of

town or the country, anywhere but here."

"What the hell's going on? You're scaring me, Dillon."

"Good. You need to be scared," I say, and explain to her the phone call with Sara. I would love to give her some bullshit reason, to say that everything is fine and dandy and I just think a vacation would be nice, but I need her to know the truth. I would never lie to her about anything, especially something as serious as this. "Just go get the pup, pack a bag, and go. You can't tell me where you're going and you can't call me. When this is all over, when everything is safe again, I'll call you."

"Dillon. I can't just—"

"Please. He's already killed three police officers and someone else I know. Now he's after me and Godfrey and I have no idea why. I don't want him coming after you too. There's no way I could live with it."

We talk a little more and eventually she agrees. She says she'll do it, but if I don't call her back within two weeks, she's coming home. I tell her that's fair enough and I guess it is. If I can't deal with this guy in that time frame, it's probably because I'll be dead.

We take a little longer to say goodbye and for a moment I'm thinking this may be the last time I talk to her. The future is starting to seem bleak at the moment, and there's a chance that whoever this person is, warlock, dark magician or something else entirely, he means to kill me, and/or Rouge. I need to find a way to stop him. I need to find Godfrey.

Before all that though, I need to go in hiding. If I stay here, I'm a target, a sitting duck just waiting to be killed. I need to go somewhere nobody will find me, yet I'll still be able to do what I need to do. Where that is, I'm not so sure right now. Not having a car makes this all the worse since I have no easy way to get around.

Damn it.

Instead of stressing out, I move around my place as fast as I can and pack things into a bag. I grab my gloves, my Tincher, the book Godfrey left for me, my laptop, my cellphone, chargers, and a stack of cash, and then I head out the door. I lock up and run down the stairs and for a moment I'm expecting the man and his monsters to be waiting for me. Instead I'm greeted with cool air as the sun sets and night begins to fall. I walk along the street until a cab comes up and I hail him. Luckily I don't look like a crack or meth head so he pulls over and picks me up without a thought.

"Where to?" he asks, and I'm not even sure. I could go to the church and see Father Ted, but that's too easy. Anyone who knows anything about me the way this one does would find me there in a second. I think also of Detective Garcia, but how would he explain me to his family. Plus, he was with me in the sewer and would be targeted as well. Since I'm going for something that's unexpected, I do the only other thing I can think to do.

"The marina at Ontario Place," I tell him, and off we go. I don't know anyone there, nor do I have a boat, so it'll be the perfect place to go. I have done a job there in the past and since most of it is sitting empty at the moment, a tourist attraction that lost all its steam years ago, there will be plenty of places to camp out and stay out of site. Once there, maybe I can put together some sort of plan, figure a feasible way out of this mess.

Maybe.

Monday

It's a little after midnight and I've thought of nothing good.

The place I'm holed up in used to be a room the lifeguards at the waterslide had for breaks and whatnot. There are pictures on the wall of girls in bikinis and men who look like they eat way too much protein. The whole place is covered in thick layers of dust and cobwebs, and it really smells terrible. It's as though there are dead rodents behind every wall. I can tell druggies had been hanging out here at some point. There are bent spoons, crack pipes and porn mags scattered here and there and I'm sure it adds to the fresh aroma around me. Still, beggars can't be choosers. I don't have a lot of options, so this'll have to do for now.

One good thing is the outlets still work. I guess since parts of this place are still open to the public they still have power running, despite the waste and cost. It reminds me of videos I've seen of River Country, an abandoned water park at Walt Disney World. The place was shut down years ago. There are all kinds of rumours as to why and in the videos people go on and on about brain eating amoebas and all kinds of fun stuff. The freakiest part about it is seeing how nature is doing everything in her power to reclaim the land and yet the old soundtrack is still playing over the speakers. Watching videos of it, seeing the green and blacks swallowing up a place that was once so full of happiness while banjo music drones on and on in an endless loop is scarier than any horror movie I've ever watched.

Creepy.

This place is running in at a close second, yet it will be my home until I see any huge bugs crawling about or that man and his monsters find me. If I have it my way I'll find them first, preferably with all the weapons I need.

I called my tattoo artist, Glenn, while on the road and cancelled our meeting. He was more than happy, since his brother and sister in-law are over at his house and he really didn't want to do it anyway. I told him I'd call later in the week and make other plans, but I'll need him to be available at the drop of a hat. He knows all about me and my line of work, so this doesn't surprise him at all. He says no problem and I'm sure it's not out of the goodness of his heart, but because I offer to pay him three times what I normally would. Money helps make loyal friends.

Once that is done, I start reading more of the book and check online for the items I need to defeat him. The only thing I'm guaranteed at this point is the hair of a northerner. Even though Rouge didn't leave me any when she was at my house I'm not out of luck there. I know she keeps bits of her own hair at home in her bathroom, which she uses to do certain hairstyles. Luckily I have a key to her house so that's accessible to me. One of three items down.

Of course once I get the tattoo from Glenn, that'll be two items down and then it's just a matter of the sceptre. So far, that item is a mystery to me. I've Googled it, gone on websites that deal with Egyptian artefacts and I even checked World of Warcraft and Dungeons and Dragons forums in case this isn't even something that really exists anymore and I need a good replica. Yet no matter how much I look, there doesn't seem to be a single mention of it anywhere other than the damn book. What are the chances of finding something that doesn't appear to exist?

After another two hours of hunting for it I give up and decide to call it a night. I know that these creatures, the Colossus, are nocturnal and won't come out during the day, so I might as well sleep and go about searching for things during the light of day when I'll have some sort of protection. I almost feel like I'm up against vampires, but that's just silly.

I make something that resembles a bed and lay down, doing

my best to sleep in the dark, grimy room. I'm trying to relax, to let myself drift off, but it's not easy. The smell alone is almost enough to keep sleep at bay. There's also the random itching I feel all over me. I'm almost sure there's a bug or twenty crawling across my arm, but every time I go to swat them away, I find nothing but my own restless mind causing the irritation. No bugs, no rats, just an over-active mind and exhaustion.

To help, I push away all the thoughts of the last few days and instead think about the last real date I had with Rouge. It was two weeks ago and we went out to eat at this sushi restaurant she loves and I let her have whatever she wanted. After that, we went for a walk down to the Harbourfront and had ice cream while we sat on the edge of the water and watched the sun set. We stayed there long after the sun went out and the moon rose. It was a quiet and simple date, but we talked and talked and I've never felt more connected to someone in my entire life than I did to her right then.

I let those thoughts take me down the spiral of sleep and I'm sure there's a smile on my face as I go.

I wake up to the loud blaring of a boat horn close by. I'd been dreaming about death, of the sound Sara made on the phone, only this time I was there in the room with her as the mystery man, the one who controls the Colossus, peeled her skin off her face and ate it. I tried to run to her, to save her from the vicious act of a man wrapped in shadows, but I felt as though my body was glued to the floor. I looked down at my feet and saw roots had broken through the hardwood floor and wrapped themselves around my lower half. Blood coursed down my legs where the wooden tentacles buried themselves into my flesh, but there was no pain. The only hurt I felt was inside my heart as I looked back up and saw Sara staring back, her face nothing but red pulp as she held her arms towards me and cried out my name.

Dillon!

Then the horn went off and I woke up nearly gasping. So, even though I'm yanked from sleep too quickly, I'm glad of it.

I sit up and my body is sore from the terrible bed I made. I really should file a complaint with the hotel manager here. This is no way to treat a paying customer. I stretch out as many of the kinks I can before I pack up my things and get ready to try and hunt down some answers. I check my phone and am glad to see that Rouge didn't call me, something I was worried about. The last thing I need is her to call when she gets to where she's going and somehow the bastard is able to find her. I have no idea what he can do or how long his reach is. I need her to lay as low as she can until this is over.

It's just after ten in the morning. It's an ungodly hour for someone like me to be up. That thought tells me where my first stop of the day will be. I'm not sure why it's there I'm deciding to go, but it's as good of a place as any. I could use a friend at the moment. I decide not to call him; after all, he doesn't have a cellphone and there's no saying he'll be near his phone. Better to just head to the church and surprise Ted and lay it all out for him. He loves puzzles, always has a Sudoku thing out, so this might be right up his alley.

I walk out carefully, not wanting to be seen in case I decide to come back again, which at the moment is the most likely scenario. Where else can I go at this point? The sun is bright to the point of being blinding and I take out my sunglasses. Once they're on I head out of Ontario Place and try to find a cab. Not an easy task in that area. I have to walk all the way up to Front Street to find one and then it costs me nearly forty dollars to get to the church. This cab thing is killing me. Maybe I should just steal a car.

In the light of day the church is splendid looking. It's very gothic, with light grey stonework, epic stain glass, and four towers that stand five storeys tall. They just don't build things like this anymore. Nowadays it's all glass and steel, not to mention ugly shapes and angles. A few years ago there was an add-on to the ROM. It looks like a terrible glass growth being born out of a wonderful historic building. Just awful to look at. And don't get me started on the Art Gallery! What are the higher-ups in this city thinking? Not much is my guess.

I walk into the dark shadows of the church and head to the

back where the alter is and the hallway which leads to the rectory. Halfway there I nearly jump out of my skin.

"Dillon?"

Father Ted's voice comes from one of the pews to my left and when I turn I see the man on his knees with a bucket and brush in hand. No wonder I didn't see him when I walked in. He was bent down cleaning the gum of his loyal flock from the undersides of seats of where they sit. How catholic of them.

"What are you doing here, Dillon? Did you help Detective Garcia out?" he asks, as he stands up and wipes his hands off on a red towel.

"Not really. It's actually why I'm here. I might need your help."

"Might?"

"No, I really need it," I admit, and he walks over to me.

"Let's go to my office and you can tell me what's going on."

I follow him through the church and feel a little better. The place is cool and quiet and I can see why people come to places like this. The sheer size of it, with the high ceiling and statues of people who we're told have been through so much makes you feel small in a way. Feeling small helps to make your problems seem insignificant in the grand scheme of things. I wish I could just sit there for a moment, meditate on it all and hope things just pass by. Maybe they will, but I doubt it.

Once in his office he offers tea, but I decline. Peel is there, huddled in the corner with a comic book, though for the most part he's looking at me as I tell Father Ted everything that's happened to date. I go through the taking of the last child, the cops dying in the sewer, the things down there with the man who knew who I was, the disappearance of Godfrey, the murder of Sara and the book. It takes longer than I thought it would, and when I'm done I feel my headache coming back. I'm starting to wonder if this damn thing will ever fully go away.

"So, you know how to kill the monsters?" Ted asks, and gets me water and some Advil, clearly seeing me in pain.

"I think so. The book says what I need, but one thing makes no sense."

"What's that?"

"The sceptre of the third Pharaoh. Nobody seems to know what that is or where to find it, so I'm kind of stuck."

Father Ted shakes his head and looks as confused as I feel. "I can't say it rings a bell for me either. I'm assuming it's Egyptian though?"

"That would be my guess," I tell him, and down the painkillers and my head continues to pulse. "I'd called Sara up thinking she'd know, but when I did, that's when she was killed by the bast...sorry, by the shadowy man."

"No need to apologize, Dillon. I can completely understand how you feel. This is not your regular work. Where's Rouge in all of this?"

"Safe. When the guy threatened to kill her if I didn't do as he told, I called her and told her to run."

"Is she somewhere safe?"

"Seeing as I have no idea where she is at all, it's the safest place to be. I have no idea what this guy can find out, if he has some way of finding things out from people or tapping phone lines, so we're not going to have any contact. I can't let anything happen to her."

"Sounds like a good idea."

I thought so too, but I really wish she was still around. Just being near her makes life so much easier in a way that doesn't really make sense. She gives me comfort just with her presence and that's something I've never known before. It's like I can figure things out better with her close by, that I see things clearer with her there. But I would never risk her life just for a bit of comfort, so I'll figure this out on my own. Well, that's the plan at least.

"And what about the book?" he asks, and sips some tea.

"It's safe. I guess as much as it can be," I tell him, seeing as it's in my bag, which is next to me on the floor. "Seeing as the shadowy man wants it so bad, I need to make sure nothing happens to it."

He nods and gives me a smile. "So what are you going to do now?"

All I can do at first is shake my head, because other than him, I'm not sure who else I can turn to that might know anything. Yet that thought brings me to something—close to it at least.

When she was on the phone, about to be killed by this unknown asshole, Sara said I needed to call the *other one...you know*, but I don't. What other one is there for me to get a hold of? She was the only person I really dealt with at the museum...

Oh damn!

I think I have it, but I can't be sure. If it is, that would make sense why she didn't want to say it on the phone, in front of the asshole killing her. Why give him another person to go after when I could just figure it out myself. I wish it hadn't taken me so long, but this has to be whom she was talking about.

"I think I need to go," I tell Ted, and try not to smile as the idea continues to brew and make sense. "Thanks for the water and the pills. My heads feeling a bit better."

"Did you think of something?" he asks, and stands with me.

"Or someone?" Peel asks, from his spot in the corner.

"Not really," I say, and I know I'm being vague, but I'd rather not pull Father Ted into this. And there might be a small part of me that doesn't fully trust the little monster in the corner. Even if I'm letting him stay here doesn't mean we're butt buddies. "I need to go try and find some way to end this. I don't want to put you out, or in any danger, Father. Thanks again." I head for the door.

"Would you like me to come?" he asks, and as nice as it would be to have someone tag along, I'd rather do this alone. The last thing I need is to see this man, a true innocent person, killed in front of me because of a need for company.

"I think I got it from here. When this is all done though I'll stop by and we'll have a chat. I'll even bring something along for your little buddy there." I laugh and wink at the Quilly who only sneers back at me. I guess he still doesn't care for me. Must be the whole monster hunter thing.

I leave the church and head to the subway a few blocks away. As I go I start to think more and more about it. Sara said I needed to see the 'other one', but there shouldn't be anyone else since there was nobody else at the museum I ever spoke to. But, the only thing I can guess is that she means her foster sister, Meg, who lives in St. Jamestown.

I have never met her foster sister or spoken to her, but Sara told me about her enough and told the woman about me too. She even tried to set the two of us up long before I met Rouge, but in the end that never worked out. Our schedules never meshed. One thing I do remember about her is that Meg is a professor of religion over at the University of Toronto and she very well could know something about the sceptre. And if the shadowy man and his monsters don't know about her, she's my best shot at gaining an advantage.

Or so I hope.

The woman answers the door and she's in tears. This has to be her, no doubt having learned of her sister's death. I wish I could've come here on better terms, but there was no time to let her have the grief she needs.

The house was easy to find, especially in this area. St. Jamestown is a strange place and has the nickname Cabbagetown. The place is sprinkled with old homes that go for one to two million dollars and high rises owned by government housing. It is densely populated with lawyers, crackheads, doctors, deadbeat dads, meth heads, bankers, and everything in between. In the daytime it looks a little haggard, but still decent. The night here, well, there's an old song from the 80's about it being when the freaks come out. In this case it's true.

When I spoke to Sara about her foster sister, she said her sister's house was one of the nicest on the street. I remembered the name, Winchester, because of the gun and seeing as the streets aren't terribly long, it was easy to spot. To make doubly sure, I opened the mailbox on the porch, pulled out a letter and saw her name on it: Meghan Beauchamp. I knocked and she answers and right away I knew she has already heard.

"Ms. Beauchamp?" I ask, and she nods. "I very sorry to hear

about your loss. My name's Dillon and I was a friend of your sisters."

"The monster guy?" she asks, and wipes some of the tears away, though more flow right away.

"Yeah. I was wondering if you have a minute. I know it's a bad time—"

"Do you know something about this?" she asks, cutting me off and already seems angry. Even through the flowing tears I see her eyes clear up a bit as something close to rage takes the place of sadness. "Is it you? Were you the one that got her killed?"

"No...please...I had nothing to do with this, not really. I only want to help get the those responsible for it."

"How are you...going...to...help?" she asks, and her tears return, turning quickly into deep sobs. "Can...you bring h-h-her back? No? Then why don't...you just...fuck off!"

"She told me to come and see you," I say, and the door is slammed in my face, but I won't stop. I lean in close and keep talking. "She told me you might know what the sceptre of the third Pharaoh is."

Nothing.

"I was on the phone with her when she died and she told me to come see you. Please. I just want to help."

I stand there on the porch with the sun on my back and hope she'll answer, that she has something to offer in this. I count to thirty and say it again, but there's nothing from inside. I guess this is a dead end too. I'm really starting to lose my cool here. How many doors can get shut on me before I realize I'm out of my depth with all of this? Maybe I should just throw in the towel and hand over the book to the shadowy bastard and his Colossus and take what's coming to me. What else can I do?

I turn to walk away and as I do, the door opens and I turn to face it. Meg is there again and pulls her front door open wide. She's wiping her face with a tissue and looks at me in a way that is totally heartbreaking. I feel this is my fault. If it hadn't been for me, the shadowy man wouldn't have had a reason to go after her. Even though he did it, how can I not take some of the credit?

"Come in then. If she sent you, I guess I can help."

She looks so lost, defeated, and I feel bad. I wish I could've waited, even a few days to come, but there's no time to lose on this. I need to do what I can and get this done.

I walk into her house and it's as nice inside as it is out. The air is cool and the scent of roses and musk hang in the air. It's well lit and decorated the way a house would in the late 1890s with ornate tables and chairs, patterned wall paper and a plush couch. She takes me into the living room and offers some water or lemonade, but I decline both. I don't want to take up too much of her time. Not at the moment.

"You were on the phone with her when she died? Why?" she asks, before I can even say anything to her.

"She wanted to talk to me about something at the museum. She thought there might be more weird things there," I lie, because it's easier than telling her I was on the phone when the sonofabitch was killing her because he wanted to get to me. If I say that, the conversation will be over.

"Have you told the police?"

"I did speak to a Detective Garcia," I say quickly, and that seems to be the right thing to say. I will tell him too, once I'm finished with all this and have a chance to call him. "I'm so sorry for you loss. Your sister was a kind and gentle person."

"Thank you. I hear people tell horror stories all the time, about growing up as an adopted kid, but my life with Sara and the Beauchamps was amazing. I wouldn't have given it up for the world. Sara wasn't my sister by blood, but she...she was my sister." I give her a second as she lets out more tears and wait to go on.

"I know her...knew her for quite a while. She helped me out so many times before. I don't even know who would do this, but I know whoever did will get what's coming to them."

"I hope so."

We sit in silence for a moment. It's a little awkward, but to be expected. The woman's grieving—or at least trying to—and here I am in her living room, a stranger, about to ask her for something that got her sister killed. I will of course leave that part out.

"What did you say you were looking for?" she asks, when she has gathered herself up enough.

"It's called the sceptre of the third Pharaoh," I say again, and a look crosses her face. It's as though she's confused.

"And Sara said to come to me about it?"

"In a roundabout way, yeah. Do you know what it is?"

"Yeah. I know what it is, but I don't know what good it'll do you." She gets up and grabs a book off her shelf and brings it over to me. She sits next to me on the couch and opens it. She zips through the pages and gets to what she's looking for. It's not what I expected. "Shortly after the death of Christ a man who claimed to be a child of Egypt moved north and came to a place in Ireland which was the home of a Druid priest. The priest found the dark skinned man intriguing and after hearing tales of Egypt, the Pharaohs, pyramids and the shrines of the dead, the leader called the Egyptian a prophet and adapted their own belief system to incorporate much of what he said. They began to mummify their dead and worship the Gods of Old as well as the great Elders of the forests and Earth. As each leader died, they named the next Pharaoh as their leader and were passed on a symbol of power. This is the item passed to the third Pharaoh, known as the third sceptre."

On the page is a gnarled branch. It's a dark, twisted thing that looks more like a root than anything else. There are things carved into the top of it, the thickest part of it, and to me they look like Runes. This can't be it though. I was expecting something grand, made of gold and jewels. Not this thing.

"Is this the only thing it could be?" I ask, and hope she's going to say she has something else.

"If it's the sceptre of the third Pharaoh, this is the only one it can be. It's said to be a holy relic, as are all other gifts given to the other ten Pharaohs who ruled that sect of the Druids, before the wild men wiped them out."

"Well, that's unexpected," I say, and sound as defeated as I feel.

"Were you hoping for something else?"

"I guess it doesn't matter what it looks like, but I can only assume something like that probably hasn't lasted the test of time. I mean, how long can a wooden stick stay before it just disintegrates?"

"There are stories that pieces of the ark and the cross Jesus was crucified on are still around," she tells me.

"Yeah, there will always be stories like that, but I need something tangible. I actually need to find this thing and without a place to start I have to assume it's gone."

"You'd be surprised," she says, and points to her bookcase. I don't see what she's pointing at. "Not the bookcase. Beside it."

And there it is, right in front of me the whole time. Beside the bookcase is a glass display that stands as tall as the other, but not as wide. Inside is an array of goodies and as I walk over I know what some of them are. One looks to be an ancient nail, no doubt used in crucifixions during the time of Christ. Another is of vial of water with Spanish writing on it, and if I'm right it's from the mythical fountain of youth. Beside that is a book bound in flesh, but it's the top shelf that pulls my attention.

"Is that really it?" I ask.

"It is. Over time the wood petrified, so it's actually stone now, but this is the same sceptre that you're talking about."

"How did you get it?"

"I used to do work in the UK and in Europe, helped a few professors at just the right time and this was given to me as a gift. Since the Druids are not nearly as respected or revered as other religions, most museums pass on items like this. Especially when they have to explain how someone from Egypt came and changed a small sect in the larger group. Easier to just forget about it."

"Well someone thought enough about it to put it in that book," I say, and point to it.

"That's because it was written by me. Guess you missed that, huh?"

I guess I did, I think, but don't say out loud. It's smaller than it appeared in the picture, but just looking at it I can feel its power. Now I need to convince her to give it to me. This might not be easy.

"When will you bring it back?" she asks, before I can even say a word. I turn to her and wonder if I look as surprised as I feel. "It's obvious you came here for it. I know what you do, Dillon. Sara told me, remember? So why else would you be here asking about it if you didn't need it for something? Just tell me this: are you going to use it to go after the fucker who killed her?"

"It's the only way to get them," I say, and nod. "The person who killed her has something with him, monsters from this world and the only way to stop them is to use that and a few other items."

"But you said her death doesn't have anything to do with you and yet you say monsters are involved. How is that possible?"

"It's hard to explain," I tell her, but then figure I have nothing pressing to get to, so I give her the whole story as far as I know it. She listens, tears up now and again, but by the end of it, she can see that I'm only a piece of the big picture, not the one painting it. That space belongs to the shadowy man. I do my best to show her there was no way I could've known what was going to happen to Sara, that it wasn't my fault, despite the guilt I feel eating away at me. All I can do is hope I get through to her.

For a few minutes after I stop talking. She says it's okay, and wipes away the last of her tears.

"Well, if you need it for that, I don't even care if I ever see it again. Just do me a favour."

"What's that?"

"Make it hurt!"

That's the plan.

Luckily the sceptre fits in my bag. It's only the length of my forearm and it's heavier than I thought it would be. I feel better knowing I have the hardest of three things I need to put an end to the Colossus so I'll be able to then face the shadowy man one-on-one. I figure the next stop should be an easy one. I've decided to head over to Rouge's house since it's not that far from here so I can grab the bit of her hair before I get the tattoo. That should mean that by this time tomorrow I can actually start to hunt them down; do what I do best.

As soon I step out of her house though, I feel nervous, as though the shadowy man might have eyes on me. He knew I'd gotten the book from Godfrey, and knew how to seek out Sara, so who's to say he isn't following me around the city, or paying someone else to. If he gets me now, with only one piece of the puzzle in tow, I'm doomed. I need to hurry and get everything I can before the bastard, or anyone he's hired, gets to me. The last thing I need is to come face to face with one of the Colossus right now.

I hit the sidewalk and I really do feel as though I'm being watched. It's a strange sensation, but I can't let that slow me down.

I take the bus since it seems the easier way to get to Rouge's, and rest my head against the window as we go. I take the time to relax and come up with a plan. When I start to hunt them tomorrow or the next day, I have to have an idea of where to start. I doubt they'll be back in the sewers, as I already dealt with them there and the shadowy man will know it'd be my first stop. I doubt he is that stupid. He's already proven himself to be a sneaky one, so I figure he's moved on to somewhere new.

Yet I also know the Colossus don't do things during the daylight hours and I assume that would mean moving about to a new location as well. So that means they'll need somewhere dark to hide, a place out of sight where the beasts can come and go in the night and they can sleep during the day. The city is full of places like that, so that'll make my job harder. Better to worry about the small details tomorrow when I have the tattoo, the hair, and the sceptre together. I will also have to try and figure out how to use them once I have them all so I can beat these things. The book wasn't very clear on that end of it.

As the bus approaches the stop closest to her house, I heft the bag up on my shoulders and groan at the weight. Who knew a petrified stick could weigh so damn much? The strain of it makes my headache return, something I thought had receded after leaving Meg's house. Great, that's just what I need. At least I know there's Advil at Rouge's house, so that'll be that. I'm a little perplexed by how insistent it is, and how just when I think it's gone away it comes back with a vengeance. I don't think I've ever been hurt like this before, and I've had a hand dangling by tendons before.

I just have to hope it'll go away sooner than later.

I pull my keys out and get her door. Damn, the house smells just like her and it makes me miss her. I remember the first time I came in, expecting something so different than what I found. I was there for a job, though, not her or to admire her place. She had some unwelcome guests in her basement and it turned out to be the best job I'd ever taken. If those creatures in their false bodies hadn't shown up, who knows if I would've ever met Rouge. It makes me feel as though fate really does exist.

I walk to her bathroom and I see it's a little dishevelled. Clearly she'd been in a rush to grab the things she thought she'd need the most and in doing so, wasn't very neat and tidy about it. I won't judge her. I know I did the same thing, though my house tends to always have a junk shop look to it. I live in a perpetual state of disorganization. No time to think about that. For now, I want to grab the hair, maybe smell her pillow, and get the hell out of there. For all I know the shadowy man is watching this place.

It takes a few minutes of rooting around makeup, hairclips and digging in her caboodle before I find some. A small ball of red hair in a bag with rollers, clips and other things for her styling I'm guessing. I tuck the wad into my pocket and head to her bedroom. I know this might be creepy to some, but if I can't have her here right now, the least I can do is get a little reminder of how her hair and skin smells when I hug her. At least I'm not hunting down used panties. Yet.

I open the door to her room and I'm knocked to the side by a blur. I grab for the wall so I don't fall on my ass. I somehow manage to stay on my feet and I quickly scan the room for what hit me. I hear feet hitting the ground and there it is to my right.

And to my left.

Two of them—this is not what I came here for. If I'd just left, maybe these guys wouldn't have found me. I guess I'm lucky though. They're not Colossus'. Instead, it's two Yerks; demons from the moon of Venus. They're big and angry looking. Their forms are made up of dirt and stone which shifts wildly as they move and breathe. I know they're not the brightest of races, but they are vicious and love violence. Guess I can add this to my string of terrible luck.

Normally, these kinds of creatures are fast to act and brutal too. They're the kind of creatures who think on the most primal level, so better to fight and kill than to talk. Strange thing is they're not coming at me. The two of them are just standing on either side of Rouge's bed, staring at me and breathing heavy.

"Look," I say, and hold up my hands, leaving my Tincher and my gloves where they are for the moment. Hopefully this will keep them at bay. "I don't know how you two got here, but I'll make you a deal. You go out that window and I'll let you both have a month on this planet where I won't even come after you. You'll be free to do whatever you want as long as you don't kill anyone of course."

They look at each other and it's impossible to tell what they're thinking. The false faces these beings have aren't always the most expressive things in the world. With them, it's like trying to get an emotional feeling from a brick wall.

"If you know who I am," I continue, "and I'll assume you do, then you know that's a pretty sweet deal. Just go out that window, and we'll dance another day. What do you say?"

"We say nothing to you, Hunter. We have a job to do," the one on the right growls, his voice like nails on a chalkboard.

"You should have given him the book, then he would have killed you quick," the one on the left says, sounding like a carbon copy of the one on the right. "Now, we get to have you for as long as we want. He said as long as we get the book, we can keep killing you forever."

So, the shadowy man might not have been following me. Instead he called forth a couple of demons through a porthole no doubt to wait out where he thinks I might go. Great. Not only can he call up ancient monsters in this world, but he knows how to get things to cross over and join him too. Perfect. I also have to wonder if there's something waiting for me at my tattoo artist's place.

I'll get to that later. For now I have to deal with the bopsy twins.

"Listen," I say, as I slowly reach towards my weapons, hoping my words will distract them enough. "I know that the man, whoever he is, has promised you all kinds of things, but do you really think he can keep those promises? Do you think this will end well for you?"

"We do. You are the Hunter, the king of lies and prince of death," number one says, while number two nods.

"Yes, he's right," butts in number two. "You aren't even of this world, yet you stay here and punish those who want to live as you do. Liar. Killer. Fiend. We'll make you see what it's like to be treated the way you treat all the rest. You'll be the hunted now."

"Listen Tweedle Dee and Tweedle Dumb, I don't really care about you two at the moment. Why not just get out of here and go find some yummy dog shit to eat?"

"We don't eat dog shit! What do you think we are, Plithers?" says number two.

""Dog shit," number one spits out. "We would never touch such vile things. It's the droppings of the cats we long for. Urine cakes and sprinkled bars of feces are a treat the likes our world never holds."

"Oh, well, my apologies," I say, and my left hand is on my Tincher, my right on my gloves. Time to end this one way or another. I'm wasting time here with these two dumb asses. "This is your last chance to go and enjoy what you like best. Take the window or else you're going home. It's really up to you?"

"The Hunter thinks he's tough." Number two laughs and takes a step towards me.

"Very, but he has no idea the pain we have in store for him, brother."

"Have it your way," I say, and as I do, number two makes his move before number one can. This is lucky for me. If they both charged at once I might have a hard time swinging the blade to get them both and no doubt I would take some damage. But one moving sooner and faster than the other gives me time.

Number two is only three steps away from me when I finally pull the Tincher free and he sees it gleam in the sunlight that is coming in from the bedroom window. He cries out just before I arch the blade and slash it across his chest. I feel the grit of the stones and dirt as the blade moves deep through him and as the cursed steel breaks free, his body crumbles to nothing more than a pile of soil and rocks. I'll have to explain that later to Rouge.

As soon as number two drops, I turn to number one who's now backing away from me with his hands up. I use this time to slip my spellbound gloves on and move towards him. He's clearly scared. One-on-one was not something he had in mind, but now that's what the odds are. I'd say even, but there's not a whole lot he can do to get rid of me now.

"I guess you're regretting not getting out of here," I say, as his back hits the wall behind him and he lets out a yelp. "Maybe I'll still let you get away if you tell me what I want to know about the man who sent you after me."

"You killed my brother. You sent him back and now he's as good as dead there. I won't tell you anything, filth!"

"Do you want to join him? Or maybe I will do something to just extinguish your light and let you die here in a body of dirt and waste instead of letting you go home."

"You can't!"

"Can and will," I tell him, and even though I could do it if I had the right tools, there's nothing on me that can do that. He doesn't need to know I'm lying though. He just needs to tell me what I want to know. "Tell me who it is that sent you, why he did it, and where I can find him."

"NO!" Number one yells, and raises his right hand. As he does, something happens I've never seen before. The dirt and rock that make up his fist and arm begin to quake and swirl, whirlpool. Then, like a geyser, the bits of him fire off in my direction and smash me hard in the chest. I grunt as the wind is knocked out of me and I get sent flying back against the wall. I hit hard and smash my head. I see stars and my brain is full of agony. I look up at him, to see if he's attacking, but I can barely see anything at all. The room looks like a blur of shapes and colours. Luckily the dummy screams as he charges at me and I have time to raise my Tincher, which he runs into like a freight train.

Behind me, I feel the dry wall buckle as the force of him hitting me pushes me back hard. I groan and push the blade in deep as his open, dark mouth moves to my face as though he means to bite it off. I need leverage so that I can get the knife moving and dispatch him. Why does he have to be so damn heavy?

"You will die, Hunter. I will eat your soul from your eyes!" he bellows, and pushes even harder, but as he does, his weight shifts just right and I can move my arm.

With all the force I can muster, I twist the Tincher and rip it sideways, pushing it straight out of the Yerk. The mess sprays Rouge's bed with black, false flesh and stones. The monster wavers and the pressure is off me as it tries to take a step back. His hand moves to the exit wound and it looks like he's trying to cover it, even though he's coming undone. He looks down at where he's coming apart, disintegrating.

The Yerk turns back to me. "You are the worst kind of evil, Hunter," he says in a low voice, and attempts to walk towards me, but his right leg turns to a pile of its former state. "There is a change coming. You will not be safe."

On this last word, the Yerk is no more than a pile of the same nothing as his brother is.

I groan as I push off the wall. My head feels like there's a metal band playing at eleven and I need them to turn it down. My chest hurts too from where he hit me, but nothing like my head. I should be resting, not doing this. Maybe when I finally get rid of the Colossus' and the shadowy man, I'll take a nice, long vacation with Rouge somewhere. Relax on a beach or go have some fun at Disney World. I think I've earned a little R and R. Especially if I make it out of this alive. If I don't make it through this, I'll get to have the longest rest I've ever known.

I take my bag with the sceptre in it, the hair in my pocket and then get ready to leave Rouge's house. I still need to find a way to get the tattoo, but I guess that'll have to wait until I'm away from here. I think if I can get a hold of my artist and convince him to meet me somewhere other than his house or workshop, it'll be better. If the shadowy man knows about him, it won't be safe to go anywhere he works out of on a regular basis.

I'm almost out the door when my phone rings and I'm worried. I'm sure it's going to be Rouge and if it is, I don't even want to think about what could possibly happen. I quickly pull it out, ready to answer it and tell her not to call back, explain it's not safe. When I see the display though, I see it's Garcia and there's a bit of hesitation. I know this isn't going to be a fun call. It can only be one of two things. He's either going to ask if I found anything out, or he's going to tell me about what happened in regards to the three officers he lost. One of those things I don't want to talk about on a cellphone, the other I just don't want to deal with. I have no idea how much trouble he's in or if he kept my name out of it—sometimes ignorance is bliss. I'd rather be kept in the dark on this.

The phone is on the fourth ring when I finally answer it. I know it'd be better to hear him out now than to wait and stress out over what it could be. Here goes nothing.

"Hello?"

"D-Dillon?" he says, and his voice is a stuttering mess. He sounds like he's crying, his breath hitched and as bad as I thought the phone call could be, this sounds as if it might be worse.

"Detective, are you okay? What's wrong?"

"I have nothing. Nothing and I...what can I do...how...what am I...you...you need to help me. Please."

"Help with what? What's wrong?"

"They came and took him...they took my boy."

Jesus! Just when I thought things couldn't get any worse, here we go.

"I'm coming there. What's your address?"

"They took him. He was in the...the bathroom and then... gone. They took him...right from me...left a note...he's gone... dead...like the others."

He's in shock. I can't believe this is the same hard, stern-faced man I met the other day. His voice is soft, weak and pathetic. I saw the way he'd looked at his son the other day and the love he had for the boy. I'm sure I'd be the same way if I lost Rouge. Well, maybe not as bad as he is. That was his child after all. I need to help him.

"Garcia? I'm coming there. What's your address?"

"There's a note…for me…"

"Okay," I say, figuring I will just let him talk until he can give me what I need. "What's the note say, detective?"

"To come to the old Distillery buildings. It says…my boy is there…to come with…a book about demons…or…or he dies…" His words melt away to sobs and I wait until they taper off before I say anything else.

"Look, I know what he's talking about. I can get the book, but I need to know where you live. I will take a cab there now and we'll go together. I'll help you, Garcia, but you have to help me too. Where do you live?"

He gives me the address and I know just where it is. I tell him I'll be there soon, and then hang up. I'm about to call a cab when I look over at the kitchen and have an idea. It's not a very good one, but it's the best plan for now.

I set my bag down on the kitchen table where I've had more than a few breakfasts with Rouge and walk to the sink. Beside it is a knife rack. I take out a sharp paring knife. I look at it and feel less than enthusiastic about what I'm about to do. This is dumb, but it's all I have for now. I turn the water on, only hot, and then head back over to my bag and pull out the book. I turn it to the appropriate page and then walk back over to the sink. I look at the knife, then the page, and let out a long breath.

Guess there's no time like the present.

I lower the blade to my forearm and push the tip of it into my flesh. I hear the skin pop, just a little, and then feel warm liquid drool from the prick. I watch as crimson drips into the sink. I'm not done though. I slide the tip of the blade up, down and across my arm, checking the book to ensure I'm doing the symbol right. White-hot pain courses through me, but I need to do this right and get it done. There's no time to get the symbol tattooed on me so scarification will have to do for now. I grit my teeth and tell myself to endure it. Pain is needed right now. On the bright side, it hurts so much that I barely feel the throbbing in my head.

That's something.

After five minutes I finish and run the raw skin under the hot water. The blood pushes out, turning thick in the flowing water. I drop the knife on the counter, and with my arms still under the tap I reach over and grab a tea towel. Once the blood flow has sufficiently stopped, I wrap the wound and turn the sink off. I feel slightly woozy. This is no doubt from the slight state of shock I'm in and the blood loss. I get something to eat and drink on the go, a pop and two bananas, and then call the cab. I want this day to end.

The cab pulls up to Detective Garcia's address and as I pay the driver I see the man sitting on the porch steps. He looks bad. He's slumped forward, his hands at his sides, his chin in his chest. Even from this distance I can see how red his eyes are and the tears staining his cheeks. Having his son taken from him must be the worst feeling in the world, just like having every hope and dream stripped from you in one fatal swoop. I know what it's like to lose so much. Everything I used to know and love was destroyed before my very eyes. The planet I come from, where the race known as Treemors lived, was the target of a war. A mad race hungry for power attacked us and I was one of the lucky few who managed to escape.

Not before I saw my family and the woman I loved killed, though. That nearly made me want to give up, to lie down and die with them, but I was pulled away by a friend and boarded on a ship that was destined for nowhere. Ten of us managed to get away, but the ship was badly damaged and we ended up spiralling into a vortex that took us into a different solar system. The shipped crashed and only I lived. So, I know about loss, yet I don't know what it must feel like to have a child, your own flesh and blood to be snatched away and their life to be swinging in the balance. My heart feels heavy for him.

Hopefully this will all work out and I can do something to alleviate his misery.

"Garcia?" I say, calling out to him, but he doesn't move or look up at me. "Detective?"

I walk right up to him and when I place my hand on his shoulder, it finally stirs him. Up close he looks much worse. He tries to smile, as though he's glad to see me, but the emotion looks limp on him and he slumps once more. Beside him, I see the note and pick it up.

Detective Garcia,

So sorry to be the bearer of bad news. It seems you have become entangled in a matter which is none of your concern. As such, I have decided to punish you by taking that which you love most, your son, Phoenix. He is a sweet, lovely boy. Such innocence in his eyes, such a bright future he could have if you are smart.

Do not fear though. It is not my goal to harm him. Instead, I will offer the child back to you, unharmed of course, in exchange for something I seek. It's a simple thing. A book.

The book is called A History of Demons, Witches and Beasts of the Earth and although you may not know it, I can assure you it will come into your life in the near future. When it does, I want you to bring it to the old Distillery buildings. I'm sure you know where they are, if not, find out. I will wait for you there so I may reunite you with your son.

Sincerely,

A friend.

P.S. Feel free to kill Dillon while you're at it and I will let you have the rest of the children too. He's a thorn in my side.

I read the last line and as I do I hear the unmistakable cocking of a gun and look at the detective. He has his service weapon in hand, and even though it's not aimed at me, the hammer is all the way back.

I didn't see this coming.

"Detective, you need to put that down, right now," I say, and don't know if I should rush him, run, or just reason with the man. I came here to help, to go where he needs to, and do my part to save his son. After all, I have everything we need, so now I need him to put the gun down so we can get to it. All he has to do is listen to me.

"He has…my boy…my son…I was supposed…I should have protected him…how could I…I fail him?"

"You didn't. You couldn't have seen this coming, Garcia. So put the gun down and let's go put an end to this. I can. I promise you that. I have everything we need to stop the monsters and the one controlling them."

"Promises? My dad promised me monsters weren't real. He told me the only thing I had to fear were death and taxes. He was so fucking wrong. Right now monsters have my son, the one thing that means more to me than the world. All I need is the book to get him back and make this right. And I need you out of the way."

"It won't end the way you want it to. Once he has the book, once there's nobody around to stop him, why would he give you anything you want? He's lying to you, Detective. He'll kill you and your son if you give in and do this."

"I have to have faith. I do. It's all I have left right now. Faith. I have to pray to God that he won't lie to me, the way my father did."

He raises the gun and points it right at me. I can see down the dark barrel of his weapon. It looks clean and well-oiled and I'm positive the thing won't misfire. Garcia is one of those people that would be so anal about his gun that he'd clean it once or twice a week no matter what. I have to be careful here. He's on edge, his son gone. One wrong word and he'll shoot me. I'm not sure I'd be able to recover from that.

"Good. Having faith is important," I tell him, and hope this will keep him from squeezing the trigger. "I tell that to a lot of people. But how are you going to keep faith, feel like a good person and look your son in the face if you kill me? Are you a murderer?"

"No, I'm not."

"I didn't think so. You don't need to do this, Garcia. He's

playing with you, trying to get you to do his dirty work. Let me go and get your boy and bring him back to you and your wife."

"My wife's dead!" Garcia growls, and the gun in his hand starts to shake. "She died four years ago."

"But I saw you at the church with—"

"My sister. Not my wife. She was taken away by cancer and now those monsters have my boy. I don't want to be alone. He's all I have, can't you understand that?"

"I do, but—"

"I'm sorry, Dillon," he says, cutting me off again. "I know God will forgive me."

"No, that's not true. Garcia, if you love your son—"

I see the flash of the barrel and instantly turn my body in a poor attempt to deke out the bullet. I think of the Matrix movies and do my best to pull off a little Neo action, but it's no good. I don't even hear the report of the gun when I see white before my eyes and my head gets rung like a bell. I'm stunned for a moment, as the white light becomes everything my world is made of. I wait for it to go away to see how bad it is, expecting a ton of pain, but all there is now is the light. It's not going away.

This time, there's no darkness.

Only light and white.

Oh no, is this death?

I have no idea, but best not to think anymore. Not that I have much of a choice.

Forever is so nice, eternity is warm and brilliant, as bright as the sun and it's not scary to be here. As I move deeper into the void I think this must be heaven, or a good facsimile of it and I try to find God and angels and everything else that supposed to be here. I've read enough to know what people say is here and I want to see it first-hand. I want the pearly white gates, the cherubs and all the perfection that heaven is supposed to be. Maybe my family will be here somewhere, just waiting for me.

There's no sound, no feel of wind, it's a vast space of nothingness, and yet I find it comforting. Even my head has stopped pulsing for the first time since I was jumped in my stairwell. The lack of a bass drum boom in my head is a blessing in itself. In fact, I feel nothing close to pain, or pleasure. It's as if every sensation has been burnt away. The only thing I can feel is the white light around me, swallowing me whole and I don't think that's such a bad thing.

I move further into the white and as I do, I think of Rouge and that's the first time I feel anything. Sadness. Sorrow at the idea I won't see her, that I've died without getting to say goodbye. There wasn't enough time for one last kiss when she left, or even a hug. and now I'm dead, shot in the head and in the great beyond. Not what I expected to happen to me, yet here I am.

Still, if this is heaven, in the way many believe the afterlife to be, Rouge should be right around the corner. I've always heard that time doesn't exist here. Not the way we perceive it on Earth or in most other realms. If that's the case, she should be here somewhere. All I have to do is find her.

I pick up my pace and pass by the same nothing as I go. There's nothing here and nothing to either side of me. It's a vast ocean of nil. I feel like I'm on the worst treadmill ever because this is just getting redundant and silly. How can I find anything or anyone here when the only thing that exists aside from me is increasingly annoying white light?

Wait, do I even exist here? Am I me or am I just light as well?

I raise my hand in front of my face and I'm relieved to see the five digits I've come to know so well. So, if I'm here and this is the great afterlife, I should be able to find someone here. Rouge has to be here.

Maybe if I call to her, she'll hear me, or be able to appear. It's worth a shot.

I open my mouth and with all the force I can muster, I yell out. "Dillon?"

That's not right. I'll try again.

"Dillon, wake up!"

That voice, it's not mine and those are my words. I go to yell again, but even before my mouth opens, I hear the same voice calling out my name and I know it. I know it so well, but my brain doesn't want to work. It's right there, on the tip of my tongue, but in the bright white of the dead, I can't find it. Is that my dad? My brother? One of the elders?

"Dillon, you're not dead. Wake your bumbaclot up!"

There it is.

Godfrey. He's here with me. Dead as well and trying to find me. At least I'll know someone else in this otherworld.

"Dillon, wake up or I swear I will lay my back hand on you!"

I don't know where you are, Godfrey, but if you call again, I'll find you. I try and say these words out loud, but I guess in heaven, words can be spoken from you mind. It's so great. Now I just need to—

Lightening shakes the world and the pain in my head wakes up. What was that? It's terrible and frightening. I go to ask Godfrey if he heard it and felt it, but before I can, the thunder strikes the world and my head again and all around me the white changes. The ground shakes and there are fissures in the perfect emptiness. Beyond the cracks I can see blue. And beyond the blue, I see my pain waiting for me—agony and a useless fight.

Oh that doesn't feel good. Godfrey, where are you? Are you feeling this too?

Godfrey doesn't answer. Instead, the thunder and pain does and with this strike the white world begins to bleed colour. There's blues, grey, red and everything else. Sound finds me, the sound of people talking, horns blowing and as the haze in front of me melts away I scream at the monster hovering over me.

"Relax, Dillon. I had to pull you inside, but it's me, Godfrey. If we stayed out there, even more people will see me."

Through the throbbing beat in my head I take a good look at the thing that's claiming to be Godfrey. It's tall and bulky, with a face that reminds me of the Lizard in the old Spiderman comics. His skin is green and bulbous, his mouth and nose more of a snout than anything, but I can tell right now he's smiling at me. There's no way I should be able to see a grin on that snout, but there's no denying it, nor is there any way to not believe who it is. The eyes give it away. I guess I never really knew what he'd look like outside the shop. This is the real Godfrey.

"What the hell is going on?" I ask, and try to sit up, but my head is on fire.

"Lay down. You were shot, but it's nothing really; more of a graze. You have bigger problems."

"Like what?"

"Like the parasite you have living in you right now."

"Parasite? What the hell are you going on about, Godfrey?" I try and sit up, but as I do, my head lights up as though someone just set off Fourth of July fireworks in here. I cry out and then feel Godfrey putting his hands on my shoulders, holding me still.

"You were hit in the head the other day, right?" he asks, and I hope it's a rhetorical question because I'm in no mood to answer him. "When you were, there must've been something on the tool used. You said it was a bat, right?" I nod. "Actually, I know for sure there was something on the bat because I'm the one who sold the damn thing."

"What?"

"It's a long story, and I'll tell you all about it, but first we need to get the fucker out of there. Now, turn your head away and then hold still."

I do as he says, biting down the pain that flares as I do, but I don't know pain until he puts one hand on the side of my face and the other hand begins to peel open the stitches in the back. I feel them popping, can sense the skin back there peeling back like a smile on some evil clown's face and before I can cry out, Godfrey, the lizard man version of him, slides fingers into me and he didn't even buy me a drink.

I try to speak, to cry, but my mouth moves and only the most pathetic sounds come out. I'm not proud of this moment, happy Rouge isn't here to see it because before long, I'm crying like a baby.

Godfrey's claws or nails or whatever is attached to his fingertips, scrape against my skull as he probes under my scalp for what he said is a parasite. My stomach is churning from the feeling, and I wracked with shivers and disgust. I can hear the wet sounds of my skin moving off my skull and there's a sensation of warmth as blood runs from the wound and pools under my ear that's pushed against the floor. I have to do something not to pay attention. If I find a special place or maybe concentrate on something in the room I'm in, maybe I can somehow forget what he's doing.

There's a vase on a coffee table full of fake flowers.

On the wall is a painting that looks as though someone might've done it by accident, then called it art.

Beside that is a framed photo of Detective Garcia and his son.

In my head I feel something shift and bite into the bone. I swear there is someone screaming inside of me.

"Got it!" Godfrey cries out, and then the pain intensifies as he tries to pull it out. The feeling of something biting into my skull intensifies and I can feel my heart beating in my brain. "You're not going anywhere, you little bastard!"

I miss that white light. The freedom and painlessness I felt was so pleasant. Maybe that was Heaven I saw for a moment and this is Hell. Perhaps all those heavy metal covers over the years were wrong and the place evil people go after they die isn't some burning pit of sulphur and horned demons, but just a ball of agony were gross looking things pull stuff from your body. I know a lot about what's out in the world and in all the universes, but death is a mystery, even to me.

Pressure. It's so intense and it feels like Godfrey's trying to tear all the hair out of my head. I wince and moan as he fights to get it loose and I hear the thing inside me, making strange cooing sounds. I hope that means it's losing this battle. Shivers run down my spine and tears have begun to roll down my cheeks from it all.

Then, as bad as the pain is, it's gone. There's a stinging in the back of my head, and a slight soreness from the open wound, but the throbbing headache and the biting shriek that had been echoing through me is no more. Godfrey let's go of my head and I sit up and turn to him to see what he's got. Clenched between his fingers is a florescent blue glob that looks a little like a ball on a string. Then I think it looks more like a weird sperm and I'm even more grossed out.

"What is that?" I ask, not sure I can remember ever seeing something like that before.

"It's a R'thuard. It's a parasite of sorts that attaches itself to the skulls of its victims and feeds off emotions and thoughts, depending on where it is. This one was harvested by a client from a Dethlore that was found on Earth years before you ever came. I've had it for a long time."

"And you sold it to someone?"

"I sold the weapon it was attached to. A bat. You're not my only customer you know."

I do know that, but selling this to someone breaks the rules, I'm sure of it. Especially a human.

"So you sold it to a human? And you told me you were scared of the consequences. What about those ones?"

"I'm not proud of what I did, and everything that's occurred since, but I'm here to help now, Dillon. If I'm going to be sent somewhere else as punishment, I think I've earned it, but for now, you deserve help. I should tell you what I know."

And he starts.

Two weeks before I was attacked in the stairwell, a man came into the shop and asked for an item. Godfrey explains that it happens now and again where a human is led to him by a source who knows what Godfrey is. Usually it's just to sell, but on occasion, it's to buy as well. The man asked for a Yourn, a type of bat that has been dipped in the blood of a Droon, which is the equivalent of a dragon, only from a distant star where it lives in a world of fire. A Yourn alone is a powerful weapon against many demons, but is just a bat against someone like me. That's unless someone also bought a Yourn with a R'thuard attached to it as this person did.

"Who was it who bought it?"

"Just a man. Nothing impressive about him. Average height, weight, with brown hair, brown eyes. Maybe thirty Earth years old and dressed as normal as people here dress, although perhaps a little dirtier than most."

"So when I came in after the accident, did you know that's what happened to me?"

"Not really. You showed me the picture of the symbol though and as you did, I saw something move under your scalp and knew the two things were no coincidence."

"So why not just tell me? You've already broken rules before. Why not just say what the symbol was and what was inside me?"

"Because this little bastard would've told its owner."

Godfrey explains that a R'thuard can and usually does have a psychic link with whoever owns it. He says he was worried that if he told me too much and acted as though he could offer me real help, he'd be killed and then there'd be no way to help as he's clearly done. I guess that makes some sort of weird sense, but it also makes me think in the end all he was doing was covering his own ass. No doubt the real reason he's helping is that I might be the only one who can stop the Colossus' and the shadowy man. If I'm out of the picture, Godfrey would have to do it on his own and that just ain't his style.

I sit there for a second and try to really put it all together. If it wasn't for what he just said, I'm not sure I'd be able to get from where it all started to here, but in a way, Rouge had been right all along. Someone is setting me up. The parasite, the attack, the kids, the killing of Sara; it's all just a strange plot that still doesn't totally add up. Whoever is doing this could have killed Godfrey and stolen the book, or if it's me they've wanted all along, why not just kill me right off the bat? It would've been easy so many different times. Is this just the crazy idea of a madman and trying to make sense of it will make my head explode? It feels that way.

"So, do you think the man who bought the R'thuard is the one behind it all, or is he a pawn like the junkie and the Colossus'?" I ask Godfrey, hoping he has a better idea than me.

"I don't know. I don't think a human could get this far, but it wouldn't be the first time. Others have done much worse with power. Rasputin, Genghis Khan and even General Lee. Humans are capable, but for this, I don't know."

I nod and know he's right. Everyone and anyone is suspect now. Even Godfrey himself. Not telling me the truth and then disappearing are just two strikes against a man who long ago struck out.

Still, he did help in the end, so I'll give him a break on that front.

"So, after it all, you left the book for me to find and skipped off until just now?"

"The book was the least I could do, but I've been following you since to keep an eye on you as best I can," he says, and I guess that explains how I've been feeling eyes on me this whole time. I really thought it was something the shadowy man had done, but since he had a R'thuard put in my skull, I guess he didn't need a spy. Godfrey was my own lizardy fairy godmother. How sweet.

"Shit," I say suddenly, and look around the room. "Where's my bag and the book? Garcia was going to take it."

"He did take the book, but good news is, he didn't know to take anything else. So we still have a chance."

"Aside from the fact that I don't know what to do with the items."

"Neither do I," Godfrey says with a smirk before he pulls out a lighter from his pants pocket and sparks it. The orange flame dances and he puts it to our little blue buddy, the R'thuard, and before long it scorches, and then turns to dust before us. It didn't make a sound.

"You look happy with yourself," I say, seeing what I'm assuming is a smile on his face.

"I am. Now that our spy is gone, I can speak the truth. I know what to do with the items and how to use them against the Colossus'."

"Seriously? Thank the stars!"

He explains it quickly and it seems easy enough, though only the first part. What we need to do after seems less fun than anything else I've ever done in my life. So, step one is to wrap Rouge's hair around the sceptre and bless it with fire as I rotate the symbol carved into my arm around it. We do it, and it seems as silly as it sounds. It also smells terrible. The odour of hair burning is enough to make me want to hack up something from my nearly empty stomach, but I hold it off.

It's done and now, it's time for the hard part.

This isn't the first rodeo I've been to in my life. There have been quite a few hairy situations in the time I've been on Earth, which is a very, very long time. Recently I went up against a Hellion, one of the most vicious demons ever made and it was right here in this world. That was a damn close call, but luckily Rouge saved my ass with some tools Godfrey sent up to me. There was also a time when I went up against two men who had called forth a female Grath, which many here might think of as a Banshee, but is a creature from three galaxies away. A Grath can call you to them with their sweet song, like a light draws in a moth, and then BOOM, your brains get turned into scrambled eggs.

The Gath cost me a friend and killed the two men who'd called her forward. I thought I was a goner too, but luck was what saved me. A scholar who'd heard rumours of her had come and distracted her just long enough for me to cut right through the mist that was her being with a tool called a Bellaham. Once the weapon touched her, she all but blinked out of existence in this world and was sent back to where it belonged. Of course the scholar was quite dismayed by the whole ordeal and called the police on me. Luckily, I wasn't charged with the murders of the three men who'd died there because no real evidence could be found as to what could've killed them. I didn't mention the lady siren and they just figured the scholar was a nut job.

Ever since I started this job I've had to face off with monsters, demons and beasts of such different sizes and shapes, so this shouldn't be any different, and it should actually be a cakewalk. Should be, but I doubt it will. I'm not that cocky. There was a time when I would have gone into this with that kind of head set, that there's no way I could possible lose, but over the years I've come to learn the very hard truth—anything that can happen, will.

"Why do you think this shadowy man and his monsters are in the distillery? Why there?" Godfrey asks, and it's something I've been thinking about since I found out about it in the note.

"I guess the dark would be the best bet. Maybe he thought we'd go back to the sewers after the cops were killed and this was his way of staying ahead of the game." I can only guess. I don't know what this guy is thinking at this point. To be honest, I've still got a lot of questions. Why did he call the Colossus' forth, why does he want the book so bad, why have the junkie and his little otherworld friend attack me and why put the parasite in me? All these questions and no real answers.

It again comes down to trying to make sense out of a madman's plot. When they live in reality their plans are just as moronic as those I've read in books over the years. Take over a world they destroy, unleash monsters onto the earth, wipe out an entire race of people, create a nuclear holocaust, but to what end? What would any of those things really accomplish? A sane person can't be expected to come up with an answer. It takes a certain kind of warped brain to make real sense out of such senselessness.

"Okay," Godfrey says finally. "I get that part of it, I guess. Makes as much sense as the rest of this does, but why there? It's not exactly abandoned."

"It's not? I've never been there. I know they film movies down there sometimes, like the opening scene in the first X-Men movie, but I just assumed otherwise it is vacant."

"No. It's become a haven for hipsters and microbreweries. They've even turned it into a tourist trap in a way."

I shake my head. I hadn't known that. I need to get out more I guess. Rouge says the same thing every now and then. She tells me I need to think outside the box, but I'm still kind of new to the whole dating thing. Everything I've learned is from old John Cusack and Molly Ringwald movies. Maybe I do need to broaden my horizons.

"Well, I guess we'll have to hop that fence when we get to it," I tell him, as I grab my bag and head to the door. I put my hand on the knob then look back to see Godfrey hasn't moved. "You're coming, right? I thought you wanted to redeem yourself."

"I do. I'm just a little worried."

"Same here, but we have the tool to beat those things, so let's get a move on."

I see him shake his head and look at me with deep, black eyes that look more like ping pong balls than what I'm used to. This whole lizard look he's sporting is still a bit jarring, I guess.

"There's more to it than that, Dillon. Something's not right here. There's been things not right for a while, haven't you noticed it?"

"Like what?" I ask, not sure I know what he's going on about.

"When was the last time you heard from *them*? Have you spoken to anyone from Head World, the offices that control the hunters? Has anyone said anything to you about the fact that you're dating a human woman? Or even made contact with you to let you know I left my shop?"

"No, but—"

"No buts, Dillon, you know that's strange. There've been rumours and mummers that things are not going well in the other worlds and realms. Haven't you heard anything at all or felt it at least?"

I think on it, and at first there's nothing there but his fear and worry. Sure, I haven't heard boo about the Hellion I killed, the Porter I killed and closed or the fact that I'm dating Rouge, but that doesn't mean anything really. There are times when I don't hear from them for a year or more so why should I worry?

I think of Rouge again and how wrong what I'm doing is. It goes so against their rules that it's weird and worrisome that nobody has contacted, or even come to arrest me. I know I shouldn't be bothered by it, maybe they're just so happy with the job I do they're willing to overlook certain things. Still, something's not right and I keep racking my brain.

And that's when it comes back to me. Not a reason why I've not been contacted or punished, but what was said to me that should have me even more worried. It's from back when I was jumped by the junkie and the Skell in my stairwell.

Since you stopped that Hellion, word is going through the universe, to every realm what you've done. Some are more scared of you and the hunters than ever before, but not everyone. There's a group out there, spanning numerous planets, realms and planes of existence, that are coming together and want you dead. They're paying any cost to get you, rid them of the last Treemor. They thought they already had, yet here you are.

I tell this to Godfrey and he looks as grim as a lizard can. "That doesn't sound good. Dillon. We need to find out if what the Skell said is true or not. What if this is connected to that or it's something far worse. Maybe these Colossus' are just proof of how much influence the Head World has lost. I don't know if we should keep going with this, or try and get answers first."

"You're kidding, right?" I ask, and hope he is. This is not the time to give up.

"No. Why fight this battle if the Head World is coming apart. We could just leave and—"

"And nothing, Godfrey. This isn't even a question. I have someone here I love and even if I didn't, I can't let this stand. This shadowy man is up to something and I can't help but feel as though it's personal." It's hard not to feel that way when you've been attacked, had a parasite put in your head, watched three cops killed, had to send your girlfriend off, listened to an old friend die, and then get shot. It feels as if this is very personal. "There's also Detective Garcia and his son to think about. They're not part of any of this, nothing more than pawns. I'm not ready to have their blood on my hands."

He's silent and I know he's never been one for fighting. Not really his thing, aside from the time he came at me with a damn sword of course. Though at this point, I have little doubt that it was all a scare tactic to make the parasite in my head report back that Godfrey wasn't helping me. I could be wrong though. Godfrey has fucked me in the past, and not in the carnal way.

"Look, you come and help me any way you can, and I'll owe you. Big time, okay?"

He's silent for a moment, no doubt trying to figure out if he should come along or leave me to my own devices. I think of saying more to him, offering some deed or object in order to seal the deal, but I think just giving him the promise of being owed should be enough. I hope it is.

"I do like the idea of you owing me, Dillon."

"Then, I'll owe you two times. Deal?"

"You better stand behind that promise, Hunter," he says, and we finally leave.

It's still sunny by the time we reach the Distillery District. We had to walk here using the sewer system. I figured it was best to keep Godfrey out of sight. It's not every day that people see a six and a half foot walking lizard fully clothed strolling down the street, so I thought best to just stay off them. It's not like we could've cabbed it or taken a bus, either. It's hard enough getting a cab in the city. In Godfrey's current state it'd be damn near impossible.

It takes us longer than I'd like to weave through the labyrinth of tunnels and I notice for the first time in as long as I can remember that I'm not even noticing or caring about the bugs here. My fear of insects has haunted me long before I ever arrived on Earth, yet as we pass by loads and loads of cockroaches and other things squirming in the water, I don't pay attention to them. I guess my mind is busy with more important worries.

After checking to make sure we're in the right area, I peek out of the sewer grate to see if it's safe to come out. The metal lid is right between two buildings and as soon as I look out I see that Godfrey was right about this place. There are people everywhere. Most are dressed in a way best described as hipster. In other words, the men are all sporting shaggy beards and oversized glasses while wearing plaid shirts two sizes too small, but the pants are even smaller and tighter. There are massive amounts of suspenders and bow ties as well, being worn by both sexes and I don't know why I see more than one unicycle in the group. Are these people off duty circus performers, or is that an actual way they want to get around?

The women look a lot like the men, but their plaid shirts are too big for them, as are their glasses; most of those are thick and black or cat-eyed. The cuffs of their pants are too high to be regular ones, and too low to be capris. There are a lot of lunch boxes here too, most with a picture of Ghostbusters or Scooby Doo on the side. Oh well, it could be worse. This could've led us to a place full of Juggalos.

"We're not going to be able to get out of here without being seen. We need to find somewhere else," I tell Godfrey, and move away from the grate.

"Is it busy?"

"Well, despite the strong odour of weed in the air, I'm pretty sure you'd still be noticed, lizard face."

"Count yourself lucky that nobody can see your true face, Treemor!" he growls, and I guess that's true. My race would have just as hard of a time fitting in.

We move along, heading what I'm guessing is south and when we come to another grate, I look up and out. What I see now is the inside of a building and I realize it must be a drain for one of the old whiskey making facilities. Perfect. I don't see or hear anyone so I push on the grate and try to get out. It's in here pretty tight, but I think I can push it open. I grunt and groan and struggle with it until Godfrey tells me to get out of the way. Once I do, he moves to it and with one good shove the metal grate is airborne. It crashes down next to the hole and he laughs.

"Guess it is a good thing I came after all," he tells me, and steps out of the sewer. I say nothing, not wanting to give him any satisfaction, but he's right. Who knows how long I would've struggled with it. I'm also thinking this might not be the last time I need his help and strength.

Ignoring the sloshing of my drenched feet, I step out and try to figure out what the next part of the plan should be. There was nothing in the letter about what building the shadowy man was in or anything that can lead us to them. For all I know, Detective Garcia is already here, having given up the book and is dead. I have to hope that's not the case. Who knows what else the shadow man could call forth once he has the book in hand.

"So, what now?" Godfrey asks, as if I have a clue.

"We need to find them. I'm guessing it'll be in a building with no windows, no real access to the public and very dark. Maybe if we go up to the roof, we can figure it out from there."

He nods and we move. There's a stairwell to the right of us and as we go, I have a weird sensation as though we're being watched. I've come to know that feeling pretty well lately, and I wasn't wrong then—Godfrey had been keeping his eye on me. Who could it be now?

I turn fast, expecting one of the Colossus to be there and when I see the shape in the shadows no more than ten feet from us, I visibly jump. I need to get a handle on that.

"Godfrey!" I call out, and the giant lizard turns.

"Holy Jesus!" the man engulfed by shadows says, and there is fear in his voice. My guess is he has nothing to do with any of this. "Is that one of those crocs that was flushed down a toilet and got all mutie?"

"What are you talking about?" I ask, and the man steps forward. It's a security guard, I think. His uniform says that's what he is, but he's very dishevelled looking. His uniform is a wrinkled mess, cat hair clings to the black pants, and his hair looks as though it's trying to flee his head in several directions. For a moment, I'm reminded of Doc Brown in Back to the Future.

"I'm talking about the monster in the slacks beside you. It looks like some mutant from the sewers, like those stories in New York back when gators and crocs were given as pets and then people started flushing them down the can. They eat all kinds of toxic shit and turn into...well, I imagine the thing beside you."

"I'm no *thing*!" Godfrey yells, and makes a motion as if to go after the old man, but I put a hand on him in hopes of calming him down.

"You sure look like one. Damn scary thing too."

"He's not. It's a...disguise is all. We're planning on pranking someone," I lie, terribly. There's no way to believe that Godfrey is in a costume, not unless Rick Baker made it for him, that is. Yet the guard nods as if he buys it completely. "I take it you're security here?"

"Yup. Came down to try and catch a nap. These twelve-hour shifts are hell on my knees. So, I come here, have a little sip of the sauce and nap. Not like anything really happens here. You're not going to rat me out are ya?"

"No. Not at all, but we could use some help."

"That's what I'm here for."

"We need to find a building. One that would be pretty dark, no windows and one the public doesn't go into."

"For the prank?" he asks, and pulls a water bottle out of the pocket of his cargo pants. He takes a fast sip, makes a face, and I can guess right there that it's not water in the bottle. Too cheap to buy a flask? Or is he smart that nobody would question a water bottle?

"Yeah, the prank," I tell him. "Maybe there's a building here you don't really patrol either?"

"There's only one and I don't patrol it. Nobody does. It was the old barrel room. I'm sure it smelled delicious at one time, but now, you don't want to even try to hang out in there for long."

"Why?"

"Smells like pure cat piss. The place has a real ammonia smell to it. They say it was from some incident in the factory, I think it's just too many Tommy Cats getting up to no good," he says, and laughs before taking another swig.

"How can we get there?" I ask, and feel hopeful.

"Easy, go up to the third floor and there's a door that says *overhang*. Open that and there's a walkway that looks kind of like a bridge. It goes right over to the one you'll want. Best way to go if you want to stay out of sight and not spoil the prank." He walks a little closer to us and points to where the stairs are and as he gets close, the smell of liquor and BO is overwhelming. "You going to post this on YouTube?"

"Sure," I tell him, and begin to walk away. "It'll be titled *Return of the Lizard King.* You like it?"

"Sounds good. I'll search for it in a week. Have fun and stay out of trouble."

"We never do," I call out, and walk up the stairs, glad to be away from him. "Well, that was fun," I say to Godfrey.

"Must be nice to get paid to sleep all day and drink," he jokes. "He thinks his job's hard, but look at him. He wouldn't know tough if it jumped up and bit off the man's balls."

I laugh at that and it's true. I know people who do security jobs. I get jobs all the time where guards work and the industry is very strange. Some of these places, the guards get to sleep or drink or fuck the dog their entire shift, and they get paid the exact same amount as guards who work in high crime areas where they're forced to patrol in areas cops won't. I once showed up to do a job in the Moss Park area and the guards there had it tough. They only have two people to work sixty-seven properties in one of the highest crime areas in the city. Drugs, guns, gangs and general criminals are everywhere and they have to deal with it all day and night long. Sure, my job isn't much easier, but at least I have the tools to protect myself. These guards get paid almost minimum wage and run the risk of getting shot or catching some disease. And everyone hates them. Criminals. Tenants. Cops. They get no respect at all.

Not my idea of a good time.

We get to the door and open it. Rusty hinges cry out as we push it open and for a second I'm amazed there isn't a lock on the thing. With a half-drunk guard napping in the basement and no locks on doors like this, this place is as secure as Godfrey is human. Then, I quickly see why.

"What the holy shit is this?" Godfrey moans from over my shoulder as he looks out the door.

I see why almost immediately and think this is going to suck. Hard.

The so-called walkway barely exists anymore. There's a steel skeleton of what once was a bridge and the odd wooden beam here and there, but not much else. I wonder if there's any way to get across this safely without plunging to our deaths.

I look down, and maybe death is too strong of a word. It's only a three-storey drop, so we probably wouldn't die. Instead, most of our bones would break and then the world would go insane as everyone pulled out a cellphone and snapped pictures of the six and a half foot giant lizard that fell from the sky. Those images would go viral and then what? Who knows how the world would react to something like that.

There are times when people in my close circle, mainly Rouge, have asked why it hasn't happened already. I have a website and commercials on late night TV. People hire me all the time to hunt down and kill monsters and demons that are in their homes and business, yet the world moves on as if nothing has ever happened. And I can only think that it's because with it being just in their house, confined to their place of business, it becomes a dirty little secret. You don't go bragging to your neighbours when you get cockroaches or bed bugs, so why would you when something crosses over from another realm or dimension? So, as long as it's a personal secret, a little embarrassment they don't want to share with the world, everything can continue to run smooth and be right as rain. Faith in everything good can continue to exist as if nothing ever happened.

But a picture of Godfrey in his current state being sent out all over Facebook and Instagram would send things into chaos. So, it's best to take this as slow as possible. That's what I am thinking when Godfrey grabs the handrail and leaps clear to the other side. Fifteen feet as if it was nothing.

Must be nice.

"Hurry," he says, and motions towards me.

"Easy for you to say, Frogger. Maybe you should've grabbed me before you jumped."

"I would've if you'd stop getting donuts at Tim Hortons," he says, and mocks having a big gut while pointing at me.

"Are you trying to say I'm fat?" I say, offended at the implication.

"Not trying. I am. Is Rouge a chubby chaser? Oh that's right, fat people like you don't run so there's no need to chase."

Oh, he's having a ball over there, trying to call me fat. I'm going to get over there and see just how my fat foot fits up his reptile ass in a second. First, I have to make it across.

There's two ways I can do this. I can balance beam on the handrail, or slowly make my way over using the skeletal frame of the bridge. Either way there's a huge risk of falling, but I need to get over there no matter what. I decide the latter way is the only safe way to go and I just do it.

It's slow and tedious work. I inch my way over and after

what feels like an hour, but is more like five minutes, I'm beside Godfrey.

"It's about time." He chuckles and slaps my back.

"Seriously, I'm about to throw you off of here."

"Maybe you can try and fight me later. For now, let's get this over with, Tubs."

I elbow him hard in the ribs and then slowly open the door into the building I'm hoping to find the Colossus'. Right away the smell hits me and I know we're in the right place. The smell is a little like cat urine, but there's more to it than that. There are hints of mould, decaying bodies of animals and sulphur. Not sure what all of that means, but it could very well have something to do with the Colossus'.

I let the door close quietly and when it does we are plunged into darkness. It's so intense, like nothing I've ever seen before and my usual keen eyes are having a lot of trouble adjusting. I close them for a count of ten, do it as hard as I can and then open and it's still thick black everywhere. That usually helps at the very least.

"You need a hand?" Godfrey asks, and I feel his hand on my arm.

"I can't see a thing," I admit.

"Hold on to me and I'll lead you down the stairs. Maybe it'll get better."

I certainly hope so.

As blind as I've ever been I hold onto Godfrey as he leads me along what feels like a hallway and then I hear the slight sound of a door opening. He warns me of stairs ahead and I carefully feel my way down. We get through three levels and find nothing. On the main floor Godfrey tells me he's having trouble finding a door to any sort of basement or cellar. I decide to let go of him and feel along the walls in hopes of finding it. Down here the smell is worse than ever, but it's only a smell. It can't hurt me.

My hands slide along the wall and it's filthy. There is grim which feels a lot like soot, but there's a slimy feel to it, very oily. I have the urge to wipe my hands off, but as I'd only dirty them again there's no point. I keep going. Through the filth and the stench I move on…and I find it.

Finally!

I get Godfrey's attention by waving my hands wildly in every direction. I have no idea where he is so I have to look like an idiot in hope that he sees me. I don't want to call out to him and alert whatever might be below, so it's arm waving or nothing. I hear his feet on the floor, clawed toes scrape along the ground and then he's beside me. It's then that panic starts to fill me a bit.

"Are you ready for this, Dillon?" Godfrey asks, and even though I can't see his face I can hear the hesitation in his voice.

"Not really, but what choice do I have? I want to end this."

"Good. Turn around so I can get the sceptre out."

Once that's done, the sceptre in hand, I reach out and push the door inwards. It's quiet, not rusty like the others, as though it's been used more recently. Once it is ajar, I see light flickering from below and I breathe a sigh of relief. The last thing I wanted was to have to face off against the Colossus' in total darkness. That wouldn't be fun.

I put the sceptre in my right hand, the same arm that has the symbol carved in it. I take a final long breath and move slow and quiet down the stairs. I'm halfway down when I can hear a voice. It's Garcia. He's here already. Damn it. I should've known, but I was hoping he wouldn't be able to find the place so fast. I stop for a second to listen.

"…no! You promised. I did everything you asked, now give me my son and I'll give you the book." He sounds terrible, like a man on the verge of tears and madness. I'm sure that stern look has melted away and has been replaced by something sad and pathetic. I can't really blame him. The man loves his son.

"This is not a place for bargains, Detective. Give me the book or my Colossus here will simply take it from your dead hands. And then, they'll eat your son. Does that sound fair to you?" It's the voice of the shadowy man, something foreign and yet so familiar. If he's here and the Colossus' are too, this can be all over in a matter of minutes. Kill them, and then him.

"I just want my son," I hear Garcia say weakly. He sounds so close.

"Then give me the book. Stop this or I will lose my patience. The book if you please."

I can't wait any longer. I have to get down there before Garcia has a chance to give him the book. I don't even know why the shadowy man wants it so bad, but the fact that he does want it at all means I have to stop it.

With the sceptre tightly gripped in my hand, I run down the stairs fast. I don't know if it's quiet or not and I don't care at this point. Time to attack.

"Don't do it, Garcia. Don't give him the book!" I yell this out as I hit the bottom of the stairs and take in the scene. The room is big, three times as wide as it is tall and it's over thirty feet in height. There are tools and machines all over, partial dismantled barrels, and a few tables scattered around us. On one of the tables is a child I'm assuming is Garcia's son. The boy is tied down and unconscious. Right behind the child, facing me, is the shadowy man. He's wearing a hood up over his head so I can't see his face, but his body language tells me just how unhappy he is to see me. That's what I was hoping.

"Give him his kid back and it'll just be us, asshole!" I yell, and move forward. I turn and look at Garcia. "Whatever you do, don't give him that book."

"In fact," Godfrey says, and comes around me towards the detective, "I'll take that for you. Keep it safe."

"Jesus Christ!" is all Garcia musters to say, as he pulls the book tight to his chest.

"No. I'm Godfrey."

"Detective, it's all right, he's with me. He's here to help us get your son back and stop all of this," I tell him, and he looks at the monster lizard with fear nearly swallowing him up. I don't know what to tell him to make him feel better, but I'd better act fast. I turn away from Garcia and look at the shadowy man who is backing away from us, nearly disappearing into the shadows.

"You told me you killed him, Detective. Now your son will pay for your lies. I'm sorry it had to be like this."

And then the shadowy man is gone, swallowed by the dark behind him.

"He's going to kill my son! You ruined it. He was about to let Phoenix go and you ruined it!"

I run over to him and grab the book from his hands. He fights for a moment, but releases it, and then I see why. From his coat he's pulled a gun, the same one he already shot me with, and no doubt means to do again. I nearly drop the book at the sight of it, but Godfrey acts quickly. He rips the gun from the man's hand and tosses it away.

"Don't be stupid," Godfrey growls. "Go and get your son and get out of here while you still can."

"But—"

"But nothing, Garcia," I say, and put the book back in my bag. "I have a sinking feeling things are about to get bad in here."

I'm guessing he knows I'm hinting that the Colossus' are about to come and he nods. Garcia runs to his son, Godfrey at his side, and they free the unconscious boy. I'm looking all around and there's no sign of the monsters; not even a sound. My heart's racing a bit and I try to calm down. I need a clear head and steady hand for the storm coming.

"You almost done?" I ask impatiently.

"Fast as we can, Dillon," Godfrey answers, and goes back to work on freeing the boy. After a minute they come back my way with the unconscious boy in his father's arms. I point to where the detective needs to go to get out. I tell him to hurry and he does, thanking me as he goes. I see him disappear in the door to the stairs, and it's a relief. That's seconds before the ground under me starts to quake.

Here they come.

"Don't let go of the sceptre," Godfrey tells me, and looks into the shadows the conjuror disappeared into. He has nothing to worry about. If I held this thing any tighter I'm pretty sure it would shatter. I'm squeezing it as tight as I can, watching and waiting.

Each second is like a beat, a pulse of time that moves with the rumbling of the approaching monsters. I take a deep breath, hold it for three of those beats and when I let it out, the silhouette of the first monster comes from the darkness and is born into the room as it lets out a terrible sound. I'm afraid. I'd be lying if I said I wasn't. The thing is terrifying and I've already seen what it can do to someone. The memory of the beast biting into Platanov is still fresh in my mind. At the thought my mouth is filling with the acidic and metallic taste of fear and adrenaline. Yet I know I have something in my hands that can defeat it, a sceptre wrapped in the one thing which can bring it down. This time, they'll get a fight.

"Get behind me," I tell Godfrey, and take a step forward.

The monster slows its charge as it scans the room. The nest of eyes on the elongated face of the Colossus fall on me, and as they do the beast charges at us with full force. The monster's mouth opens, webs of mucus hang from broken, browned teeth. The muscles in the arms of the thing are rippling and the scent of the long buried monster hits my nose as it closes the gap. There's little time left before it's do or die and I know I'm not ready to die.

Not today.

Not yet.

Now it's picking up its pace, charging at me like a runaway freight train. All perpetual motion. I hold steady until it is about ten feet away from me, knowing it won't be able to stop at this rate. I have inertia on my side.

It's fifteen feet away.

Ten feet.

Five feet.

Two feet.

That's when I raise my hand, lift the sceptre up and allow its own force to provide me what I need to strike it. The Colossus' weigh slams into the sceptre and its eyes fall on it seconds before contact is made. I wish I could say there was fear in one of its numerous onyx eyes, but there's no way to know. It does try to stop, attempts to put on the brakes and avoid the inevitable, but it's much too late for that. The monster moves as though it wants to veer right, and it almost does, but the sceptre still hits it straight in the face and blinding green light explodes from the beast's face. I thought for a moment it would pierce the creature, that the monster would be impaled on the cylinder of petrified wood, but it doesn't. As the two touch, the green light comes and knocks it backwards a full two feet.

It mewls and cries as fissures erupt across the black haired head of the Colossus. I watch as the beast falls to its side and its hands shoot up to his face as though it can stop what's happening. More light bleeds from the cracks spreading across its body and from the splits in the ancient flesh—I can see thick, black liquid seep through looking like molasses. It bubbles out, pooling on the floor as steam rises from it and I know I'm watching it die. I'm so thankful this worked, that the beast is stopped by it, but before I can watch it die and celebrate, I catch sight of the other two out of the corner of my eye.

Damn it.

"Dillon," Godfrey says, and taps me on the shoulder in case I didn't already notice the obvious.

"Yeah, don't worry, I see them," I say, and turn to them.

Neither is as quick to run at me now that they see the remains of their fallen brother. I watch as they look from me to the one on the ground and back at me again. I wonder if they're afraid. I'm curious if they know one of their number is dying on the floor and soon they'll be joining him. I'm feeling confident about this. Killing the first wasn't nearly as hard as I thought It'd be, so these two will be easy. I've faced worse.

Or maybe not.

I think I might've been too cocky. The monsters speak to one another in a language that sounds like people talking underwater and then they move towards me and Godfrey, but not straight on. They're circling up, one coming up the right, the other on the left and now I'm worried. If they attack at the same time, this might not turn out so well. We only have one sceptre and there's no way to do anything about that.

"I hope you have a good plan, Dillon," Godfrey says, and they're so close now.

"Not a good one at all. Wish I did."

"I see. Well, if we don't make it, I hope you rot in whatever hell you end up in. Damn fool. You should've stayed out of this. I told you that, didn't I?"

"I know. I don't think I had much of a choice though. One way or another, I think ending up here was inevitable."

They attack.

It's amazing how fast these giants are. Over twice the height and width of me, but I don't even think I could move quite as quick. They manage to cut the distance between us in seconds and it's all or nothing now. I want to help Godfrey, but there's no time. All I can do is hope to hit the one close to me, and then quickly strike at the other before it hits my friend.

The sceptre arches through the air; I think I can almost hear it whistling as it goes. I definitely feel it strike home and I silently cheer to myself at the great shot. I could've easily missed, but there's no missing the way the sceptre feels when it whacks the muscular form. Knowing the way the sceptre instantly destroys the Colossus, that I only have to touch it and the deed is done, I spin around in hopes of helping Godfrey. When I do, I notice something's wrong. My hand feels too light and when I look over at it, I am surprised to find it empty. The sceptre is gone.

I look at the Colossus I just hit and can't believe it. The damn thing sacrificed itself, grabbed the sceptre as I hit it and pulled it from me. The thing cries out as it falls to the ground, holding it close to its disintegrating body, and that's when I see crack and then hear it shatter. My one weapon against them, destroyed.

Great.

I turn back to Godfrey in time to see the monster's arm slam into my lizard friend's chest and send him sailing through the room, where he disappears into the shadows. There's a dull thud as he hits what I'm guessing is either the wall or ground, but I can't worry about him now. I absently call out to him, but I know he's not going to answer. I hate to think it, but I'm pretty sure he's dead.

Again, there's no time to worry about him because the last surviving Colossus is inching towards me. I need to move, to figure out what to do, but there's really nothing left for me to do but run. It's not like I have the sceptre any more, and I can't fight this thing with my bare hands or even my Tincher. There's no way to win this, so I have to flee. With my bag on my back, I turn quickly and run at the stairs I'd come down and hope I have enough adrenaline in me to out run the thing.

My feet just miss a pool of black, tar-like blood as I go. The monster cries out a sound that's a bit like a cross between a thousand bees and metal scraping on metal. I wince, but am close to the stairs. They're narrow, so I hope that'll play to help me get away. The big thing right now is I can't fall. No movie clichés here please. I just need to run and keep on running until I can get somewhere safe and find another way to kill this thing. Luckily I still have the book, so I will hold onto hope there'll be some alternative answer in it.

Less than halfway up the stairs I hear the cracking and crumbling of the walls behind me. My hope it wouldn't be able to follow me up the close quarters are dashed, so I dig deep and find a little more strength to help me get up the steps. I use the fear and need to survive to help me run even faster.

I can feel the monster's hot breathe billowing up the narrow quarters and I do not want to feel it any closer than that. I don't want to feel it at all, to be honest. I just want to be at home with Rouge and to have this whole nightmare behind me. Safe and sound, in my own apartment; not here at all.

I get to the top of the stair and try and figure out how to get out of here. I look around quickly and there it is. When Garcia and his son fled, they must've left the door open. I can see it on the far side of the room, the waning sunlight is coming bleeding in and I know that's my holy grail, my sanctuary. I run straight to it.

The next few seconds are like a dream. Not one of those good ones where you're a superhero flying or laying down with some perfect beauty. This is one of those nightmares you have where you're running at something, trying to get away from whatever is chasing you, and yet no matter how fast you go, the goal just stays the same distance away. You cry out and run faster, but you get no closer to your goal. It's how I feel as I try to get out to the light of day, hoping to escape the Colossus that wants to eat me.

The bag on my back feels as though it weighs a ton; it slams against me and bounces up and down painfully, but I won't toss it aside as my only real hope lies in there. The crashing behind me gets louder, but I can't stop and don't dare to look back. Even as the world behind me explodes with a sound of demolishing brick and drywall, I don't stop. Bits of debris hit the backs of my leg and my head, but they're nothing compared to the way I'll feel if I let the Colossus get me. So feet, don't fail me now.

The door is right there, in arms reach and that's when I feel a gust of wind rush behind me and know the beast is right there and it just took a swipe at me. It cries out again and I'm sure it's close enough to make contact this time, but I'm at the door, finally at it and I should be fine. I'll be out in the open with more places to run, so I should be able to get away.

That's my hope, anyway.

I get one foot out the door and suddenly my feet aren't on the ground anymore. I'm flying through the air for a split second and then my body slams on the cobblestone walkway. The wind is knocked out of me and my body is pinned there with the weight of the monster on me. Damn it! I can't let its skin touch mine. I do remember that they're poison. I can't let it—

My head feels a little light and I'm having trouble breathing. It's the heaviest thing I've ever felt, how I imagine a car would weigh if it was on me. I start to gasp for air as I struggle to get free without letting it touch my bare skin. There are people all around. I can't see them, but I can hear their screams of terror as the monster lies there, no doubt about to bite my damn head off. I need to get out. I have to use my size as an advantage and wiggle through some spot. I pull my hands into the sleeves of my shirt and decide to move backwards, knowing the thing has small legs.

"Get your phone out and film this, bro!"

I hear the voice of some idiot calling out for an Instagram or YouTube moment and hate that. Sure, don't help, video the fucking thing.

I get half a foot down from where I was and it's only then that I notice the Colossus hasn't actually attacked me. It's not really fighting or doing much of anything. That is until it starts to scream like a banshee and thrash around. My right leg gets battered under the gyrating motion, but I use this time to figure out a trail of escape and move. It's a close call, nearly getting my head crushed by the tree trunk thick elbow of the monster, but I get out in one piece. I jump to my feet, check to make sure I'm fine, and then look back at the Colossus.

It's not good for the monster.

The flesh of the creature is bubbling, hissing as it goes from black to a grey and moving closer to a clear white. It's as though someone coloured him in with a marker or crayons and now it's playing in reverse. Clear foam boils from the monster's mouth and its eyes begin to pop and drool down its colourless face, moments before it finally turns to dust. When it's all done the remains look like nothing more than an old fire pit.

The last of them are dead.

Finally.

"You okay, dude?" someone asks to my left, and all I do is nod absently. "What was that thing?"

"Special effects," I tell him without really thinking about it. "We're filming a movie here."

"Really? Cool!" he says, not bothering to wonder where the camera is. More than likely he's a big stoner who'll forget about this in a week or two. Around him I hear murmurs of *bullshit* and *what a liar*. A woman close by says something about a government conspiracy, but since there is nothing else to prove otherwise, no evidence left of the monster other than what they have on their phones, what are they really going to say?

For me, I stare at the ashes a little longer, trying to work out what happened. I should be dead. There's no way I should be alive while the Colossus' are all dead. Normally I give credit to planning and knowing what I'm doing, but this was all dumb luck. Every bit of it. There's no way I should be standing there when I don't even know how the thing died.

I don't know how long it takes me, but out of the blue, as I look at the faces of the crowd in the fading light, I get it. It was right there in the book.

If all else fails to fall them, the winds of the dragon wing or the fire of Ra will extinguish the life of a Colossus

I wish I had just done this for all of them. Would've been much easier and maybe Godfrey would still be alive. Man, that kind of hurts just to think about. Sure, we've had some issues in the past, times where I was sure he'd sold me bogus goods and nearly got me killed, but I've known him for so long. He was one of the real constants in my life, and now he's gone.

The crowd slowly thins out as there's nothing left to see. The monster is gone and the action is over, so it's back to having a good time and drinking for them. Once they've all moved on, only a few lingering close by, I decide to go back into the old warehouse. I can't just leave Godfrey there. Not only will it raise way too many questions if he's found, but in the end he was a friend and I can't let him just rot there.

I head in and carefully walk down the nearly ruined stairs. Seeing the destruction the Colossus made has me in awe. In a way, I feel bad for them. Here these creatures were, ancient beings that lived on Earth long before humans started to walk, and in the span of a few minutes they're wiped out by me. It's not their fault that some asshole called them up and they were forced to fight for him. They had no free will in the matter and that makes me feel for the creatures. I'd kill them again if put in the same situation, mind you. When it comes to live or die, I always chose the selfish way.

Still, I can't imagine what it's like to just do because you're told, never letting your own choice guide you. Even with my job there have been times when I've bent and broken the rules. There's always the chance that I could get in trouble, but I won't do anything that doesn't feel right or will do more harm than good. In the end, I listen to my heart as well as my obligation when doing anything.

Once I get downstairs I'm hit by a horrid smell. I walk through the room and find the smell is coming from the boiling ooze of the dead monsters. There's a smell of sulphur and dirty feet, all mixed with the overwhelming reek of cooking cabbage. I cover my face and head over to where Godfrey fell. I'm guessing when I get to him I could try to carry him up the stairs, but not only is he too heavy, but I won't get two feet out the door before more people come running over with their cameras and stupidity.

"They dead?"

His voice finds me before I find him and I can't help but smile. I move quickly to where he is and find him leaning against a wall holding his side, clearly in pain.

"How bad is it?" I ask, as I kneel beside him.

"Bad, but I've been through worse. You get them all?"

"Yeah. Last one burnt up in the sun."

"Good. And the shadowy man?"

I shake my head. "No luck there. He's long gone."

"Well, at least you got Garcia's kids and the rest of them."

"Rest of them?"

"The kids. They're here, alive."

"Where?" I ask, and look around, but see nothing.

"There's a false wall over there," he says, and points to his right. "I can hear them breathing so they're alive."

"That's a neat trick."

"I have a ton of them. There's a lot about me you don't know, Dillon."

"Okay, well, I need you to get out of here before we do anything about them. You think you can walk?"

"I guess I'll have to try."

Godfrey gets up and I see he's bleeding from a few spots, but at least the cuts appear superficial. That's a good thing. It takes him close to ten minutes to head back up to where the terrible bridge between the buildings is. I give him a few more minutes before I head back to where the kids are. As I go down, I pull my phone out and dial Garcia's number. He answers it right away.

"Dillon!" he yells out as he answers, and I can tell he's been crying. "Are you okay?"

"I'm fine, but—"

"Thank you so much! You saved my boy, and I'll never forget this. Never in a million years. I will—"

"That's all well and good, but you need to listen. I need you to get back here as fast as you can, bring EMS with you, too."

There's a pause and I know why. I'm no psychic, but he has to be terrified at the idea of returning to this place. After what he's seen and the fact that his son was nearly killed, coming back here is the last thing he must want to do.

"The kids are still alive. They're here," I tell him, knowing that'll get him into gear.

"All of them?" he asks, and his voice cracks.

"I don't know. I'm about to find out. Now, get back here and be the hero of the day."

He hangs up and I head over to find where the kids are. The false wall has a door and after a bit of a struggle, I manage to open it. They're all here, alive. I breathe a sigh of relief and go about untying, ungagging and waking them up. The kids are scared, but appear unscathed. No cuts on them, they seem as though they'd been fed and given water. I'm sure all their scars will be mental, but there's not a whole lot I can do about that.

Fifteen minutes later, I've led them up to the first floor and Detective Garcia shows up. He's arrived before EMS and that's good. It means I can slip away before anyone sees me. Less questions to answer. I'm sure there'll be a whole lot of questions too, especially when a forensic team shows up and finds the goop in the basement that used to be the Colossus'. That's not my concern though. Right now, I'm only thinking about the shadowy man who I still need to find.

I say goodbye to Garcia and head out. He says he'll call later and let me know how it all went and then I'm off. I think about where I might find the shadowy man, but first things first. I need to get home and rest. It's been a long day.

Unlike Godfrey, I can use the front door to leave, and I do. Nobody around knows what's going on, but in a few minutes the whole Distillery District is going to turn into a circus of cameras and flashing lights. I know someone might bring up the video of my fighting the monster outside of the building, but who's really going to take that seriously? I'm sure if someone shows it to the cops, it'll look like nothing more than some bad video reminiscent of Big Foot or the Loch Ness Monster. After all, we all know that monsters and demons aren't real. Humans feel safer thinking they're the only evil in the world.

Tuesday

I open my eyes and see it's a quarter after three in the morning and groan. I thought it was later. I'm so tired and want nothing more than to close my eyes and sleep, but my brain is going a million miles a second, and there's no way I'm going back down. I'd come home, had a shower, and got into bed just after ten at night, and five hours shouldn't be close to enough sleep for me, but it's all I think I'm getting today. There's still the shadowy man to deal with, and I can't afford to let him walk around and possibly call forth some other demon or monster to take me on. So I might as well get out of bed and try to figure out what to do next. All I can think is to see if Godfrey is up and about. Maybe he might have some ideas as I feel as I'm all out of fresh ones.

I call him and he's awake.

"Sure. I'd be happy to have some company," he says, and then I hang up and head out.

I take a cab to his store and as I walk towards his shop I see a line of homeless people close by. A few call out and ask for change, but I don't have time for them. Not at the moment.

The door opens even before I get to it and Godfrey's there, looking the way I remember him, reminiscent of a young Peter Tosh. He looks tired, worn out and I'm sure that's just because he's still hurting from the strike he took from the Colossus. I let the door shut behind me and follow him to the back room. He's limps as he goes and holds his side.

"How bad is it?" I ask.

"Feels a little like every rib's broken and my guts are bruised and crushed, but otherwise I'm fine," he says, and tries to laugh, but when he does he takes in a sharp breath and I can tell how much it hurts him to laugh. I know that feeling all too well. "So, what's your next move?"

I sit down and he does too and I hold my empty hands up, a great example of what choices I already have.

"All I know for sure is that I need to find him. Who knows what else he's going to try and pull. He could call up something just as bad, or worse. He could even find a way to get to Rouge. I don't want to sit around and play that game."

"I know. Maybe if we can figure out what he has planned, why he's doing all this, it'll be easier. Clearly stealing the kids wasn't his ultimate goal, or they'd all be dead. But they weren't. I saw that much on TV."

"Not only were they alive, they were fed, hydrated and unscathed. What was the purpose of taking them at all?"

"Maybe to get you there, or at least to get you involved," Godfrey suggests, and I feel a sense of déjà vu going on. This is what Rouge said and even though it seems like a long shot and overly complicated, I'm not sure what else it could be at this point. I'm still hesitant to accept it as the only possibility, and I tell him just that. He nods and continues, "Well, say the ultimate goal was to get the book, the only copy left in existence that I'm aware of. If this shadowy man knew I had it, maybe he used you to get to it, knowing monsters are your thing. You do have all those ads on late night TV and online as well."

"Seems like a stretch. Why not just come after you?"

"How would they know I had it already? If they knew I did, they'd come straight at me, but if they thought I could at least get it, they use you as the middle man."

"I see your point." Sort of, but still, it comes off as such a roundabout way to get from point A to point B. Still, there's so many loose ends that don't really tie together, but it's a starting point. It doesn't really help us get any closer to the shadowy man, but if what Godfrey's saying is true, then we have a way to get this asshole's attention. "At least we still have the book."

"On you?"

"No, it's at...shit!"

I jump up from my seat and run for the door. The book's back at my place and there's nobody and nothing there to protect it. If an otherworldly monster or demon were to show up, sure, they'd never get in through the door with all the curses and spells I have guarding it. But the shadowy man and the monsters he already called are earthbound. There's already a chance he called other creatures of this world and they'd be immune to all of my charms. Not sure why I didn't bother to think of that.

It takes a few minutes to find a cab and I offer him an extra twenty to get me back to my place as fast as he can. He smiles and drives like the devil through the night. If Godfrey's right and the ultimate goal was the book, I may already be too late, so I have to hope this shadowy man had no idea the book's there. Hopefully he just assumed I had it on me, figuring I knew what he's up to.

Maybe I shouldn't get my hopes up too high.

I'm feeling panic set in. Even though the cabbie is driving at near warp speed, it's still not fast enough. I go back and forth looking from the time on my phone to peering out the window to see how close we are, and each time it's as though time is my enemy. I need to get to my place yesterday. All I want is to see the book and know I didn't make some stupid mistake.

After what feels like an hour, but is less than ten minutes, the cab comes to a stop out front of my building. I hand him a fifty and get out. I run through the front door, leap up the stairs and for a moment, struggle with the keys to my apartment. It's a cliché. One of those scenes in a horror movie where someone is trying to get inside, to flee a murderer, but they suddenly can't remember which keys unlocks it. I feel as though I'm going to make matters even worse, that I'll drop the keys and in that split second it'll be too late. The fact that the door's locked means I should relax a little. People don't normally break into a place and then lock the door as they leave.

Finally the door's open. I throw it wide and don't bother to shut it as I rush to the bedroom and grab my bag. I can tell from the weight of it that the book's still there, but I won't feel better until I'm holding it. I undo the bag and there it is. Safe and sound. I pull it out, flip through the pages quickly to ensure it's what it is, not a bait and switch. Once I do I close it and breathe a sigh of relief. I feel a bit silly, as if I over-reacted, but really, better safe than sorry.

With the book in hand I head back out into the living room, wondering if I should head back over to Godfrey's or not. It'll cost me even more money to do it, but I think I'd rather have company and an extra head on this, than to be alone. When I step out of the bedroom, the book nearly falls from my hands and I jump a little.

"Give me the book, Monster Hunter!"

In front of me is someone I know.

He's dressed the exact same as the shadowy man, the same as the man in the basement of the Distillery warehouse, the hood of his sweater up just as it had before. The man looks smaller thought, not as strong or menacing as he had in the basement or the sewer, but there's little doubt this is the bastard. He reaches up though and pulls it off and when I see his face, I'm in utter shock.

"Give it over and I may let you live," he says again, his voice the same as it was the first time I saw him in my stairwell and the second time I saw him outside of Godfrey's store the day I found the book. It's the junkie. The one who hit me and infected me with the parasite.

"It's you! The whole time it's been you?"

"Just give me the book, Hunter, and maybe I'll even let you live."

"Why should I? What do you even want it for?" I ask, as I subtly look around the room for a weapon to use on him. He's human, of this earth, so really almost anything I grab will be enough to kill him. I just need to get close enough to do it. And I do plan on ending him here and now. He might be pretending to be a junkie, acting like a homeless man, but if he has the ability to call forth ancient monsters to work for him, I'd hate to see what else he can do. Especially if he has this book.

"Yours is not to question why, yours is but to do or die," he says, and smiles. "My dad used to say that to me. Any time I questioned him, asked him why I should do anything he asked me to do, he'd say it. Now I get to say it to you. Give me the book, Dillon, or I will end you here and now. Make it fast."

He has nothing in his hands. No weapons, no tools or talismans, so I'm not so sure how he plans to do anything to me. Yet, he's clearly clever, a tricky bastard who has done something most humans can't. I'd rather just walk up to him and bludgeon him to death with the hefty book, but I have to be cautious. I need to attack at the right time.

"Are you upset that I killed your little pets?" I ask, hoping to egg him on a little, make him mad so he attacks first and loses his edge.

"Not really," he says plainly, not moving at all. "Things die. That's life. And if you don't want to die either, if you don't want your little redhead queen to follow shortly after, you better hand over the book."

"Shut your fucking mouth. Don't even mention her!" I growl, and feel my hands squeezing the book hard. "You even think about hurting her and I will turn your face into the same bubbling mess I left your pets in."

"Then give me the book or not only will I kill her, I'll give her a little of my—"

I don't let him finish.

I throw the book in the air, send it flying towards him and he looks straight at it. His eyes are wide and his arms reach out to catch it, but he'll never get the chance. While he's distracted by the flying book, I rush him, grabbing a used butter knife off the table and I pounce on him. He cries out and we hit the ground. Before he has a chance to struggle, I use the blunted steel to tear into him. It's not easy, but with enough force I manage to bury the knife into him over twenty times, ripping through his clothes and flesh sloppily.

"Please…no…it's not me…please…I wouldn't hurt…"

He gargles the words as blood fills his lungs and stops his lies as the knife goes into his windpipe. His hands stop flaying against me, fingers lose their strength, and fall to his sides. Blood drools from the corners of his mouth. I pull the knife from his throat and there are a few weak arterial sprays as the heart comes to a stop. I wait a moment, ready to stab again in case he's still alive. After a minute there's nothing at all, just a pathetic man in a spreading pool of his own gore.

He's dead.

It's finally over.

I stand up feeling good. Normally, a person would be shaky after a thing like this, but I'm used to death at this point. Killing him, even though he's human and it's a little out of the norm for me, is still just part of the job. Now, I need to do something so that nobody sees the dead man just inside my doorstep.

I grab the junkie's leg and pull him a little further into my apartment. Blood smears on the floor as I shut the door and pull out my phone. I make a quick call, figuring I need to handle this fast. I know exactly who to call.

There's a knock at my door.

I call out for him to come in. I walk out into the living room with a cup of coffee as Detective Garcia steps into my apartment for the first time. I'm glad to see he's alone. When I called him and told him what happened, I hoped his family duty would come before his work. This dead man was the one responsible for the kidnapping of his son, the very person who threatened to bring down everything that Garcia knew. I figured it would be enough to make him push aside what was proper, to do what was right for his boy, and for me.

"Jesus," Garcia says and shuts the door. "You sure did a number on him."

"Would you've done any less?"

"If it'd been me, you wouldn't even know he was human," Garcia answers, and gets closer to the body. "What did you use on him?"

"A butter knife. It was the first thing I saw. Grabbed it as I ran at him and that's that."

"Not sure I've ever seen anyone killed with one before. Shit."

"So how should we handle this?" I ask, seeing as I've never had to get rid of a dead man before. Since I called him, I had images of carrying the shadowy man, the junkie to my bathtub and sawing him up into pieces, and then putting the small bits into garbage bags. It's not a pleasant thought, but it's one of many things that went through my mind while I was alone.

Garcia stands up, walks over to my couch and sits down. He looks a little stressed, no doubt he's trying to figure out how best to deal with it. I think of telling him about a few of the ideas I had, but he's a trained police officer, a detective that has dealt with homicides. If anyone knows how to dispose of a dead body and get away with it, it should be him.

"You have any more of that coffee? I could use a cup," he says, as he leans back, eyes closed.

"Sure. How do you take it?"

"Lots of cream, lots of sugar."

I head to the kitchen and go to work, waiting to hear what he might offer. When he says nothing, I decide to ask him about the kids and his son.

"Everything is fine. The kids were returned to some very happy parents, my son is currently with my sister. All them are shaken up, but no doubt the whole situation will be buried deep in their subconscious before long, where it can grow and fester until they are adults with ruined lives."

"That's a dark way to look at it," I say, and grab the cream from the fridge.

"It's not a Disney story. This is messed up."

"How about with your bosses? Did you spin it so they bought how you found the kids?"

"I didn't even try. I just said there was reports of some sort of strange things going on there and boom, I found the kids. When my superiors showed up and spoke to a few people, they went on about a movie shoot, monsters and all kinds of bizarre things. I think everyone is just happy to be able to tell the media the kids are home safe tonight."

"But you're in the clear, right?" I ask, and come out with his coffee.

"Sure. I'm the hero. And now I get to call this in and hope my hero stature is enough to make everyone buy the bullshit I'm about to give them." He takes the coffee and reaches into his suit jacket. From there he pulls out a pocketknife. "Wipe my prints off this. Use the cloth to carry it over to him and put it in his hands. Make sure you squeeze his hand around it or they'll be able to tell it's a plant."

"Then what?"

"Then we call it in. You're going to say he attacked you with that while you were eating and you defended yourself."

"And that'll work?"

"Look, it sounds like bullshit, but I'll take the call and then it's really only you, me and my bosses. With everything else, hopefully this will slide by with no issues." He sips the less than hot drink, colder than it should be thanks to all the cream, and he gives me the thumbs up. "Nobody is going to give a shit about him. Especially not me. Not to mention I owe you big time. This I guess is just the first payment."

That's what I was hoping to hear.

Wednesday

After the police left yesterday and took the junkie/shadowy man's dead body away, the first thing I did was call Rouge. I was excited to and hoped she'd come right home to me. When she picked up on the fifth ring, I was worried I'd caught her sleeping in.

"I was just out in the backyard with my friend, Tanya," she told me. "I take it things are back to normal?"

"As normal as they can be. Can you come home tonight?"

"I don't think so. I already made plans, but I will be back tomorrow afternoon, promise," she'd told me, and that would have to do.

I told her about everything that had happened, right up until the moment the police left my house. She said little on the phone. There were a few *wows*, and *oh my God* or two, and more than a handful of gasps. When I was done, she told me she hoped this wasn't going to be a frequent thing.

"I should hope not," I'd told her, and tried to laugh it off, but it's been getting harder and harder to find this funny. Not only was this one of the hardest things I've ever faced, seen more people killed than I'd ever cared to, had to kill a human myself, but Rouge's life was in some kind of peril. This was the second time since I met her that someone threatened harm to her, and I can't help but question how long I can do this for. Not that I plan on leaving her. I'd leave the job before that ever happened. But if I do quit, there's no way I can stay on this planet, and so I'm stuck between what I want and what I have to do.

We spoke for a little while after that and then only sent a few text messages through the night. We agreed to meet at her house for noon.

It's a little afternoon when I get out of the cab in front of her house and I'm so happy that I can finally see her again. It feels like it's been forever. I pay the cabbie and as I walk up to the door I wonder what we should do to celebrate the whole thing being over. Before I can even get to the door, it flies open and Rouge runs out into the yard to greet me. Her arms wrap around me, squeezing me tight and I return the gesture. Our lips meet and we kiss long and hard right there on the lawn. I don't even know how long this goes on for, but if feels so good I don't want it to end. She pulls away slightly, kisses my neck, and whispers things in my ear that get my blood pumping.

I guess I know how we're celebrating our reunion.

After we lay in her bed for a few minutes following some very active *catching up* we head out into the living room for snacks and TV. She's telling me all about the fun she had up at her friend's cottage, of how she went fishing, swimming in a terrifying dark pond and roasted marshmallows during a meteor shower, and goes to the YouTube app on her PlayStation. I'm too busy watching her, looking at the way her skin looks with her flushed afterglow, that I don't even notice right away what she put on.

But then I hear a sound I remember all too well and my blood runs cold.

I turn and there on the screen is a video of me and the Colossus out in the Distillery. There are people everywhere as I struggle to get away, looking all spastic as I do, and then like a moth to the flame, the damn beast is up in flames. It's a terrible sight. I hear Rouge gasp. Even though it's over fast, the asshole that posted it put it on a loop so we get to see it over and over again. As it fades out it says *Fact or Fiction* in ridiculous, bold lettering. I look at it again and see that even though it was posted yesterday, it already has over a million views.

That sucks.

"Can you pull up the comments?" I ask her, not having any idea how this thing works. She does, saying nothing at all at this point and we scroll through them.

So fake.

I call bullshit.

Who dresses like that anymore? Are those boot cut or relaxed fit jeans? This guy's from the 90's.

Monsters are real. They are created by the government and this is one that obviously got away. I bet that guy's actual a Nobody Man and there's a black helicopter close by.

Photoshop.

Look closely at it. You can tell that it's CGI. How lame!

Dumbledore6969, why post this bullshit? You're such a dickbag!

The comments go on and on like that. Either people think it's fake, or they sound like a conspiracy nut. Either way, I feel like I'm in the clear. I look over at Rouge and she doesn't look too happy.

"What's wrong?" I ask.

"This can't be good for you, can it?"

"How so?"

"Couldn't you get in some serious trouble? I mean there's video of you involved in killing that thing. Didn't you say something about that?"

"It'll be fine. I didn't have a choice. You can tell it attacked me. To anyone that watches it, I didn't do anything against the rules. Not really." I'm not totally sure about that, but hey, I have to stay positive about these things.

"Are you sure?"

"Yeah, darling, positive."

She leans over and kisses my cheek and I feel a round two coming on. "I can't believe how many people think it's fake though. There's not a single comment by a sane person that questions it."

"I know. Even when I was there, people pretty much accepted the bullshit excuse I gave them that we were filming a movie."

"How could they? It sure it looked pretty real in person."

"Smelt nasty too." I laugh. "But people will believe what they want to, or what they need to. It's easier that way. It's hard for someone to see something like that and accepted it as the truth, no matter how obvious it is. Better to just call it fake and move on, than it is to face the craziness."

"This is that whole faith thing again, isn't it?"

"Sort of," I say, and lean in for another kiss. "Maybe we should find a way to forget about that video. I think there's something in the bedroom that could help."

"And what's that?"

"Me all naked and sexy like," I say with a bad Scottish accent, as I rub my chest and act like a fool. "You know you want this sexy beast."

"Damn right I do, monster slayer."

The rest of the day we spend in bed. The night looks the same. Life can be good.

Sunday

I don't know what made me do it, but I decided to come out to the church today. I spoke to Garcia on the phone and he said he was coming out for the last mass of the day, which was set for eleven-thirty in the morning. I show up and there are people milling in with smiles on their faces and greetings for everyone. It's kind of nice. Living in the city you don't always get to see this kind of friendliness, so in a way, it's refreshing.

I don't see Garcia or his son anywhere around so I head in to find a seat. I sit next to an elderly woman with a lilac dress and a head full of platinum hair, and when I do she smiles at me. I can't help but return it. After all the bad things that have happened over the last little while, this is what I need. Nice, genuine people.

The crowd whispers quietly among themselves and I scan around for the detective. There's no sign of him. Maybe he came to an earlier mass or decided not to show up at all. I consider leaving right then, but the organ starts to play and everyone is rising. Too late now.

Father Ted and a group of altar boys come walking down the aisle. Ted is nodding to everyone he passes as a boy beside him swings a Thurible full of incense. When the priest's eyes meet mine, he smiles brightly and mouths *hello, Dillon*, to me. I nod back.

Once on the altar, mass starts and it's quite interesting. Father Ted reads a sermon about change and it has everyone listening.

"Today, like every day before it, and the ones still to come; is a new day. And with a new day, comes the chance to change things. Every day we wake up, get ready and head out to face the world, usually doing things as a routine, following the order as we think we must. But in order to grow and learn, we must challenge ourselves and force change in our own lives and the world. There are so many stories in the bible that teach us about this, but I'd rather you think of your own lives, your own experience and how change did, or could've made your life and the lives around you better. Did you take a walk instead of a bus, and that bus was in an accident? Did you decide not to go into work and had a wonderful day connecting with your children? Or maybe you refused to follow rules that you thought were unnecessary and unneeded and found true happiness at the end of the day."

The words sound like they're aimed right at me. I know all about that, change. I took a chance and said no to following the rules, the status quo, and found Rouge. I've never been happier. I could've stuck to the laws and regulations given to all hunters, but then where would I be? Unhappy is where'd I be. Hearing the words come out of Father Ted's mouth, and finding a connection to them brings another smile on my face on a day already filled with so many. Once again I'm glad I came out here for this.

He continues, and I listen, though I'm distracted by my own thoughts. I want to get back to Rouge's house after this and enjoy another well-deserved day off with her. We earned it.

The sermon is followed by a few hymns, and then communion. After that he says a few more nice words about loving one another and finding peace in God. When it's all done, Father Ted comes down off the altar, and walks to the main doors of the church to say farewell to his parishioners. I stand close by, watching just as I had not long ago and wait for him to finish. He set the altar boys off and finally comes walking over to me with a smile and his arms held out in greeting.

"Dillon, so glad you came out. If ever I was surprised to see someone in the pews, it was you. What brings you by? Looking for a little faith in God?"

"I actually came by to see Detective Garcia. He said he was stopping by and I thought I would come see him and his son, and since I was here I'd come see you too. If you're not too busy of course."

"Dillon, I'm never too busy for you. Let's go have some tea."

We walk to the back of the church and head towards the rectory. "Did you see the detective here earlier?" I ask.

"I'm afraid not. I was hoping to. His son could use all the help he can. What an awful thing to have gone through," he says, and I agree. "I mean, no child should be forced to see things even a grown man or woman couldn't handle. Children are resilient, but their minds are still so frail and easily scarred."

"I know. Poor kid." We walk into the rectory and he leads me to his office. "When did you speak to Garcia last?"

"Last time the two of you were here. When I saw what happened, I was hoping he would come by with his son and there'd be a chance to talk after. I would like to offer the boy some solace. What kind of tea do you want?"

"Earl Grey," I say absently, thinking about a few things, mainly what I saw in the warehouse. It was a disturbing thing, seeing all the kids the way they were, especially the detective's boy who was strapped to the table. I'm lost in thought and almost don't hear Father Ted come back into the room. He sets the tea down in front of me.

"How've you been, Dillon? This job was probably hard on you even."

"It was," I say, and give him a few details, right up until the junkie/shadowy man died. "I didn't really have a choice. He was a threat to the woman I love and to God only knows how many others. I've never done that before, taken a human life, and to be honest, I'm struggling with it. It's hard on my conscious."

It hasn't been that hard, to be honest, but I am talking to a priest, so it seems like a good thing to say. It's better than what I want to say, which is *I'm glad the bastard is gone and can't hurt anyone else.* I bite back those words for good reason.

"There's a reason murder is a sin. Even a righteous murder weighs on a good heart, Dillon. How's your tea?"

"Just how I like it. Earl Grey. Hot," I say with a smile and mimic Jean Luc Picard, even though I haven't bothered to drink any of the tea. "Where's your little friend, Peel? I thought he'd be here too. I really like the way that guy smells."

"He's down stairs. Sometimes he goes down there when church is in session just in case I bring people back here."

"Want to go down and tell him it's okay to come up? I can come to."

"After," Father Ted says, and lifts his cup up. "Let's finish our tea and talk some more. It's a while since you were here, and so much has happened."

"Okay," I say, and look around the room.

"So, how come you were hoping to talk to Detective Garcia?" the priest asks, and leans back in his chair, his face frozen with a perma-smile.

"Well, it's been a few days since I killed the shadowy man at my apartment and I just wanted to touch base with him. He seems so different lately. So..." my voice trails off, but my lips keep moving.

"Different? How so?"

"He...he seems...so...oh wow."

"Are you okay, Dillon? You sound strange."

I shake my head and open my eyes wide. I lean over and try to put the tea cup down and it misses the table. The china shatters on the floor and warm tea hits my shoes. They've seen worse days.

"I'm...kin...kinda ti...tired."

"You look it," Father Ted says, and puts his own cup down with ease. "That must be the poison working already."

"Wh...what...poi—"

"Don't try and talk, Dillon. There's no real point. Just sit back and relax, let the poison go to work and you'll be dead in no time."

I give him a look to show him I'm confused, and he smiles.

"You have no idea what's going on, do you? Is this the part where I tell you the whole thing, where the evil villain finally reveals the master plan that you fell prey too? I'm not too up on these Earth things so, I think I'll just sit back and watch you die. It's really for the best, Hunter."

"T…Ted…why?"

"Ted! Ted! Why me, Ted?" the priest mocks, and then laughs. "Well, the least I can do is give you that one. Father Ted is dead. He died nearly five months ago. He was sitting right here in this chair, drinking this shitty, hot beverage and then, off to the land of his little God he went. Peel was the one who found him, you know. He'd crossed over a few days before, came over as a bit of a scout to see if you or the priest was around. When he found this dead body, he almost went in it himself, but knew it'd be better to call on me, so I could come and claim it.

"The universes are changing, Dillon. If you go out into the universe, you can sense it, smell it in the stars. The people you work for are on the way out. Our group, our organization feels now is the time to do what we want, to use the Earth and be free to come here on our own. Why should we listen to these stupid laws made by beings who are beneath most of us? To protect this world? Have you seen what this place is? Earth is a cesspool and a realm of gluttony and degradation. Why shouldn't we be allowed to come?"

My eyes slump a little and he chuckles at the sight of it. He must be loving the fact that he defeated me.

"I took your priest's body and set this all into motion. I raised the Colossus', earthbound monsters that are much worse than my own race, and set up a plan to get you to bring me the book that would allow me to call every monster, demon and being from here to the surface. Better to prepare the world for what lies beyond here by showing them what's right in their own backyard, right?

"That's why I came to the hospital and introduced you to Detective Garcia. I knew you would help him and knew your friend, Godfrey, would be able to get it. That lizard bastard has a way of getting his filthy claws on anything he wants. And he did. It seemed so easy. All I had to do was get the book from you, remove the great monster hunter from the equation, and it would all come together. My group, the organization, they want you dead so bad. So many feel you are going to really get in the way. But I had the Colossus', so how hard could it be?

"Everything seemed so perfect, but you are a tough bastard, Dillon. I will give you that. You live up to the stories I've heard of Treemors. Even killing the homeless man I managed to convince to attack you not once, but twice, came as a bit of a surprise.

"And yet, here you are, sitting in my chair, dying just as you should. Not as tough as you thought, are you?"

"Not as stupid as you thought, either," I say, and sit up, done with the act. I've heard enough to know this imposter needs to die. Guess my days of killing humans, even ones with otherworldly beings in them, isn't over after all. "Don't look so surprised. I knew you weren't Father Ted before you even brought me the tea."

I reach behind me and pull out my Tincher and my gloves. The fake Ted fumbles his way out of the chair he's in. He knocks his tea over and is crying even though I'm not even approaching him yet.

"How? How could you know?"

"You said you felt bad for Garcia's son," I tell him plainly. "Bad move."

"So? It was all over the news."

"Was it? The kids being found was all over the news. Garcia never reported his son missing and had taken the boy out of there before coming back to get the rest of them. So, there's no way the real Father Ted could know that without talking to the detective first. You should learn to lie better."

"Wait...please...I can tell you things!"

"Of course you can. I hear that all the time. But to be honest, you'll say whatever you can to get out of this. I won't believe a word you say. I have no faith in your kind. The only thing I have faith in, is this."

I raise the Tincher and head after him. It's not a hard job. The faker cringes in the corner of my dead friend's office and I simply plunge the blade into his chest. He convulses once and I feel the familiar vibration run up the blade of the knife as it comes into contact with the visiting soul inside. I look away though as I free the blade, and send the spirit back to where it came from. Even though it wasn't Ted in that body, it's still the face of the man I once cared a lot about. I look up at the ceiling, his body quakes again, and then slowly slumps to the floor. I draw my knife back and walk to the kitchen to wash the blade off.

That didn't feel as good as I would have liked it to. I know it wasn't the real Ted in there, I've been doing this long enough. There've been times when I've had to do the same thing to another creature that took over a dead human, but this is different. This felt personal. It was far worse than killing the junkie I'd thought was the shadowy man. Worse by a long shot.

Once the blade is clean, I dry it and walk out of Father Ted's office. I need to do something about his body, but not yet. There's still work to do.

I've been in the basement of the church more than once. I know the place well. I don't even bother to turn on the extra light on the stairs, I just walk down and halfway to the bottom I see candle light flickering.

"Is he dead already, Kenta?" Peel asks from below. "That seems to have gone fairly easy if—"

His words die on his false lips as he sees me standing at the bottom of the stairs, my Tincher in hand. I still feel sick from what happened above, but there's rage here too. And determination. I've been played, made to feel like a fool and I don't like it.

"You're here," Peel says, and backs away from me, but there's nowhere to run. "Does that mean Kenta is dead?"

"Yes. I killed him, the bastard hiding in my friend's body. Were you really expecting to come out of this on top?"

"It was worth a try. So, I guess now you're going to send me back as well?"

"Maybe. Or maybe I rip you open until I find your centre, your spirit, and I'll just put it out altogether. I haven't decided yet."

"What can I do or say to help? I don't want to die. I don't mind going back, but I don't want to die. I didn't do anything wrong."

I can't help but to laugh, though there is no humour in it. I'm pissed off and the sound is bitter and sarcastic.

"Nothing wrong? You stole kids, killed three police officers, murdered another friend of mine, stole the body of someone close to me, and for what? The book? For some stupid plan to get the world ready for your kind? You've done nothing but what's wrong."

"It's not that simple, Hunter. You have to know that."

"Really? The one up there, Kenta, sure made it sound simple."

"That's because Kenta is a Creel. You know their kind. They're rash and harsh, from a world of pain and misery. What else do you expect from them? But I'm telling you, there's more to it all. A bigger picture. You can either understand it, or just get in the way. Either one you choose the future will happen regardless. Things are evolving."

I shake my head and slowly begin to walk towards him. He's afraid. I can tell by the way his fake shoulders slump as he backs into the wall and raises hands made of old tea bags.

"I've been hearing that way too often. An organization is coming, one that wants to put the powers that be in their place and destroy the hunters right? Is that your plan?"

"It's more than that, Hunter. For too long the kind you serve has controlled everything, keeping the rest of us in their shadow, but we refuse to stay there. Why are the universes and realms free to them, but barred for the rest of us, the ones they don't deem fit?"

"To protect the worlds chosen, the ones not ready for what is out there," I say, and that's just how it is. My job is to protect the Earth and humans from the truths beyond the stars that they're just not ready for. They can barely handle the things on their own planet, day-to-day lives. How would they react to what is out there?

"And who decides who's ready for what?"

"Not you, and not those you follow."

"Keep thinking that way, Hunter, but you can't stop what's coming. If it takes a war, there'll be a war. And then, how will you manage to win, to walk away? Soon, you'll be on the other end of a Tincher and I wonder how much mercy there'll be."

"About as much as I'm going to show you."

I move in closer and there is no mercy, not from me, not today. I don't send him to his home world, there's no point. If there's a war coming, maybe I should start snuffing the lights out of them all, just like I did these two.

"My God, Dillon!" Garcia says, as he looks down at Father Ted's body. "You killed him too? What in God's name is wrong with you?"

"He was already dead," I tell him, and explain everything that happened. "It was Kenta and Peel from the beginning. He put us together so that I would help find the book and then they set you to kill me when they took your son. All so getting the book would be even easier. Saying it out loud sounds like something way too complicated, full of too many ways for it to go wrong, but it almost worked. I did get the book and you shot me and left me for dead. But it's over for now."

"I don't even know what to say. Father Ted was a good, honest man. How long had he been dead for?"

"Five months."

"Five months?" he says the words, as though he doesn't believe them. "All this time, every Sunday I saw him, it was all a lie? How could that thing lie so well?"

"Who knows. Maybe it was a preacher on his own world."

"And my son's first communion, I guess that was nothing too. How am I going to explain it to Phoenix?"

"Why would you?"

"Because it wasn't real. He'll have to do it again."

I shake my head and walk over to Garcia, pulling him away from Father Ted's lifeless body. "That's the problem right there, detective. In your son's eyes it was very real. He doesn't need to know this to feel as though it was. Telling him will make his already shaky faith crack a little more. The real Father Ted told me a lot. In the end it comes down to this: having belief and faith that something is true is more powerful than finding out something is false. You can build a foundation on trust and hope. Nothing can be built on knowing the world you live in is a lie."

And as those words leave my lips, I think about everything that just happened and what I'm here to protect. This world lives under a blanket of falsehoods and lies. People live in a cocoon of safety they don't really have. If the truth finally comes out and everyone wakes up from the dream they've lived in of a perfect world, how long will it be before the walls around them crumble and fall. How can a place built on nothing by fairy tales and lies stand up to the tidal wave of truth that's threatening to wash in?

Time will tell.